THE PRIEST WHO WAS NEVER BAPTIZED

STORIES

THE PRIEST WHO WAS NEVER BAPTIZED

Stories factual and fictional of
Russian life in the
nineteenth century

by Nikolai Leskov

Translated and edited by
James Muckle

Bramcote Press
Ilkeston 2004

First published 2004 by
Bramcote Press,
81 Rayneham Road,
Ilkeston DE7 8RJ,
Derbyshire,
United Kingdom

Printed in Great Britain by
Biddles Ltd., Guildford

British Library Cataloguing in Publication Data
A catalogue record for this book is available from the British Library

ISBN 1 900405 12 1

Contents

Foreword

IT is a matter for regret that many fine works by Nikolai Leskov (1831-1895) are not available in English translation. This volume fills a few gaps, and its contents, as far as can be ascertained, appear here in English for the first time. Several did not make it into the Collected Edition of Leskov's works which appeared in the 1950s, perhaps because they did not match Soviet prejudices about Christianity and morality. It was certainly not because they lack quality.

These stories were all written between 1876 and 1890, after Leskov's 'intellectual crisis' of 1875, when he confessed to having 'wavered in his [religious] views'. The 'wavering' and questioning were there from the start of his writing career in 1860, but it is certainly true that from the mid-1870s onwards Leskov appears more strongly as a moralist, a thoughtful critic of the Orthodox Church—in particular of the contemporary interpretation by clerics of its doctrines, its role in society and the like—and the emergence of a 'Protestant' tinge in his way of thinking. At the same time, Leskov's humour, the gloriously colourful language to which I have been able to do scant justice in these translations, the rich portrait of Russian life, especially village life, and the vivid characters flourish in these tales in the highest degree.

In terms of their subject matter and style these stories are a mixed bag. Leskov's works *were* a mixed bag, and that is of their essence. The pleasure of browsing through his stories is partly due to their variety, the fact that we never quite know what to expect next. None the less, these stories are united by their strong spiritual and moral message. 'The Priest Who was Never Baptized' has a distinctly 'Protestant' feel to it, as Leskov's opponents were quick to point out; it is set in rural Ukraine, or 'Little Russia', as it was often termed in those days. The expression is perhaps regarded as offensive in the present century, when we can take offence, it seems, at almost anything in language: Leskov certainly meant no disparagement by using it, so I have retained it in translation. The story is full of humour, incident and colour; but there is also much superstition and cruelty and even an incident of brutal murder. 'Rebellion Among the Gentry in the Parish of Dobryn', which as far as I can discover has never yet been republished since its first appearance, purports to be a learned article and appeared in a much respected historical journal, but it is one of the funniest of Leskov's stories—true or false, and who knows which? Yet the implications of the story for office-holders in Church and society are strongly underlined. 'Selivan, the Bogeyman' is—or claims to be—a reminiscence of the author's or narrator's childhood: the viewpoint of a child, recollected in maturity, adds spice to an already fascinating tale of rural life with all its wrong-headedness, prejudice, hard-hearted disregard of the suffering of others, and near-idiocy, as well as the variegated comedy of character, manners and slapstick.

'A Pygmy' is a short tale with a clear moral, a sharp character-study, and a sketch from St Petersburg life at the time of the Crimean War. 'Wrong Done at Christmas' and 'Vexation of Spirit' were both intended for children. Lev Tolstoy took over and adapted the first of these as 'The Thief's son' and, to my mind, spoilt it by over-simplification of the ethical issue. The pious tone, especially of some parts of the latter story, may be thought dated and even sanctimonious for children today, but it would not have been thought so in 1890, and certainly not in Russia, where the 'stiff upper lip' had little place in a religious context. I include 'Vexation of Spirit' in this collection also because it seems to me to illustrate Tolstoy's biblical precept against oath-taking, 'swear not at all', far more poignantly than anything comparable which Tolstoy himself ever wrote, and also because it contains a notable character portrait of the idealistic, only partly coherent, but saintly and inspirational 'Goat'. Finally, 'A Response to "The Kreutzer Sonata"', is included because it illustrates another aspect of Leskov's debate with Tolstoy's views, and also because it has the fascination of a work which starts really well but is unfinished: readers may like to consider how the author intended to complete it, or how they would do so themselves. There is an incident in it which is striking for its drily contemptuous depiction of the vacuous chatter of the upper classes and illustrates that these people's stereotypes, superstitions and conventional attitudes are in no way superior to the peasants' credulity and cruel indifference to the predicament of others.

The subtitle chosen for this volume of translations is intended to raise explicitly the question of how far these stories are reminiscences of real life, and how far pure imaginative invention. In relation to every one of them, Leskov claimed or strongly implied that they were real-life events, or authentic experiences from his own childhood. The bizarre antics of the protagonists in the supposed historical study of Dobryn are highly improbable, but apparently true; the tale of the unbaptized priest could well be based on fact; the narrator of 'Selivan', 'Wrong done at Christmas' and 'Vexation of spirit' shares much biographically speaking with Leskov himself and his family, and his own name is used in one place; we are unquestionably meant to think that the narrator of 'A Response' is Leskov himself. Does it matter how much of this is the literal truth? What we may term the 'imaginative reader' will not think so. Early biographers of Leskov were fooled into using his stories as sources of accurate information on his life-story. Later writers, being much more conscious of the distinction between 'author' and 'narrator', have been more circumspect—to the point of believing little he said about himself unless information external to the works confirmed it. Leskov's contemporary readership, however, clearly recognized his portrait of their own country and society as an utterly convincing one, and if they were taken in by some of his claims to literal accuracy in matters of history and biography, then this simply illustrates his superlative skill.

Leskov's writing is particularly rich in topical references to persons and events, many of which are puzzling to the modern reader, even the Russian reader. There are many scriptural or half-scriptural quotations (and misquotations) which I have tried to identify. He provides some of his own annotations, and these are given here as footnotes, sometimes slightly adapted for the sake of clarity. The notes at the end of the volume are intended to help the modern English-speaking reader to make sense of matters in the text which require elucidation today. I have done my best to trace every recondite point, but even the availability of a university library and the resources of the much-vaunted and overrated Internet have not enabled me to achieve complete success. I am grateful to friends for valued help: Alan Richards (for an ingenious explanation of a knotty point of translation), Michael Pursglove (for identifying the poetry quoted in 'Dobryn'), Professor Grigory Kliucharev and colleagues (for advice on difficult points particularly of Orel dialect), and Dr Alan Suggate (for help in tracing biblical references). The remaining information gaps are entirely my responsibility.

J. M.

A note on the spelling of names. There is no system of transliteration which will enable non-Russian-speakers to pronounce Russian names unfailingly correctly. This book uses the British Standard system (which is perhaps the easiest to grasp, but which is no longer used in scholarly contexts) with some adaptation: the soft sign is ignored, in the endings of names Vasily is preferred to Vasiliy, Pidnebesny to Pidnebesnyy, and -sky to -skiy. In cases where Russian names have widely accepted English spellings, these are used: Nikolai and Alexei (rather than Nikolay and Aleksey).

The names themselves. Non-Russian readers sometimes complain of confusion resulting from the various forms of the characters' names. There is little to cause real difficulty or confusion in this collection of stories; the general idea is actually given by the author himself on p. 62, where he discusses the versions of village people's names. Savva and Savka are clearly the same name, as are Nikolai, Nikola and even Mikola. Ladies and gentlemen were frequently known and invariably addressed politely by their name and patronymic (that is, their first two names rather than their surname). This applied also to Tsar Nicholas I, widely known in Russia and referred to in these stories as Nikolai Pavlovich. Whereas in standard Russian a female Leskov or Dukachev are Leskova or Dukacheva, the peasants dub them in these stories 'Leschikha' and 'Dukachikha'. The ending *-ikha* is often used to denote the female in the animal kingdom: these have therefore been rendered 'Leskovess' and 'Dukachess'.

The Priest Who Was Never Baptized

An improbable story

(and a modern myth)

To Fedor Ivanovich Buslaev

THIS short record of an actual, although improbable, event I dedicate to a scholar eminently worthy of respect, a connoisseur of the Russian language. I do this not because I claim the story to be worthy of attention as a literary work. No; I dedicate it to Mr Buslaev because the highly original event it recounts has, even now, in the lifetime of its central character, come to be accepted among the people as a perfectly formed myth; and it seems to me that to trace the formation of a myth is no less interesting than to investigate 'how history is made'.

I

ONE day I was sitting with a circle of friends when we came across this newspaper report:

'A village priest was celebrating the wedding of his daughter. Needless to say, the banquet was of the very best, everyone got thoroughly tipsy and was enjoying themselves as village and family people do. In due course, the Deacon of the parish turned out to be a lover of choreographic art and, carried away by the general rejoicing, went so far as to exercise his "merry legs" and was moved to launch himself into the *trepak* in front of all the guests. Alas, also present at the feast was the Rural Dean, who chose to find the actions of the Deacon highly offensive and worthy of the severest punishment, and, filled with zeal, the said Rural Dean penned a denunciation to the archbishop, declaring that at the wedding of the priest's daughter the deacon had 'burst into a trepak'. Archbishop Ignatii received the denunciation and noted the following decision:

> Deacon N. 'burst into a trepak'.
> The *trepak* has not complained.
> Why, then, is the Dean complaining?
> Summon the Dean to the Consistory and question him.

'The affair concluded with the tale-bearer, who had to travel a hundred miles and expend a good deal of money on the trip, returning home having been told that it was his job to rebuke the Deacon on the spot instead of telling tales about one isolated incident.'

We were all unanimous in expressing total sympathy with Archbishop Ignatii's characteristic resolution, but one of us, Mr R., who knew a very great deal about clerical life and who had an immense store of anecdotes drawn from this unique section of society, interjected:

'This is fine, gentlemen, I'll admit it's fine: the Dean really shouldn't have "told tales about one incident, and moreover an isolated one", but there are cases and cases, and the one we've just read about reminds me of another, when a Rural Dean told tales to his archbishop and put that cleric in a much greater dilemma, but, none the less, the matter turned out well.'

Needless to say, we asked our friend to tell us about the dilemma, and this is what he said:

'The affair I shall tell you about, since you ask, began in the early years of the reign of Emperor Nikolai Pavlovich, but wasn't concluded until the end of his reign, in the very frantic days of our fiasco in the Crimea. Against the background of these momentous events, which so inevitably occupied the attention of the whole of Russia, the complex issue of the 'priest who was never baptized' was played out in obscurity and is remembered only by those still alive who played a part in the intricate story, which has taken on the status of a fascinating myth of recent provenance.

'Since the affair was in its own time and place known to many and the central character flourishes to this day, you will forgive me if I do not indicate the scene of the action with strict accuracy and if I avoid giving the people concerned their real names. I shall simply say that it all happened in the South of Russia, among the Ukrainian population, and it concerns an unbaptized priest,

Father Savva, one of the best, an honourable man, who still thrives, who practises his priestly calling, and who is greatly loved both by his superiors and by his rural parishioners.

'Apart from the name of Father Savva himself, for which I see no need to provide a pseudonym, I shall change all other names of persons and places.'

II

AND so, in a certain Cossack village in Little Russia—shall we call it Paripsy?—there lived a rich Cossack named Petro Zakharovich, who was known as Dukach. He was a man of mature years, very rich, childless, and very intimidating indeed. He was not a *parasite* in the Great Russian sense of the word, because extortion after the Russian manner was not known in Little Russian villages, but he was what people called a *dukach:* a churlish fellow, peevish and defiant. Everyone was afraid of him and would cross themselves when they encountered him; they would cross to the other side of the road to avoid being cursed by Dukach, or even, if the mood took him, assaulted. His real name, as happens fairly often in village communities, had been thoroughly forgotten by everyone and replaced by the sobriquet or nickname of 'Dukach', the Boor, which reflected his unpleasant personal characteristics. This offensive nickname, needless to say, did nothing to soften Petro Zakharovich's manner, but rather angered him all the more and drove him to a state in which, despite his high natural intelligence, he would lose his self-control and all reason, and would hurl himself on other people like a madman.

Children playing outside only had to see him coming and they would scatter in fright, shouting: 'Look out! Trouble! Old Dukach is around!' Their fears were not groundless, for old Dukach would set off in hot pursuit of the fleeing children with his long stick in his hand: it might be one that any sober Little Russian Cossack might carry, or one that he had happened to pull from the hedge. Yet it was not only the children who were afraid of Dukach: grown-up people tried to give him a wide berth, as I said, 'so as not to get mixed up with him'. That was the sort of man he was. Dukach did not like anybody, and no-one showed him the slightest goodwill, neither to his face nor behind his back; on the contrary, everyone thought that Heaven had been inexplicably slow in omitting long ago to have sent down a thunderbolt on such a boorish Cossack so as not to leave even his innards behind, and everyone, according to his ability, would have been glad to put right this omission of Providence, only Dukach, as if to spite them, never seemed to give them the chance. He was a very successful man—everything did well in his iron hands: his huge flocks of sheep multiplied like the flocks of Laban under Jacob's watchful eye. There was not enough space for them in the neighbourhood; Dukach's red oxen with their sharply angled horns were powerful and immense and were transported in new carts by the hundred to Moscow, or to the Crimea or to Nezhin; the apiary in his lime-grove in a warm fold in the hill was such that the hives ran to hundreds. In short, in Cossack terms, his wealth was incalculable. And why had God been so good to Dukach? People could only wonder and console themselves with the thought that this would all lead to no good, that God was probably 'tempting' Dukach to become ever more mighty so that He could 'smite' him in the end, and smite him so hard that the whole village would hear the crash.

Good people impatiently awaited this reckoning upon the evil Cossack, but year on year passed and God did not smite Dukach. He got richer and strutted around, and nothing ever seemed to offer the threat to his ferocity which it deserved. The public conscience was greatly troubled by this. This was all the more so because no-one could say Dukach would suffer through the actions of his children: he did not have any children. But then, all of a sudden, Dukach's old wife began avoiding people. Dukachess, as she was known, was embarrassed, or, as the locals said, 'ashamed': she did not go out in the street, and after this the news got around that Dukachess was 'not empty'.

Everyone's heart beat faster, and tongues began to wag; the public conscience which had been exhausted by long expectation now awaited imminent satisfaction.

'What sort of a child will it be! It'll be a Child of Antichrist! It'd better never be born; it should die in the womb and never see the light of day!'

They eagerly awaited events and finally their waiting was at an end: one frosty December night in Dukach's spacious house, the mother suffered the sacred pains of labour, and a child appeared.

The new inhabitant of this world was a boy, and moreover he lacked any bestial deformity, as all good people had wished; on the contrary, he was unusually well-formed and handsome, with black hair and big blue eyes.

Kerasikha, the peasant woman who brought this news to the public and who swore that the child did not have horns or a tail, was spurned and nearly beaten up, but the child remained very, very pretty, and very well-behaved into the bargain: he even breathed quietly and seemed to be ashamed to cry.

III

WHEN God granted life to this infant, Dukach, as mentioned above, was already starting his decline. His age at that time was probably something over fifty. It is well known that older fathers passionately welcome news of the birth of their first child, particularly if it is a son and heir to their land and their wealth. Dukach too was delighted by the happy event—but he expressed his delight in the manner that his stern character allowed. First of all he summoned the homeless nephew who lived with him, Agap by name, and warned him he could give up any false expectations he might have of inheriting his uncle's goods, because God had now sent his estate a real heir, and then he instructed Agap to dress up in a new long caftan and cap, and to prepare at crack of dawn to make his way to the visiting district magistrate and the priest's young daughter to fetch them to act as godparents.

Agap too was already getting on for forty, but he was a downtrodden man with the air of a chicken with a wizened head; he had a comical bald patch on one side, which was the handiwork of Dukach.

When Agap had lost his parents as a youth and was taken into Dukach's household, he had been a lively and even a bright child and had the great advantage for his uncle that he could read and write. So as not to keep his nephew free of charge, from the very start Dukach began to send him with his ox-cart drivers to Odessa. And once when Agap returned home and gave an account of his expenditure on a new cap, Dukach flew into a temper at the notion that Agap could have incurred this expense on his own initiative, and beat the boy so cruelly about the neck that he was ill for a long time and afterwards never walked quite straight; Dukach took the cap away and hung it on a nail to be eaten by moths. Agap with his twisted neck went without a cap all year and was a laughing stock to all good people. At this period he often wept bitterly and had plenty of time to think about how to ameliorate his plight. He had long since become resigned to the persecution, but people used to tell him that he could have settled matters with his uncle, not simply and directly, but by 'politics'. What they meant by political methods was to be subtle, for instance by buying a cap and not telling his uncle, but by 'ascribing' the money in small portions to other things. And on top of that, in case the worst came to the worst, he should wrap a long towel round his neck when he went to see his uncle, so that if Dukach turned violent at least it would not hurt all that much. Agap took all this advice to heart, and a year later, when his uncle despatched him to Nezhin, he left without a cap and came back with the account and with a cap which did not appear among the expenses. Dukach did not notice at first, and was inclined to praise his nephew, saying: 'I beat you, but all for nothing!' But the devil tempted Agap to show his uncle how unjust on this earth is the justice of men! He checked that the towel was firmly wrapped round his neck, as it was to serve for his political discussion, and, finding his uncle in a good mood, he said to him:

'Hey, uncle, that's good! You beat me for nothing! So is there justice in this world?'

'What sort of justice?'

'This sort—look, uncle,' and Agap flicked the paper he was holding and said: 'No cap here?'

'No,' replied Dukach.

'But there is!' boasted Agap, and placed on the side of his head his new fancy cap, made from the best rams' fleece produced in Reshetilovka.

Dukach looked at it and said:

'It's a fine cap. Let me try it on.'

He put the cap on, went to the fragment of mirror set into the wooden wall, shook his grey head and spoke again.

'Just look at what a splendid cap it is—I'd look fine in it.'

'That's right, it'd be good.'

'And where did you pinch it from, you devil?'

'Oh, uncle! Why do you think I stole it?!' said Agap. 'As God is my witness, I've never stolen anything in my life.'

'Well, who did you scrounge it from, then?'

But Agap answered that he didn't scrounge the cap: he simply just got it by politics.

This struck Dukach as so amusing and so unlikely that he roared with laughter and said:

'Oh, come on! What do you know about politics?'

'Well, that's what I did.'

'Tell me how.'

'It's true, I did.'

Dukach merely wagged his finger at him but Agap stuck to his guns, insisting that he had 'done it by politics'.

'What conceit did the devil put into your head,' said Dukach, 'that gave you the idea that a chattering clod like you could diddle somebody in Nezhin?'

But Agap stuck to his story and said that he had carried out a political trick.

Dukach got him to sit down and tell him everything about the political trick, exactly as it happened. He poured some plum brandy into a dish, lit his pipe and got ready to listen for a long time. But there was nothing to listen to. Agap simply repeated his story all over again, and said:

'Is there anything about a cap on this paper?'

'No,' said Dukach.

'But I've got a cap!'

And he revealed just exactly how many kopecks he had added under each heading of expenses, and he said it all cheerfully, open-heartedly, relying entirely on the towel wrapped round his neck; but then what he had least expected happened: Dukach, instead of beating his nephew about the neck, said:

'Damn you and your politics! You rob me and wrap your neck up so it won't hurt! I'll give you politics!' and he pulled out a clump of Agap's hair that he just happened to have in his hand.

Thus ended the political struggle between uncle and nephew, and when it became known about the village, it confirmed Dukach's reputation as a man 'made of stone'—there was no way of getting round him, neither directly nor by political means.

IV

DUKACH had always lived a lonely life: he visited no-one and nobody had any desire to be friends with him. But this did not appear to trouble Dukach one little bit. It may even be that he liked things that way. At least, he used to say with some satisfaction that in his whole life he had never had to kowtow to anyone and never would—and moreover he could not imagine any circumstances in which he would be forced to do so. And indeed, why should he ever need any friends? He had plenty of oxen and plenty of property, and if God should punish him in some way—if the oxen should drop dead, or if some of his buildings were to burn down, well, he had plenty of land, plenty of fields—everything was in order, everything would come right again and he would make good his riches as before. And if it did not come right, there was a place in a distant forest where there was a prominent oak tree with an old cooking pot buried beneath it containing some old rouble notes. He only had to fetch it from there and he would be able to live for a hundred years without spending the lot. What did other people matter to him? To help baptize his children? But he had not had any children till now. Or to pacify his wife, who used, as women will, to complain:

'People are afraid of us and they're jealous—it'd be better if somebody came to like us.'

But what attention should a self-respecting Cossack pay to a woman's nagging?

And so year upon year passed, bringing all the events and misfortunes of life onto Dukach's head without doing him very much harm, but the need to kowtow to other people none the less had not entirely escaped him: people were now urging him to have the baby baptized. Any other man less proud than Dukach would have taken this in his stride, but for Dukach to go around calling on people and asking a favour was not his style at all. And, anyway, who should he call upon and ask? — Well, certainly, not just anybody, it would have to be the very foremost citizens: the priest's young daughter who fancied herself as being in the height of fashion, and the magistrate who lodged at this time of year with the Reverend Father Deacon. Let us assume that these personages were of high status—but what if they refused? Dukach recalled that he had paid little regard not only to the common folk, but that he had shown no respect to Father Jacob, and as for the Deacon, he had even once had a set-to with him on the dyke because he would not give way and turn off into the mud to let Dukach pass. Who knows, they might not have forgotten this even now—now that this proud Cossack needed their help, they would probably remember. Well, there was nothing for it. Dukach descended to a stratagem: rather than have to face a refusal himself, he called in Agap to invite them to be godparents. And as a special inducement, he provided him with some offerings of a rural nature which he took from a secret hiding place: for the magistrate's wife a tortoiseshell comb decorated with a fruit and vegetable design, and the magistrate himself a gilt phial in the shape of a cockerel with some German writing on it. But it was all in vain: the intended godparents would have nothing to do with it and refused the gifts; they even, according to Agap, laughed in his face, and said, 'What's Dukach worried about? Does he think the children of a devil like him can be baptized?' And when Agap pointed out that the child had been unbaptized for a week now, the priest, Father Jacob, is supposed to have said prophetically: 'What's a week, when he's going to stay unbaptized for the rest of his life?'

Hearing this, Dukach cocked a snook with his right hand in his nephew's face and told him to take the same message back to Father Jacob in return for his prophecy. To make him feel further inclined to go, he took the other hand and helped him on his way with a clout on the back of his head.

V

AGAP of course did not regard this as the worst possible outcome he could have expected from his unsuccessful embassy, and taking refuge from his uncle's presence in the inn, made such a good job of telling the tale, that within half an hour the whole village knew about it, and everyone from the youngest to the oldest was delighted that Father Jacob had 'read it in a book that the little Dukach was doomed to remain unbaptized.' Even if old Dukach had then swallowed his pride and invited the lowest of the low in the village to be a godparent, he would not have found anyone to agree, but Dukach knew that: he knew he was in the position of a wolf which had fouled the territory of all the others, and he had therefore nowhere to go and no-one to support him. Having sent Agap off to deliver the rude gesture to Father Jacob, he knew what he had to do; he decided to dispense with the cooperation not only of all his fellow-villagers, but even with the services of Father Jacob himself.

To spite them all, but perhaps most of all Father Jacob, Dukach decided to have his son baptized in the next parish, in the village of Peregudy, which was only about five or six miles from Paripsy. And so as not to put off the day for too long—he wanted to have his son baptized at once, today, in fact—to silence the gossip by tomorrow; on the contrary, he wanted everyone to know by tomorrow that Dukach was a real Cossack who wasn't going to put up with mockery from anyone, and who didn't need anyone's help. He had already chosen the most unlikely godfather: Agap. It was true that this choice would surprise many, but Dukach had an answer to that: he was choosing 'people met by chance', since there was a belief that such were sent by God. It was true that Agap was the first 'chance encounter' whom the rich Cossack cast eyes on when he heard of the birth of his son; and the first woman 'chance encounter' was the peasant woman Kerasivna. To ask her to be godmother was a little awkward, because Kerasivna did not have a completely spotless reputation: she was without any doubt at all a witch; there was so little doubt of this that even her husband did not deny it. He had been an extremely jealous old Cossack called Kerasenko, but his crafty little wife had beaten all his insufferable jealousy out of him. Once she had turned him into the most downtrodden simpleton imaginable, she lived just as she liked—serving in the tavern sometimes, working sometimes as a midwife, sometimes selling wheaten bread, and finally, simply 'gathering the flowers of pleasure'.

VI

HER being a witch was known by old and young, because the eventuality which established the fact was of the most public and scandalous nature. Even before her marriage Kerasivna had been a fearlessly wilful girl. She had lived in towns, and she owned a somewhat elaborate glass drinking vessel in the shape of a horned devil, which had been a gift brought by a Rogachev landowner from the banks of the River Pokot, who used to make devilish goods like this in a nearby glass-blowing workshop. And Kerasivna used to drink to her heart's content from this vessel, and it did her nothing but good. And, as if that were not enough, she displayed the most considerable daring by agreeing to marry Kerasenko. No-one could have done this other than a woman who was absolutely fearless, because everyone knew that Kerasenko had driven two wives to their graves already, and when he could not find a third anywhere in the neighbourhood, then it was that Khristya inflicted herself upon him and married him, making only one condition: that he would always believe what she said. Kerasenko consented to this, but thought to himself:

'This woman is a fool! Do you think I'm going to trust you? Once we're married I shan't let you go a step away from me!'

Anyone else in Kerasivna's position would have foreseen that, but this bright young maiden seemed to have turned stupid: not only did she fearlessly marry a jealous widower, but she set about reforming him, so that he would stop being jealous of her and let her live her own life in freedom. This, of course, was arranged by an act of the most cunning witchcraft and with the undoubted help of the Devil himself, who had once actually been seen in human form by Kerasivna's neighbour, Pidnebesnaya.

This happened soon after Kerasenko married his bold young Khristya, and even though a good ten years had passed, the poor old Cossack well remembered the satanic event. It happened in winter, one evening, during the Christmas festivities when no Cossack, not even the most jealous one, could stay at home. But Kerasenko was adamant and would not let his wife out of his sight, and this led to a battle between them, when Kerasivna said to her husband:

'Now, then, since you have gone back on your word, I'll give you what for!'

'What for? So you'll give me what for, will you?'

'I'll do for you once and for all.'

'What'll you do if I don't let you out of my sight?'

'I'll cast a spell on you.'

'A spell? So you're a witch, are you?'

'You're about to find that out.'

'Well and good.'

'You'll see. You'll be surprised what I'll do. You keep me here, and I'll do for you good and proper.'

And she set a time limit:

'Three days,' she said, 'and it'll happen.'

The Cossack sat at home for one day, sat for two days, and sat all through the third day right until the evening, and then he thought: 'The time's up, and I don't care if a hundred devils come and fetch me away, I'm fed up with sitting here on my own at home. Pidnebesnaya's tavern is right opposite my hut; from there I'll be able to see everything if anyone comes to my door. And at the same time I'll have two or three, or even four quarts...I'll hear what people are saying around the town...I'll dance a bit—have a good time.'

So he went. He went and sat down, as he had intended, by the window so that he could see his own hut, could see the light burning; he could see his wife hanging around. Was it such a marvellous idea? And Kerasenko sat and had a drink and spent all the time looking over the road at his hut; but then widow Pidnebesnaya saw what he was doing, and thought she would have a little joke at his expense. 'You're an old fool of a Cossack,' she said, 'why are you bothering to look? You'll never see what's really going on.'

'Well, all right, we'll see!'

'You can't see much: the more men keep their eyes on us women, the more it is that the Devil helps us.'

'You can talk if you like,' said the Cossack. 'If I keep an eye on my wife, there'll be no damage done.'

At this everyone in the inn nodded in agreement.

'That's no good, Kerasenko, no good at all! Either you're an unbaptized heathen, or you've gone so far to the bad that you don't believe in the Devil any more.'

Everyone was so exercised by this that someone even called from the crowd:

'Don't look at him any more: make him turn around three times and be a good Christian again!'

And actually they nearly set about giving him a beating, in which action, as he noticed, a certain stranger played a particularly strenuous part. Kerasenko for some reason got hold of the idea that this was none other than the landowner from Rogachev who had given his wife the drinking glass with the devil on it, and about whom he and his wife had held a frank discussion before their wedding, which ended with the condition being imposed that nothing more was to be heard of this man ever.

The condition was sealed by a fearsome oath, that if Kerasenko ever so much as mentioned this landowner, he would be handed over straight to the Devil. And Kerasenko recalled this condition. Only now he was drunk, and could not resolve his puzzlement: what was the landowner doing here? So he hurried home, but his wife was not there, which struck him as even more absurd.

'He wasn't to be mentioned,' he thought, 'we agreed not to mention him, so what's he doing around here, and why isn't my wife at home?'

And while Kerasenko was engaged in these thoughts, he suddenly got the idea that on the porch outside the door someone was kissing. He started, and listened...He heard another kiss and some whispering, and then yet another kiss. And all this was happening right outside his own door...

'A thousand devils!' said Kerasenko to himself. 'Either that vodka of Pidnebesnaya's has gone to my head (since it's so long since I had any) that I'm imagining the devil knows what; or has my wife sniffed it out that I want to have a row about the Rogachev gent, and she's already cast a spell on me? People have told me more than once that she's a witch and that I just haven't seen it yet, and now...listen! They're kissing again...Oh, oh, oh!..., again and again. Just you wait—I'll catch you!'

The Cossack got down from the bench where he was lying and crept quietly to the door. He put his ear to the keyhole and listened: a couple were kissing, no doubt of it, kissing—smacking their lips, what is more...Then he could hear talking, and it was undoubtedly his wife's voice; he heard her say:

'And as for that husband of mine, heathen that he is: I'll kick him out and let you into the house.'

'Oho!' thought Kerasenko, 'so she's boasting she'll get rid of me and let someone else into the hut...That's what *she* thinks.'

And he stood up, intending to smash the door open with a mighty blow, but the door opened of itself, and there on the doorstep stood Kerasivna—looking fine, calm, though perhaps just a little flushed. She immediately flew at him, as any Little Russian wife might. She called him a son of the Devil, a drunkard, a dog, and many other names, and in conclusion reminded him of the condition that Kerasenko was not to dare be jealous. And to prove he trusted her, he was to let her go to a party. If he didn't, she would teach him a lesson he wouldn't forget in a hundred years. But Kerasenko was nobody's fool, and to let her go out after seeing with his own eyes the Rogachev landowner at Pidnebesnaya's tavern and hearing his wife kissing someone and telling him that she would let him into the house...That would, of course, be nothing short of flagrant idiocy.

'No,' he said, 'you can try it on a bigger fool than me somewhere else, but I'm going to lock you up at home and go to bed. That'll be safer; then I shan't have to fear your spell neither.'

When Kerasivna heard this, she turned pale; her husband had never before taken this tone with her, and she realized that she had reached the most serious crisis in her marital politics, and she had to win whatever the cost: or else everything she had achieved so far with such skill and perseverance would be lost without trace, and might even put her back a very long way.

And she leapt up, snapped to her full height, made a highly offensive gesture in his face, and made as if to sweep out through the door, but he had anticipated her intention and averted it by fixing the door by the chain, and, dropping the key into the immensely deep pocket of his baggy trousers, said with disconcerting calm:

'You're going nowhere except from the doorstep to the stove.'

This made Kerasivna's plight even clearer to her: she accepted her husband's challenge and flew into such an indescribable and fearsome state of frenzy that Kerasenko became quite alarmed. Khristya stood in the same place for a long time, trembling and flexing herself like a snake, while her arms contorted, her fists were firmly clenched, a rattling noise came from her throat, and on her face there appeared in turn livid and crimson patches. Meanwhile her eyes, which were trained point blank on her husband, turned sharper than knives and suddenly appeared to flash with red fire.

The Cossack found this so frightful that he did not wish to see his wife in such a rage, so he yelled:

'Curse you, you damned witch!' and blew out the light.

Kerasivna merely stamped her foot in the dark and hissed:

'You'll find out I'm a witch all right!' The suddenly she leapt up to the stove like a cat and shouted ever so resonantly up the chimney:

'Ooooh! Suffocate him, the swine!'

VII

THE Cossack was truly even more alarmed at this frenzy of his wife's, but so as not to let her escape, witch as she was, and since she obviously intended to fly off up the chimney, he seized her, pinned her arms to her sides, flung her on the bed with her back to the wall and immediately lay down beside her on the outside edge.

Much to her husband's surprise, Kerasivna offered no resistance; on the contrary, she was very calm, like a submissive child; she did not even upbraid him. Kerasenko was very relieved at this, and with one hand firmly clenched around the key in his pocket and the other grasping his wife's sleeve, he fell fast asleep.

This blessed state did not last long: he had scarcely dropped off, and his brain, bursting with alcoholic vapour, had gone all soft and lost all clarity of perception, when all of a sudden he received a jolt in the ribs.

'What is it?' he thought, and experiencing several more jolts, he muttered:

'What are you poking me for, woman?'

'If I didn't poke you, you wouldn't hear—what's going on in the yard?'

'What *is* going on?'

'Just listen!'

Kerasenko raised his head and heard a frightful squealing noise outside.

'Aha,' he said, 'someone's dragging off our pig.'

'Are they, now? Let me out at once and I'll go and see. Is the sty door locked properly?'

'Let you out? Oh, yes...!'

'Come on, give me the key or they'll get our pig, and we'll have no sausage or lard all over Christmas. Everyone else will be eating sausage and we'll just have to sit and watch them...Oho-ho-ho... Listen, you can hear they've got him. Oh, poor little thing, listen to him squealing! Let me out now and I'll go and snatch him back.'

'Oh, yes, so I'm to let you out! And where in the world is a woman supposed to do jobs like that—snatching a pig from some robbers?' said the Cossack. 'I'd better go and do it myself.'

And indeed, he did force himself to get up, though the last thing he wanted to do was go out of the warm hut into the freezing weather; but he did not want to lose the pig, so he got up, threw on his coat and went out. But then occurred the inexplicable event which provided the most indisputable evidence to confirm Kerasivna's reputation as a witch, and which made everyone from that time onwards be afraid to have her in their house, never mind ask her to be godmother, as the arrogant Dukach did.

VIII

KERASENKO had scarcely managed to open the pigsty door, where the pig, which was not at all happy with the trouble it was causing, was wailing dolefully, when something broad and soft, like a bale of sackcloth fell on top of him from out of the impenetrable darkness. At the same moment something struck the Cossack between the shoulder-blades, knocking him to the ground. He picked himself up and made sure that the pig was unharmed and lying in its usual place. Kerasenko locked it up again more firmly and went back to the hut to resume his slumbers.

But it was not to be. Not only was door of the hut firmly locked, but the porch was too. He tried here, he tried there—all locked. What devilry was this? He knocked and knocked, shouted and shouted for his wife.

'Wife! Khristya! Quick! Open the door!'

Kerasivna gave no answer.

'Damn the wretched woman! What does she mean by locking the door and going off to sleep straight away? Khristya! Hey, woman! Open the door.'

Not a sound: it was as if everything had died inside; even the pig was asleep and was not grunting.

'Here's a pretty mess!' thought Kerasenko. 'Curse you for going to sleep! Oh, well, I'll climb over the fence into the street and go to the window: she sleeps near the window, she'll hear me then.'

And that is what he did: he went to the window and knocked on it, but what should he hear? His wife said:

'Go to sleep, husband, sleep, don't you bother with whoever's knocking, it's just some wretch hanging around.'

The Cossack knocked even more loudly and shouted;

'Open up now, or I'll break the window.'

At this Khristya lost her temper and replied:

'Who's that disturbing honest folk at this time of night?'

'It's me, your husband.'

'What do you mean, my husband?'

'You know very well—Kerasenko.'

'My husband is here inside. You take yourself off, whoever you are, don't wake us up; me and my husband are asleep in bed together.'

'What's all this?' thought Kerasenko. 'Am I asleep and having a dream, or is it really happening?'

So he knocked again and shouted:

'Khristya, hey, Khristya! Open the door, there's a good girl!'

He kept on and on in this vein; but she kept silent for a long time, without answering at all; then she said:

'Take yourself off, whoever you are; I tell you my husband is at home, he's here in bed with me, here he is!'

'But Khristya, you must be imagining it.'

'Ha! Thank you for that idea! Do you think I've lost my wits, that I'm so senseless I don't know what's what? No, I'm the best judge of what's real and what isn't. Here he is, here's my man, he's right close by me...Here I am making the sign of the cross over him: Lord Jesus Christ, and now I'm kissing him, and now I'm embracing him, and kissing him again...We're perfectly happy together, and you, you evil old lecher, beat it off to your own wife, and don't stop us sleeping and kissing. Good night, and God bless!'

'Curse you, the Devil take your man: what the hell's going on here?' said Kerasenko, shrugging his shoulders. 'I suppose when I crossed the fence I got the wrong house. But no, this *is* my hut.'

He crossed to the other side of the street and set about counting houses from the well with a tall lever over it.

'One, two, three, four, five, seven, nine... It *is* mine, the ninth.'

He went back, knocked again, shouted again, and the same thing happened: again and again the woman's voice, and every time it got angrier and angrier, always to the same effect:

'Go away, my husband's here with me.'

And it was Khristya's voice, unquestionably her voice.

'Well then, if your husband is there with you, why doesn't he speak up for himself?'

'Why should he? We've said all there is to say.'

'Because I want to hear if there really is a man with you.'

'Well, there is: you just listen to us kissing!'

'Damn the pair of them! They *are* kissing, and they tell me I'm not who I am, and they're sending me off home to somewhere else. But just wait: I'm not quite mad—I'll go and get some people together and they'll tell me if it's my house or not, and if I'm my wife's husband or if someone else is. Listen, Khristya, I'm going to wake some people up.'

'Well, go on, then. But leave us in peace: we've had a good kiss, the pair of us, and we're lying here side by side and having a really good time. And we couldn't care a fig for anyone else.'

Suddenly another voice, unquestionably male, chipped in and said the same:

'We've been kissing, and we're lying side by side. So you clear off and go to the Devil!'

There was nothing else he could do: Kerasenko was sure that someone else had slipped into his place by his wife's side, and he went to wake the neighbours.

IX

WHETHER it took a long or a short time matters little, but Kerasenko, who was frantic by this time, managed to come completely to his senses and assemble twenty or so Cossacks outside his house together with a crowd of curious Cossack women who had come along with their husbands without being asked. Kerasivna, however, stayed where she was and continued to assure everyone that they were all under a false illusion, and that her husband was at home with her, was lying close by her, and to prove it she more than once let them all hear her kissing him. All the men and women heard this and thought that it could not possibly be a deception, because the kisses were genuine, and also they could hear from outside the window, though not particularly clearly, the voice of a man that Kerasivna assured them was her husband. And they all heard this voice once when it came to the window, and to everyone's alarm said:

'What do you poor deluded fools think you're doing? Here I am at home in bed with my wife; and you're all being led astray by a hallucination. Everybody give it a good hard clout, and it'll just fall apart.'

The Cossacks crossed themselves, and the man standing closest to Kerasenko struck him on the back of the head as hard as he could, and then took to his heels: all the others followed his example. And so Kerasenko was thumped by everyone, and in the space of a minute had been locked out and cruelly abandoned on the doorstep of his bewitched hut, where some cunning demon had so zealously replaced him in his own marital bed. He made no further attempt to relieve his suffering, but merely sat on a heap of snow weeping bitterly, as no real Cossack should, while all the time he could hear his wife Kerasivna kissing someone else. But, happily, all human torments come to an end—and so did Kerasenko's—he fell asleep and dreamed that his wife picked him up by the scruff of the neck and took him to his own very familiar warm bed, and when he awoke he really did find he was in his bed, in his hut, and he could see, pottering around at the hearth cooking dumplings, none other than his sprightly wife Kerasivna. In short—all was as it should be; there was nothing to remind him of the pig, or the nightmare. Kerasenko dearly wanted to talk about this, but he did not know how to introduce the matter.

And so the Cossack dismissed it all from his mind, and from that day on lived in peace and concord with his wife Kerasivna, letting her do just exactly as she liked, of which freedom she made the very best she could. She sold goods and went where she liked, and domestic happiness did not suffer in consequence, well-being and experience increased. On the other hand, Kerasivna was condemned by public opinion: everyone knew she was a witch. The cunning Cossack woman did not dispute this notion, as it gave her a certain prestige: she was feared and respected, and when people came to her for advice they would bring her either a basketful of eggs or some other little domestic gift.

X

KERASIVNA was known to Dukach too, and he knew her, needless to say, as an intelligent woman, whose advice was always worth seeking, despite her being a witch, in any awkward situation. And since Dukach himself was not a popular person, he was not particularly reluctant to approach her. People said they had seen them more than once standing together beneath the dense willow tree which grew entwined into the wattle fencing which separated their vegetable patches. There were some who were even inclined to think that there was something sinful in this, but that, of course, was pure malice. It was simply that Dukach and Kerasivna, having something in common as far as their reputations were concerned, were acquainted and found things to talk to each other about.

So it was now, in the annoying predicament consequent on Dukach's unsuccessful search for godparents, that he remembered

Kerasivna, and called her in for counsel, telling her all about the offence people had been causing him.

She listened to all this, considered it briefly and with a shake of her head cut in abruptly:

'Well, then, Mr Dukach: let me be godmother!'

'You be godmother?' Dukach repeated, considering the proposition.

'Yes—or perhaps you believe I'm a witch?'

'Hm! People do say you're a witch, but I see no sign of it.'

'And you won't.'

'Hm! You as godmother...What will people say about that?'

'What, those people? The people who wouldn't come into your house even to spit on the floor?'

'That's true, but what will my old woman say? She thinks you *are* a witch.'

'Are you afraid of her?'

'Afraid?..I'm not such a fool as your husband: I'm not afraid of women or anybody else: it's just...You aren't really a witch?'

'There you go, Mr Dukach, you're a fool like all the others. Go on then, you'd better ask somebody else to be godmother.'

'Now wait, wait, don't be angry: be a witch if you like. But, look here, do you think the priest in Peregudy will perform the baptism if you are godmother?'

'Why shouldn't he?'

'God knows—he's a bit of a scholar—works from the Bible all the time. He'll say it's not his parish.'

'Don't worry—he won't say that: he may be a scholar, but his wife's all right...He may work from the Bible, but in the end he'll be like everyone else—he'll do as his wife says. I know him well, and I was with him once at a party, where he wouldn't drink anything. He said: "It says in the Bible, be not drunk with wine, wherein is excess", and I said, "Excess it may be, but go on, you have a glass," and he had one.'

'He had one?'

'Yes.'

'That's all right, then, but just watch out in case a glass of wine does some harm to our little lad: gets him christened Ivan instead of Nikola.'

'Very well, then, I'll see he's christened Nikola. Unless you think I don't know that's a Moscow name?'

'That's right, it's Moscow as can be.'

There was one other matter, concerning the fact that Kerasivna did not have a big enough sheepskin to take the baby to Peregudy, and the weather was icy in the extreme, real St Barbara's Day cold, but Dukachess had a magnificent nankeen-lined coat. Dukach took it and gave it to Kerasivna without asking his wife.

'There you are,' he said, 'it's yours now, but don't dawdle. I don't want people saying Dukach didn't christen his baby for three days.'

Kerasivna made some difficulties over the coat, but in the end took it. She turned up the fur-lined sleeves a long way, and everyone in the village watched as the witch, provocatively setting her colourful bonnet on the back of her head, got into the sledge with Agap. It was harnessed to a pair of Dukach's powerful stallions, and they set off to Father Jeremiah in the village of Peregudy, about six miles away. When Kerasivna and Agap departed, the curious onlookers noted that both godfather and godmother were sober enough. And what if Agap, who was driving, was seen to have a little cask of brandy in his lap? That was obviously for the entertainment of the clergy of the parish to which he was bound. Kerasivna had the baby wrapped in the front of her newly-acquired dark blue hareskin coat. This was the child whose baptism was destined to give rise to the strangest turn of events, a fact which many knowing people keenly foresaw. They knew that God would not allow the son of such an evil man as Dukach to be baptized, least of all with an infamous witch as godmother. It would bring faith in the sacrament of baptism thoroughly into disrepute!

No, God is just. He could not and would not allow such a thing.

Dukachess held the same belief. She bitterly lamented the wilfulness of her husband in choosing an undoubted witch as baptismal sponsor for this long-awaited child.

Surrounded by these circumstances and predictions Agap and Kerasivna departed, with the Dukaches' child, from the village of Paripsy to Peregudy where Father Jeremiah was priest.

This all happened in December, two days before the feast of St Nicholas, around two in the afternoon, in fairly fresh weather with a strong 'Moscow' wind, which, as soon as Agap and Kerasivna had departed, whipped up into a fierce snowstorm. The sky above was leaden, lower down the snowflakes whirled and a cruel blizzard set in.

Everyone who wished ill to Dukach's infant saw this, crossed themselves devoutly and felt fully satisfied: there could be no doubt now that God was on their side.

XI

THESE premonitions made Dukach himself uneasy: however strong-minded he was, he was none the less prone to superstitious fears and—he was a coward. It was true, for whatever reason, that the storm which was now threatening godparents and child had burst out exactly as they passed the village boundary. But the most disturbing thing of all was that Dukach's wife, who had spent her whole life in servile silence before her husband, suddenly opened her usually wordless mouth and said:

'In our old age and for my consolation, God gave us a child, and now you've eaten him alive.'

'What is all that?' Dukach interrupted. 'How have I eaten him alive?'

'You gave him to that witch. Where in the whole of the Cossack Christian world have you ever heard of giving a child to a witch to take it to be baptized?'

'But she'll *have* him baptized—that's what she's gone for.'

'It's never happened, and it never will; God wouldn't ever allow an evil witch to approach a Christian font.'

'Anyway, who told you Kerasivna was a witch?'

'Everybody knows it.'

'It's all very well for people to say that, but no-one's seen a tail on her, have they?'

'They haven't seen her tail, but everyone saw how she tamed her husband.'

'Why shouldn't she tame a fool like him?'

'She stopped everyone from buying Pidnebesnaya's white bread.'

'Because Pidnebesnaya is too fond of her sleep and doesn't knead the dough at night, her bread is worse.'

'There's no point in arguing with you, but ask anyone you like, any *good* people, and they'll all tell you the same thing: Kerasivna is a witch.'

'Why trouble other good people when I'm a good person myself?'

Dukachess turned to face her husband and said:

'What? You're a good man, are you?'

'Yes, what do you think? Are you telling me I'm not?'

'Of course you aren't.'

'Who told you that?'

'And who told you you *were* good?'

'And who said I wasn't?'

'Who have you ever done any good to in your life?'

'Who have I ever done good to?'

'Yes.'

'The Devil take it, it's true I can't think of anyone I've ever done good to,' thought Dukach, unaccustomed to being argued with like this, and so as not to have to listen to any more of this conversation, unpleasant as it was for him, he said:

'I can do without talking to a woman like you.'

So saying, and so as not to have to stay in the same hut as his wife, he snatched the astrakhan cap that he had taken from Agap long ago and went for a walk outside.

XII

DUKACH must have had many uncomfortable thoughts on his mind, seeing that he spend a good two hours outside, because it was sheer hell in the open air: a violent storm was raging, the dense snow was driving and whirling and it was impossible to draw breath.

If it was like that near people's dwellings, in a sheltered spot, what must it have been like in the open steppe, where the full fury of the storm must have been raging around the godparents and the child? If conditions were overwhelming for a grown-up person, did it need much to suffocate a little baby?

Dukach realized all this, and doubtless gave it a good deal of thought, because it was certainly not for pleasure that he dragged himself through the fearful snowdrifts towards the dyke which ran outside the village and sat there for a long time in the half-light—he sat so long, obviously desperately impatient to see something where nothing could possibly be seen. Dukach stood for ever such a long time in the centre of the dyke, until it was quite dark—there was no-one to shift him from his position, and he saw no-one, except that it seemed a wild round-dance was going on above his head and peppering him with snow. At last he tired of this endless hallucination, and as nightfall approached and the darkness intensified, he uttered a croak, extracted his feet from the drift which had covered them by now, and set off home.

Finding his way slowly, painfully and uncertainly through the snow, he stopped several times, lost his way and found it again. He went on again, moved forward and stumbled on something which he felt with his hands and realized was a wooden cross—a very, very tall wooden cross of the sort that are placed by the roadsides in Little Russia.

'Aha, that means I'm outside the village! I'd better go back,' thought Dukach and turned in another direction, but he had scarcely taken three steps before the cross was again straight in front of him.

The Cossack paused, took a breath, and correcting himself, went another way, but here too a cross was barring his path.

'What, is it moving ahead of me or something, or what's going on?'—and he felt around with his hands and investigated the cross, and another and yet another alongside it.

'Ah, now I see where I am: I've strayed into the cemetery. There's the light in our priest's window. That bastard wouldn't let his daughter be godmother. Well, I didn't need her. But why the devil isn't Matveiko the sexton here?'

And Dukach set off to find the sexton's hut, but suddenly fell into a pit and struck something so hard that he lay senseless for some time. When he came to, he saw that all was calm around him and he could see the star-covered sky.

Dukach realized he had fallen into a grave and set to work with hands and feet, but it was not easy to get out, and it was a good hour before he could scramble out. He spat in irritation.

Some considerable time must have passed, an hour at least—the storm had noticeably quietened, and the sky was clear and starry.

XIII

DUKACH made his way home and was very surprised to see that neither his house nor any of his neighbours' were showing a light. It was obvious that it must be very late. Surely Agap and Kerasivna must have returned by this time with the baby?

Dukach felt a tightening of the heart which he had not experienced for a long time, as he opened the door with an uncertain hand.

It was dark in the hut, but in the far corner behind the stove he could hear plaintive sobbing.

It was his wife weeping. The Cossack realized what the matter was, but he could not refrain from asking:

'Aren't they back yet?'

'By this time the witch will be eating my baby,' burst out Dukachess.

'You're a stupid woman,' replied Dukach sharply.

'Then it's you who made me stupid; but I'm not so stupid as to give my own baby to a witch.'

'Oh, drop dead, you and your witch; I nearly broke my neck falling in a grave.'

'Ah, in a grave...well, it's her that led you into a grave. You'd do better to go off and kill something.'

'Kill what? What are you on about?'

'Go and kill something, if it's only a sheep,—or else the grave will have swallowed you up for some good reason, and you'll die soon. And why not: it's all people like us deserve—everyone will say we gave our child away to a witch.'

And she continued to expatiate on this theme, whilst Dukach was thinking all the time: where *is* Agap, where has he got himself to? If they'd got to Peregudy before the blizzard really blew up, they'd have waited there until it died down, but in that case they should have set off again for home as soon as it improved, and they should have been here by now.

'I wonder if Agap drank a bit too much from the cask?'

This idea seemed quite possible to Dukach, and he hastened to pass it on to his wife, but she simply moaned:

'There's no point in speculating, we're never going to see our child again: that witch Kerasivna has eaten him, and she caused the bad weather, and now she's flying away with him over the hills and drinking his scarlet blood!'

This infuriated Dukach so much that he cursed his wife roundly, and he grabbed his rifle from one shelf and his fur cap from the other and went out again, intending to shoot a hare and throw it into the grave where he had fallen, while his wife stayed behind to bewail her misfortunes by the hearth.

XIV

THE Cossack was angered and upset in a most unaccustomed way for him, and he had no idea what to do with himself, but since he had blurted out his intention regarding a hare, he found his way more automatically than intentionally to the barn, where there were mischievous hares running around. He sat down by a bale of oats and meditated.

He was tormented by premonitions, and sadness entered his heart and aroused troublesome memories. However unpleasant his wife's words had been to him, he admitted that she was right. It was true that he had never done a good action to anyone in his whole life; rather had he done a lot of harm to a lot of people. And now, because of his obstinacy, his one and only, long-awaited, child would perish, and he himself had fallen into a grave, which according to the universal belief could bode nothing but ill. Tomorrow the whole world would know about all this, and the whole world was his enemy. But...perhaps the child would be found yet, and so, to distract his mind, he would stay up all night seeking a hare to kill, and by so doing would avert the threat of the impending grave.

Dukach sighed and began to peer around: was there a hare hopping around the steppe or scratching around under the stacks of grain?

There was indeed. A hare awaited him as the ram awaited Abraham: near the last bale of oats, on the wattle fence covered with snow, level with the top, was a fully-grown grey hare. It was clearly surveying the area and it occupied the most superb position for Dukach to aim at.

Dukach was an old and experienced huntsman; he had seen many sights when hunting, but he had never before had a sitting target like this, and so as not to lose his chance, he took aim and fired.

The shot rang out, and as it did, a strange feeble groan came through the air, but Dukach had little time to think: he ran forward to stamp on the still-smoking wad, but having stepped on it, he stopped in the most uneasy surprise: the hare, which was still a few paces in front of Dukach, went on sitting where it had been and did not move.

Dukach again took fright: in truth, was the Devil playing tricks on him? Was it a werewolf before his eyes? Dukach made a snowball and hurled it at the hare. The snowball hit its target and shattered, but the hare still did not move—only a groan again sounded. 'What witchcraft is this?' thought Dukach; he crossed himself and cautiously approached what he had taken to be a hare, but it was not and had never been a hare: it was simply a sheepskin cap sticking out of the snow. Dukach grabbed the cap and by the light of the stars saw the lifeless face of his nephew which was covered with something dark, sticky and with a damp smell. It was blood.

Dukach trembled, flung down his shotgun, and returned to the village, where he woke everyone up and told them the dark deed he had done; he repented before everyone, saying: 'The Lord is just to punish me,—go and dig them all out of the snow, and tie me up and take me to the magistrate!'

Dukach's request was granted: they tied him up and locked him in another hut, and the whole community went in the direction of the barn to dig out Agap.

XV

BENEATH a heap of snow which had covered the sledge they found the bloodstained body of Agap, and—unharmed, though nearly frozen stiff—Kerasivna, on whose breast the baby was sleeping, completely unharmed. The horses were standing here too, up to their bellies in snow, with their heads drooping over the fence.

Once the horses were freed a little from the drift they began to move and brought the frozen godparents and the child back to the village. Dukachess did not know what she should do: bewail the misfortune of her husband or rejoice at the salvation of the baby. She took the little boy into her arms and brought him to the fire; when she saw he was wearing a cross, she burst into joyful tears, and then carried him before the icon and with passionate delight, in a deeply emotional voice said:

'Lord! for saving him and bringing him beneath Thy cross, I shall never forget Thy goodness to me; I shall bring up this child and give him to Thee. Let him be Thy servant.'

So was the oath sworn which came to have such significance in our story, where so far we have heard nothing of an 'priest who was not baptized', while actually he *is* here, just as Agap's famous cap seemed not to exist, but really did.

But I continue with the story: the baby was in full health; by simple peasant remedies Kerasivna too recovered, though she seemed to understand little of what was going on around her and repeated over and over again:

'The child is baptized,—call him Savka.'

That was enough for such a stressful occasion, and even the name was to everyone's taste. Even Dukach in his disturbed state approved it and said:

'Thanks to the priest at Peregudy for not spoiling the lad by calling him Nikola.'

At this point Kerasivna came to and said that the priest had wanted to call the child Nikola: 'He said that's what it should be according to the church book', only she disputed this reasoning: 'I said, thank God for church books in their place, but you can't call a good Cossack child by a Moscow name like Nikola.'

'Those were good Cossack words,' said Dukach, and he told his wife to give her a cow, and he promised that if he got through this, he would find some way of repaying the good turn she had done them.

The business of the baptism ended there, and the long and gloomy funeral period began. Agap never recovered his senses. His head, wounded by a thick piece of small shot, turned black even before it could be cleaned, and in the evening of the following day he gave up his greatly-suffering soul to God. That same evening three Cossacks, armed with long staves, took old Dukach away to town and handed him over to the authorities, who put him in jail as a murderer.

Agap was buried, Dukach was sentenced, the child grew, and Kerasivna almost recovered, but never quite 'regained full strength'. She changed markedly—she walked around as though she was simply not herself. She became quiet, sad and often pensive; she gave up quarrelling with her husband Kerasenko, who could not make head or tail of what had happened to his little wife. His life, which had so far been totally dependent on her obstinacy and self-will, became peaceful in the extreme: he never heard the slightest objection to anything from his wife, and no reproach, and—never seeing nor dreaming of the gentleman from Rogachev—he could not believe his luck. This astonishing change in Kerasivna's character was long and vainly discussed on market day: even her friends—loud-mouthed fellow-stallholders—would say that she had 'gone all kind'. And, to tell you straight, with the possible exception of one or two of the male customers of the market stall where she sold bread, she never called down the Devil on anyone's father, their mother or on any other of their relations. There was a rumour going around that the landowner from Rogachev had twice appeared in Paripsy, but that Kerasivna would have nothing to do with him. Her rival, the baker Pidnebesnaya, even she, not wanting to harm her immortal soul, used to say that she heard once how this gentleman came up to Kerasivna to buy a loaf, and got these words in reply:

'Clear off, and don't let me ever see you again. I've got nothing for you: nothing to give, nothing to sell.'

And when the gentleman asked what had happened to her, she said:

'It's hard: I have a great secret.'

The incident upset old Dukach's life too. Under the good old legal dispensation he was sentenced to three years and was confined in prison on the suspicion that he might have killed his nephew deliberately, and then, his good behaviour not having been vouched for by the other inhabitants of the village, he narrowly escaped being exiled. But the matter ended when his fellow-villagers took pity on him and agreed to have him back just as soon as he had expiated his sin in a monastery through the penance imposed upon him by the church.

Dukach was able to live at home only by the grace of the very people he had despised and hated all his life...This was a terrible lesson to him, and Dukach accepted it in exemplary fashion. Having served his formal term of punishment, after five years he arrived in Paripsy as a man of advanced years, confessed his pride to all and asked everyone's forgiveness, and left again for the monastery where he had done penance by the court's decision. He took with him his tin box full of roubles to pay for prayers 'for three souls'. Which three souls these were Dukach himself did not know, but this was what Kerasivna had said to him: that because he was such a dreadful character, it was not just Agap who had been lost, but two other souls that were known only to God and herself—to Kerasivna, that is, but she could not tell it to anyone.

All of this therefore remained a mystery, and a box in the monastery full of thick old rouble notes had something to do with it.

Meanwhile the child, whose appearance in the world and whose baptism had been accompanied by the events described, grew a little older. Brought up by his mother—a straightforward but very good-natured and tender woman—he rejoiced in her tenderness and good nature. I shall remind you that when this child was returned to his mother from Kerasivna's bosom, Dukachess had 'promised him to God.' Such 'promises' were usual in Little Russia until very recently and were punctiliously observed—particularly if the 'promised' children had no objection. Even so, cases of objection if there were any at all were very rare, and this was doubtless because 'promised children' were brought up from their earliest years in such a way that their character was of the appropriate cast. When the child reached a certain age in this frame of mind, not only did he not resist the parental 'promise', but even strove on his own account to fulfil the promise with a pious sense of submission, of a type which is only attainable to living faith and love. Savva Dukachev, as he came to be properly known, was raised precisely in this manner and early in his life discovered a real desire to fulfil the promises made on his behalf by his mother. In his very earliest childhood, being of a rather tender and gentle constitution, he was remarkably God-fearing. Not only did he never destroy birds' nests nor attack frogs with a stick, but he was the protector of all gentle creatures. The word of his tender mother for him was law—sacred, as much as delightful—because it agreed in all respects with the requirements of his own tender child's heart. To love God was for him both a requirement and his greatest pleasure, and he loved Him in everything which reflected God in himself and made Him both understood and invaluable for the person to whom He came and in whom He made his abode. Everything that surrounded the child was religious: his mother was pious and prayerful; his father lived in a monastery and was repenting of something. The child knew from a few hints that his birth was connected with something or other which had changed their domestic lives,—and all of this took on a certain mystical character in his eyes. He grew under the protection of God and knew that from His hand no-one should ever pluck him. At the age of eight he was sent to school with Pidnebesnaya's brother Okhrim Pidnebesny, who lived in Paripsy in a back street behind of his sister's tavern, but had no connexion with that establishment, and led an unusual life.

XVI

OKHRIM Pidnebesny belonged to a very interesting new Little-Russian type which began to be defined and shaped in the settlements beyond the Dnieper around the first quarter of the present century. At the present time this type has emerged quite clearly and is readily recognizable by its powerful influence on the religious spirit of the local population. It is really astonishing that those who study our society and others who love the common people and occupy themselves poking around some of the more trivial aspects of rural life have either overlooked or do not consider worthy of their attention those ordinary folk in Little Russia who have set a completely new stream flowing in the religious life of the people of southern Russia. I have no time to repair this omission here, and it is beyond my powers; I shall simply tell you that they were a sort of *hermit in the world*: they built little shacks onto their family homes in a secluded corner, they lived clean and chaste lives, both internally and externally. They avoided none of their fellows and did not keep themselves apart; they worked and laboured alongside their family members and were models of industry and thrift, they did not avoid social intercourse with others, but introduced a special, rather puritanical, character into all their doings. They greatly respected 'learning', and every one of them without exception was literate; but their literacy was used for the study of the Word of God, which they undertook with passionate zeal and reverence, but also with the presupposition that it was preserved in a pure form only in the single volume of the New Testament, while in the 'tradition of men' followed by the clergy all was distorted and corrupted. It is said that these ideas have been instilled in them by German colonists, but in my opinion it is irrelevant who instilled it; I know only that from all this developed the so-called 'Shtunda'.

Pidnebesnaya's unmarried brother Okhrim the Cossack was one of these people: he had taught himself to read and write and to read the Scriptures, and he considered it his duty to teach the same to others. He taught anyone he could, and always for nothing, expecting no more payment for his work than was promised to 'whomsoever shall do and teach'. This teaching usually decreased in summer when there was a great deal of work to do in the fields, but it increased in autumn and continued through the winter until the spring sowing. The children came for lessons during the day, and later people assembled at Pidnebesny's for 'evenings', social gatherings of working people, as they might anywhere else. Only at Okhrim's they did not sing vapid songs or engage in empty chat, but the young girls spun flax and wool, and Okhrim, having placed a plate of honey and a plate of nuts on the table to entertain his visitors 'in the name of Christ', would seek permission in return to 'speak of Christ'. The young people allowed him to do so, and Okhrim treated his guests to honey, nuts and Gospel teaching, and soon he so caught their interest that not one of these young lasses and lads had any desire to go to gatherings elsewhere. The discussions would sometimes take place without honey and nuts.

Okhrim's evening meetings also led to friendships, the consequence of which turned out to be marriage, but here a very strange thing was observed which worked mightily to advance Okhrim's reputation: all the young people who fell in love at Okhrim's evenings and later got married were happy with each other. Needless to say, the reason for this was most likely because their friendship came about in the peaceful atmosphere of spirituality, and not in the turmoil of passion and debauchery—when choice is led by the desires of the blood rather than the sensitive attraction of the heart. In a word, as the Scripture says: 'God setteth the solitary in families...but the rebellious dwell in a dry land'. Thus Pidnebesny's reputation grew, and, despite his simplicity and undemanding nature, he gained in Paripsy the most honourable position: that of a man pleasing to God. No-one came to him for censure, merely because he never judged anybody, but everyone wished to learn from him if they 'hope towards God that there shall be a resurrection of the dead.'

XVII

AT that time a few men like Okhrim Pidnebesny had emerged in Little Russia, but they lived unobtrusively and long remained unobserved by any but the peasant community.

Twenty-five years later these people drew more attention to themselves, appearing in that wide and closely-knit religious community which is known as the 'Shtunda'. I was very well acquainted with one of their leaders: he was an open-hearted, good-natured unmarried and unattached Cossack. Like the majority of his fellows, he had taught himself to read and write, and he single-handedly taught all the local children and young women. These last he taught at the evening meetings, or, as the Great Russians would say, at informal 'sit-down gatherings' in his hut, to which they would bring their work: the girls would sew or spin, and he would speak of Christ.

Their discussions were of the simplest, totally foreign to any consideration of dogmatics or institutions of worship, and they had as their almost exclusive aim the moral education of the individual according to Christ's teaching. My Cossack preacher friend lived, however, on the left bank of the Dnieper, in a place where there is not yet a Shtundist community.

At the time our story took place, moreover, this teaching had still not been clearly worked out, even on the right bank of the Dnieper.

XVIII

DUKACH'S little boy Savka was presented for instruction to Pidnebesny, and he, noting the boy's quick mind on the one hand and his passionate religious spirit on the other, took to him very strongly. Savva repaid his sincere teacher in the same coin. Thus a bond formed between them that was so strong and tender, that when old Dukach took his son to enter him in the monastery and thus dedicate him according to his mother's promise to the service of God, the boy was very homesick, not so much for his mother as for his open-hearted teacher. And this feeling so affected the boy's weak constitution that he soon fell ill and took to his bed. He would doubtless have died if Pidnebesny had not come to see him quite by chance.

He realized the reason for the illness of his little friend, and when he returned to Paripsy found a way of persuading Dukachess that an offering to God should not amount to infanticide. He therefore advised that the boy should not be confined in the monastery any longer, but that he should be made 'a living sacrifice'. Pidnebesny proposed a means which was not entirely strange or unknown to the Little-Russian Cossack mind: he advised that Savva should be entered in a 'spiritual college', from whence he could go on later to a seminary—he might then become a village priest, and every village priest may do a great deal of good to poor and uneducated people, and therefore become a friend to Christ and a friend to God.

Dukachess was convinced by Okhrim's arguments and the adolescent Savka was withdrawn from the monastery and entered in the spiritual college. Everyone approved this step with the single exception of Kerasivna, who, probably by reason of her advanced years, had been possessed of a gloomy spirit of contradiction, which expressed itself in frenzied behaviour where the affairs of her godson were concerned. It was as if she both loved and pitied him, but at the same time, God knows how, she caused embarrassment on his account.

This began when he was a very little child: Savka would be taken up to receive communion in church, and Kerasivna would cry:

'What are you doing! Don't do that, don't take him forward... a child like that...he can't receive communion.'

They took no notice of her—she would turn positively green in the face and either laugh or demand of the congregation:

'Let me out—so my eyes can't see him receive the blood of Christ.'

When they asked what her objection was, she would reply:

'It's a burden I have to bear,' from which they all concluded that when she had transformed her life ceased to practise witchcraft, the Devil had found in her heart a house empty, swept and garnished, and had entered in and dwelt there, taking with himself several other demons which did not love the infant Savka.

And indeed, the 'demons' made a terrific fuss when Savka was taken off to the monastery: they so inflamed Kerasivna's mind that she chased after the sledge for more than two miles, shouting:

'Don't endanger your immortal soul! Don't take him to the monastery. It's not a sacrifice well-pleasing unto God.'

But, of course, she was not heeded,—and now that there was talk of sending the boy to the college 'to turn him into a priest', Kerasivna suffered a great misfortune: she had a stroke and was paralysed. She lost the power of speech for a long time, and it did not return until the boy had been sent away.

It is true that when Savka was entered in the college there was one other slight difficulty, which was that they could not find his name in the official registers of the church at Peregudy. This would have been a disaster for a secular school, but in a church college it was treated more flexibly. In church colleges they know that the clergy often forget to write even their own children's names into the registers. After the christening they do not stint on the drink and are afraid to write because their hand is trembling; the next day they have a hangover, and the day after that they have forgotten about it. Such cases are well known, and of course this is what must have happened here, and therefore, although the Warden cursed the clergy concerned for a crowd of drunkards, he accepted the boy anyway, since his name did appear in the record of confessions. Savka's name appeared here very clearly and indisputably, and more than once a year at that.

This factor put everything to rights,—and the excellent boy worked admirably: he passed out of the college and then out of the seminary; he was destined for training for the episcopate in the theological academy, but to everyone's surprise refused to go and expressed the desire to be an ordinary priest, and in a country parish too. The young theologian's father, old Dukach, had died by this time, but his mother, now an old woman, was still living in the same place in Paripsy, where just at this very time the priest died and there was a vacancy. The young man took his place. The unexpected news of the appointment delighted the Cossack community in Paripsy, but the aged Kerasivna completely lost her reason.

Hearing that her godson Savva was to be the village priest, she shamelessly rent her skirt and tore off her beads; she flung herself down on a compost heap and wailed:

'O, earth, earth, swallow us both up!' But then, when this mood had somewhat left her, she stood up, crossed herself and went off into her hut. An hour later she was seen, dressed all in black with a stick in her hands marching along the high road to the provincial capital, where Savva Dukachev's ordination was to take place.

Several people met Kerasivna on the high road and all saw that she was walking in great haste,—not sitting down to rest and not conversing with anyone on the way. She looked as if she was marching to her death: her eyes were turned upwards and she was whispering continuously,—doubtless, praying. But God did not hear her prayer. Although she reached the cathedral at the very moment when the deacons were tapping the ordinand on the shoulders and shouting, 'Is he worthy?' no-one heeded the village woman in the crowd who cried, 'He is unworthy, he is unworthy!' The candidate was ordained, and the peasant woman was expelled from the church and eventually released after she had spent ten days or so in the police station washing the clothes of the whole staff and chopping up two barrels of cabbages. Kerasivna was only interested in one thing: 'Was Savva a priest?' And discovering that he indeed was, she fell to her knees and crawled six or seven miles on her knees back to Paripsy, where the new 'Father Savva' was already in residence.

XIX

THE Cossacks of Paripsy, as I said, were very glad that they had been granted a priestly father from their own Cossack breed, and welcomed Father Savva with great warmth. They were particularly well-disposed towards him because he was very solicitous of his old mother, and straight away on his arrival asked after his 'godmother',—although he had doubtless heard that she had been, well, one thing and another—and a witch. He did not allow this to poison his attitude in the slightest. In all, everyone thought that this man promised to be a very good priest, and indeed this is just what he turned out to be. Everyone loved him, and even Kerasivna had nothing to say against him, but only sometimes frowned and sighed, whispering:

'Aye, he's all right, but if only there was some fish in the fish soup!'

But she seemed to think there was no fish, and you cannot have fish soup without fish. Therefore, however good Father Savva was, he was worth nothing, and one day that would be revealed.

And indeed people did begin to notice some oddness in him: first of all he was poor, but was totally indifferent to money. Secondly, when his wife died, as she very soon did, he did not make a great song and dance, and did not employ a pretty young housekeeper, and thirdly, when a group of the village women came to him and said they were going on a pilgrimage to Kiev, he advised them to change their minds and promise to serve the poor and the sick, and most important of all to make sure that they lived a good life at home among their families; as for the oath they had sworn to go on a pilgrimage—he demonstrated unheard-of audacity—he absolved them from it and took the obligation upon himself. 'To release someone from an oath sworn to the saints'...! To many this seemed like sacrilege of a sort scarcely possible for a baptized Christian. But here the matter ended—Father Savva soon gave even greater cause for concern about himself:

during his first Lent when people came to him for spiritual counsel, it emerged that he did not forbid anyone to eat whatever God sent, and did not instruct anyone to perform penitential bows before the icons, and if he did impose any penance, then there were oddities here too. For example, in the case of Gavrilka the miller, who was known to take payment in kind for the milling using a very deep scoop, Father Savva ordered him immediately after confession to cut the top edge off this ladle so as not to take too much grain. I not, he would be barred from communion—and Savva gave him good reason from the Scriptures, showing that 'a false balance is abomination to the Lord' and may incur punishment. The miller obeyed and everyone ceased to resent him; they brought grain to him to be milled without ceasing. He confessed to everyone that this was the result of the penance Savva imposed upon him. A young and very irascible woman, married for the second time, took against the children of the first marriage. Father Savva intervened in this matter, and after she had performed her penance for the first time, the young stepmother changed and became loving to her stepchildren. He did accept money in expiation of sin, but did not spend it on incense or candles; it maintained two homeless orphans, Mikhalka and Potapka, who lived with Father Savva in the space below the bell-tower.

'Yes,' Father Savva would say to a woman or a girl, 'God grant that your sin will be forgiven and that you will sin no more; but you see to it that you serve the Lord earnestly.'

'I'm glad of it, Father, but I don't know how to serve Him... Perhaps go to Kiev on pilgrimage.'

'No, you shouldn't go away,—work at home and don't do what you were doing before; and now you can go and measure up the orphans Mikhalka and Potapka, and make them a pair of breeches each, short ones, and a couple of shirts. They're growing fast and they're embarrassed to be showing people their bare midriffs.'

The sinners were glad to carry out this penance, and Mikhalka and Potapka lived under Father Savva's protection as if in the bosom of Christ—and not only did they not show their bare midriffs, but scarcely noticed that they were orphans.

Penances like this were not only within everyone's power to carry out, but in many cases very much to people's liking—they were even a consolation. Only, in the end, Father Savva did something which cost him dear. People not of his parish started coming to his little church from Peregudy, where he had been baptized and where another priest was now serving, not the one with whom Kerasivna in her youth used to go drinking, and to whom, on the strength of this acquaintance, she had taken Savka Dukachev to be baptized. This marked the beginning of a certain animosity towards Father Savva on the part of the priest at Peregudy, and a very damaging event took place. A parishioner of Peregudy, a rich Cossack called Oseledets, died, and as he lay dying he announced his intention of leaving what he called 'a heap of roubles for a great tocsin', that is, to buy a large bell for the church, but suddenly, having had a talk with Father Savva as he lay dying, he sharply changed his intention and left nothing for the 'great tocsin', but summoned three good farmers and declared that he would give them the heap of money to be used for 'whatever work of God Father Savva should say'.—Oseledets the Cossack died, and Father Savva used the heap of money to build a light and airy hut with opening windows, where he assembled the children and taught them reading, writing and Holy Scripture.

The Cossacks thought this was probably a good thing, but they did not know if it was 'pleasing unto God'. The priest at Peregudy explained it to them in such a way that it seemed unpleasing. He promised to enter an official complaint, which he did. The Archbishop summoned Father Savva, but dismissed him with his blessing, and he continued his good deeds: he worked and taught in the school, at home, in the fields and in his little wooden church. A few years passed. The priest at Peregudy, to compete with Father Savva, had a stone church built at this time, far better than the one at Paripsy, and he obtained a valuable icon, to which various miracles were ascribed, but Savva did not envy him his miracles, and continued to go about his work in his own quiet way. He went on conducting worship and reading the Word of God, and the same old little wooden church was at times full to overflowing, while the Peregudy priest in his stone temple had so much space that he and the sexton had the place to themselves with scarcely anyone else; he could walk around and see the church mouse come out from under the ambo and then run back and hide there again. And finally this became a great irritation to the Peregudy priest, but he might be as enraged against his neighbour in Paripsy, Father Savva, as he liked, because he could dig up nothing to Father Savva's discredit, and the Archbishop too defended Savva, even for persuading Oseledets to change his mind so that the pile of money went not to a new bell for the church, but for the school. For a long time the priest at Peregudy put up with this, contenting himself with constructing various nonsense of the type that he was a sorcerer and his godmother had been known as a loose woman in her youth and remained a witch to this day, because she would not go to confession and could not die, because it says in the Bible 'God desireth not the death of a sinner, but rather that he may turn from his wickedness and live.' But she doesn't turn from her wickedness,—she fasts, but she doesn't go to confession, he maintained.

This was indeed true: old Kerasivna, who had long since renounced all her sinful ways and even lived honourably and in the fear of God, did not go to confession. And, well, rumours emerged again that she was a witch, and that maybe Father Savva was 'giving her some comfort'.

This gossip got around, and then there was another trivial occurrence: the cows began to yield less milk...Whose fault could that be, if not a witch's; and what greater witch was there than old Kerasivna, who, as everyone knew, had cast a spell on the whole village, who had tamed her husband with the help of the Devil, and who had now outlived all her contemporaries, had not been to confession, and did not seek to die.

They really had to bring both these matters to a head, and a few good people undertook this, agreeing between them that whoever should first meet old Kerasivna in a dark place would strike her—as any decent Orthodox Christian should strike a witch—once, with the back of the hand, and say to her:

'Die, or I'll hit you again.'

And one of these God-fearing people, who was in this little conspiracy, was lucky: he met Kerasivna in a lonely place and managed to treat her to one good blow, so that she fell over backwards and groaned:

'Oh, I'm dying, fetch the priest, I want to confess.'

So the witch knew at once why she had been attacked!

But they had scarcely got her home, and Father Savva had rushed to her in alarm, when she changed her mind and began to play for time:

'I can't confess to you,' she said, 'the confession will be no good. I want another priest!'

The good Father Savva immediately, lending his own horse for the purpose, sent to Peregudy for his deadly rival, the priest there, and feared only one thing, that he would play the fool and refuse to come; but this fear was not realized: the priest from Peregudy came, went in to see the dying woman and remained with her for a very long time indeed. He then emerged from the hut onto the back steps, put safely away the travelling case in which the sacred elements were kept, and, well, he just burst out into a positively indecent fit of laughter. He laughed so much that he simply could not stop, and the people stood around wondering how this could be possible.

'Come on, now, Father, that's enough of that; you're laughing so much, we're getting alarmed,' people were saying to him.

And he replied:

'Oh, you have every reason to be alarmed; everybody should be alarmed—the whole Christian world, for something so foul has been going on here such as hasn't been heard of in all the history of Russia from the days of Saint Vladimir the Prince.'

'Have it your own way, but don't frighten us like that, please go and see Father Savva and tell him all about it: he'll think what can be done for the best,—to comfort good Christian souls.'

But the Peregudy priest just laughed all the more, but then he suddenly went green in the face, his eyes bulged and he said:

'You are all fools—ignorant and uneducated: you set up a school, but you see nothing.'

'Then will you go and see our Father Savva,—he's waiting for you over there in his hut; sit down and have a chat with him, he'll see what to do.'

'He'll see that, will he?' the Peregudy priest yelled. 'No, he won't see anything; that one doesn't know anything, he doesn't even know the sort of man he is himself!'

'We all know the sort of man he is—he's a priest.'

'A priest!'

'Yes, a priest.'

'And I'll show you that he isn't a priest at all!'

'What do you mean, not a priest?'

'Just that, not a priest, not even a Christian.'

'Not a Christian? What are you blithering about?'

'I'm not blithering—he's not a Christian.'

'Well, what is he, then?'

'What is he?'

'Yes.'

'The Devil alone knows what he is!'

The people recoiled and crossed themselves, while the Peregudy priest got into a sledge and said:

'I'm going straight to the Rural Dean, and I'm going to tell him such a story, that will shame the whole Christian world, and then you'll see that your priest isn't a priest and isn't even a Christian, and your children are not Christians, and those of you who are married might as well not be married at all, and those who have been buried have died like dogs, without remission of sin, and they're being tormented in hell, they'll go on being tormented, and nothing can ever save them from it. Yes, and everything I say is the plain truth, which is what I'm going to tell the Rural Dean, and if you don't believe me, go to Kerasivna at once, while she still lives,—I've told her on pain of the most frightful curse that she's to tell you everything, including what sort of person the man you call your priest Savva is. He's done enough harm to people's immortal souls: a magpie is sitting up on his roof and crying: "Savka, throw off your cassock!" Very well, I'll soon be back. Boy! Straight to the Rural Dean, and you, magpie, croak louder: "Savka, throw off your cassock!" I'll be back with the Rural Dean.'

At that the priest from Peregudy drove off at speed, and the people present, all of them, wanted to rush off into Kerasivna's hut to interrogate her and find out what she had been saying about her godson, Father Savva; but after a very little thought, they decided to do it differently, and send two Cossacks so that the third could be Father Savva himself.

XX

THE Cossacks and Father Savva went in to see Kerasivna. She was lying beneath the icons and weeping bitterly.

'Forgive me,' she said, 'my love, my dear but unfortunate one,' she said to Savva, 'I've kept my secret in my heart, and for over thirty years I've been afraid I would reveal it or say something to someone about it, or talk about it in my sleep, and that's why I haven't been to confession for all these years, but now that I have to reveal all to the Most High, I have spoken out.'

Maybe Father Savva was a little fearful because the secret concerned him too closely, but he gave no sign and said calmly:

'But what is this great matter?'

'I have committed a great sin, against you especially.'

'Against me?' asked Father Savva.

'Yes. I have spoiled your whole life, because even though you've studied the Scriptures and been made a priest, you aren't fit for that, because you haven't ever been baptized.'

It is not difficult to imagine what Father Savva must have felt when this was revealed. At first he was inclined to take it as the delirious ramblings of a dying woman. He even smiled at what she said and said:

'That's enough, Godmother, how can I not be baptized if you are my godmother?'

But Kerasivna displayed total clarity of mind and logic in the story she told.

'Forget all that,' she said. 'How can I be your godmother? No-one ever baptized you. And who's really responsible for that, I don't know and I haven't been able to work it out in the whole of my lifetime: was it because of our sins, or was it because of Nikola's Moscow cunning. But here come the priest from Pere-gudy and the Dean—stay while I tell them the whole story.'

The Dean did not want Father Savva and the Cossacks to stay and listen to Kerasivna's confession, but she insisted, threatening that unless they stayed she would refuse to tell the story.

This is what she said.

XXI

'SAVVA the priest,' she said, 'is neither a priest nor Savva, he's an unbaptized person, and I'm the only one in the world who knows it. This all came from the time when his late father, old Dukach, was very cruel: no-one liked him and they were all afraid of him, and when his son was born no-one was willing to be god-parents to stand by the child at his baptism. Old Dukach even invited the magistrate and the daughter of our late priest, but they wouldn't agree. Then old Dukach got ever so furious with every-one in the village and the priest, and didn't want to ask him to perform the baptism. "I'll do without him and his holy orders." He called his nephew Agapka, an orphan who lived with him and who was kept in ignorance of everything, and told him to have a pair of horses harnessed to the sledge. He summoned me to be godmother. "Kerasivna, go with Agap to the next village and see that my son is baptized." And he gave me a fur coat, for all the good it did me—I never wore it again after that day, it's still hanging on the hook thirty years later as good as it was then. And Dukach gave me one particular instruction: "Watch out for Agap, he's stupid, he can't do anything properly; so you make sure that everything's all right with the priest, in case—God forbid—for some evil reason he gives the lad a name that's not Christian, or that's difficult, or too much like a Moscow name. It's St Barbara's Day, and that's very dangerous, because Nikola's Day is very close to it in the calendar, and Nikola is too Moscow-like for me; he does nothing to help us Cossacks, but favours the Moscow folks over much. Whatever happens, I want him to be one of us, or he'll go and pray to God all in favour of the Moscow people, he'll help them out of any old mess and justify them, and the Cossacks will suffer. God forbid our children should have *his* name. And here's the name of St Savka in the calendar. He's one of us Cossacks, and he'll favour us twice as well. He may not be all that famous a saint, but he's on our side."

'So I said:

'"All right, but he's not a very powerful saint, isn't Savva!"

'And Dukach replied:

'"He may not be, it doesn't matter. But he's twice as crafty; if his power doesn't take him somewhere, he gets there by cunning, and he'll stand up for us Cossacks one way or the other. And we'll help to give him some extra clout: we'll burn candles and sing services to his glory: God'll see that honest people respect St Savka, and He'll support him all the more in his position, and he'll grow all the stronger."

'Everything that Dukach asked, I promised. And I wrapped the baby in the fur coat, placed his little cross around my neck, put the cask of plum brandy on the floor of the sledge, and we left. But we'd only gone about a mile when the blizzard blew up—we just couldn't drive: you couldn't see the road.

'I said to Agap:

'"We can't go on, we must go back."

'But he was afraid of his uncle and didn't want to turn back.

'"If it's God's will, we'll get through," he said. "And I'll either freeze to death or my uncle'll kill me—it's all the same to me."

'And he drove the horses on; he just dug his heels in and insisted.

'By this time it had got dark and you couldn't see a single thing. We drove and drove, and hadn't any idea where we were going. The horses turned this way and that, going round and round in circles, and we got nowhere. We got terrifically cold, and so as not to freeze to death we drank out of the cask we were supposed to be taking to the priest in Peregudy. And I looked at the baby and thought, "God preserve him, he mustn't die." But no, he was lying quite warm and breathing, and there was even steam coming off him. I made a hole in the snow around his little face, so he could breathe all right, we drove on again, and we drove and drove, but could tell we were just driving around in circles, and there wasn't a glimmer in the darkness, and the horses were going wherever they felt like. By this time the idea of going back home and waiting out the storm there was just as impossible as going on,—we'd no idea which direction to go in for Paripsy or for Peregudy. I told Agap to get out and lead the horses by the reins, but he said, "A fine idea of yours that is! I'm freezing." I promised him I'd give him some money when we got home, but all he said was:

'"What good's money to me if we're both going to die? But if you want me to do it for good will, let me have another good drink from that cask." I said, "Drink as much as you like," and he did. He took a drink and then he got out and went to take the horses by the bridle, but instead he came straight back, all shaking.

'"What's up?" I said, "What's the matter with you?"

'"Get away with you!" he said, "how can I go against Nikola?"

'"What on earth are you talking about, you stupid fellow: what do you mean—go against Nikola?"

'"Why do you think he's standing there?" he said.

'"Who's standing where?"

'"Just there," he said, "right by the sledge, ahead of the horses."

'"Shame on you, you fool!—You're drunk!"

'"Aha! It's a good job I *am* drunk," was his reply, "but your husband wasn't drunk when he saw things, and I can see something now."

'"All right, then," I said, "now you mention my husband; I know better than you do what he saw, so just you tell me what you think you can see!"

'"There's something absolutely huge standing there in a golden Moscow fur-trimmed crown, and there are sparks coming from it."

'"That's just you: you're drunk and you've got spots before the eyes!" I said.

'"No," he said, "It's St Nicholas in a Moscow crown. And he won't let us get past."

'And it occurred to me that this was probably not true, but on the other hand it might be true, since we weren't going to have the boy christened Nikola, but Savka, so I said:

'"Let him have his way: he won't let us pass, and we don't need to—we'll give in to him today, and tomorrow we'll do what *we* want. Let the horses go where *they* want; and you drink the whole barrel full if that's what *you* want."

'Agap was embarrassed, so I said:

'"Have a bit more, but then keep your mouth shut and leave it to me; I'll spin such a yarn that no-one will dream it's not true. We'll say we had the child baptized and given a good Cossack name, as Dukach wanted—Savka—we'll put the little cross round his neck; and on Sunday we'll say: the good Father told us to bring the child to communion—and when we take him we'll both have him baptized and taken to communion—and everything will have been done as it should for good Christian folk."

'I had another look at the baby. He was doing fine, sleeping, and warm as anything; even the snowflakes on his forehead were melting, so I made the sign of the cross with the melted snow on his brow and said, "In the name of the Father and of the Son," and I put the cross round his neck, and we just let ourselves be taken, by God's will, just where the horses fancied going.

'The horses walked on and on. Sometimes they went, sometimes they stopped, then they moved on again, the weather got worse and worse and the frost crueller and crueller. Agap was dead drunk, at first he muttered nonsense, then his voice gave out—he just collapsed in the bottom of the sledge and began snoring. And I got colder and colder, and didn't come to until people started rubbing me with snow in Dukach's house. When I came to my senses, I remembered what I had intended to say, and so I said it: I said the baby was baptized and called Savva. Everyone believed me, and I was quite relieved, because I thought I would put it all right, as I said, on the first Sunday. But at that point I did not know that Agap had been shot and would soon die, and that old Dukach had been taken off to prison; and when I did find out, I wanted to make a clean breast of it to old Dukachess, but I couldn't bring myself to, because the house was so full of trouble. I thought I would tell the whole story later, but it was hard to do it even long after, and I kept putting it off from day to day. And time passed, and the lad grew; and everyone called him Savka, and he was sent for a scholar,—and I simply couldn't bring myself to tell the secret, and it worried me a lot, and I always intended to say he hadn't been baptized, and then, when I suddenly heard he was going to be made a priest,—I was intending to go off to town and let it all be known, but they wouldn't let me near enough, and there was no-one to talk to. From that time I've not had a moment's peace—I've been tormented by the thought that all Christian folk in my home village were going to be a laughing stock with their priest who'd never been baptized. Then, the older I got and the more I saw that people loved him more and more, the worse my anguish became, and I was afraid the earth would not take me. And it's only now, in the moment of my death, that I've been forced to tell the story. I hope all Christians will forgive me, for damaging their souls with an unbaptized priest, and if you have to bury me alive I'll gladly accept that punishment.'

The Rural Dean and the priest from Peregudy listened to all this, wrote it all down and they both signed the document, read it to Father Savva, and then went to the church, placed seals everywhere and left for the provincial capital to see the Archbishop, taking Father Savva with them.

At this point the people became very agitated. There were earnest discussions: what is all this about our Reverend Father, where's it all come from and what has it to do with anything? And can what Kerasivna says possibly be true? Is it safe to believe a witch?

And they put together a scheme, which went something like this: it was all St Nicholas's fault, and the best thing they could do was to 'strengthen' St Savva before God and go to the Archbishop themselves. They forced open the church, lit all the candles they could find in the box and burned them before the icons of the saints, and then they sent six good Cossacks in hot pursuit of the Rural Dean to ask him not to dare touch their Father Savva, 'because we don't want to hear anything from anyone but our own Reverend Father, and rather than that we'll go over to another faith, if not the Catholic, then the Turkish religion, only we'll not be left without Savva.'

And so here the Archbishop had a far sharper dilemma than anything about a deacon who 'burst into a trepak, the *trepak* has not complained, why, then, is the Dean complaining?'

Kerasivna died, having confirmed all that we know in her burst of repentance, and the chosen Cossacks went to the Archbishop, thinking all night about what they would do if the Archbishop would not listen to them and took away their Father Savva.

And they became even more firm in their intention that in that case they would return to the village, immediately drink up all the liquor in all the taverns, so that there would be none left for anybody, then they would each take three women, the richer ones four, and they would become real Turkish Mohammedans, for the one thing they insisted upon was that they would have no other priest while their good Savva was alive. And how could it be allowed that he should not have been baptized when he had christened, confessed, married and buried so many people in the Christian world? How could all these people possibly be in a 'state of heathendom'? The one thing the Cossacks agreed they would grant the Archbishop was that, if Father Savva could not be a priest for the moment, then let the Archbishop baptize him secretly, wherever he liked, only this should mean he could still be their priest...or else they would 'go over to the Turkish faith.'

XXII

THIS all again happened in winter; evening was drawing on and it was around the same time of year, St Nicholas's or St Savva's Day, when thirty-five years previously Kerasivna had set out from Paripsy to Peregudy to have the little son of Dukach baptized.

From Paripsy to the regional capital where the Archbishop lived was about thirty-five miles. The deputation whose aim was to retrieve Father Savva thought that they would make about ten miles and reach the large inn run by the Jew Iosel, where they would obtain sustenance and warmth, and then set out again next morning to see the Archbishop.

It did not turn out quite like that. Conditions have a habit of repeating themselves, and they played the same trick on the Cossacks as they had on Agap and Kerasivna thirty-five years previously, and the whole group of Cossacks found themselves wandering lost across the steppe; they lost the track, and having left the road inadvertently, had no idea where they were, when all of a sudden, perhaps no more than an hour before sunrise, they saw a man standing, not in an ordinary place, but above an ice-hole in a frozen water-course.

'Hello there, lads!'

They returned the greeting.

'What brings you here at this time? You can see, you very nearly fell in the water.'

'Yes,' they replied. 'We're in great trouble, we're going as fast as we can to see the Archbishop: we want to get there before our enemies, so he'll take our part and not theirs.'

'And what do you want to persuade him of?'

'To leave us our unbaptized priest, or else if he doesn't we'll be so unhappy, we'll go over to the Turks.'

'What, go over to the Turks and be Mohammedans? Turks can't touch strong drink.'

'We'll drink it all up before we go over.'

'You cunning beggars!'

'Well, what can we do at such an insult—to take away our good priest?'

The stranger said:

'Come on, then, tell me the whole story.'

And they told him. And so, one way and another, standing by the ice-hole, they simply told the whole story from the start, and again added that if the Archbishop wouldn't leave their Savva alone, they would all 'change their faith'.

At this, the stranger said:

'Don't worry, lads, I have every hope the Archbishop will make a good decision.'

'That's just what we think,' they said, 'a man with such a high-up rank must be able to decide it properly, since the Good Lord knows him well...'

'He'll decide it right, he will. And if he doesn't, I'll help.'

'You will? Who are you, then?'

'Tell us what your name is.'

'I'm called Savva,' he said.

The Cossacks nudged each other.

'You can tell—his name's Savva.'

And this Savva said to them next: 'Look, you've arrived just at the right place,—that's the monastery on the hill over there, that's where the Archbishop lives.'

They looked, and it was true; it was just getting light and before them, beyond the river, stood the monastery.

The Cossacks were very surprised that they had managed to cover thirty miles without resting in such severe weather. They climbed up the hill, sat down at the monastery gates, got out whatever they had to eat from their bags, and set about fortifying themselves with food. They waited until the bell rang for matins and the gates were opened.

They waited, they entered, they attended the service and then presented themselves at the Archbishop's quarters to request an audience.

Although the senior ranks of our church hierarchy are generally reluctant to converse with simple folk, these Cossacks were immediately admitted to the Archbishop's residence and placed in a reception room, where they waited for a long, long time, until the Peregudy priest, the Rural Dean, Father Savva and many other people all appeared.

The Archbishop came out and held conversations with everyone except the Rural Dean and the Cossacks, to whom he said not a word, until all the others left the room, and then he addressed the Cossacks directly:

'Well, now, my good fellows, you have a grievance? You very much want to keep your unbaptized priest?'

And they replied:

'Be gracious and pity us, your Holiness: it's not a grievance... Such a priest as he is, there isn't another like him in the whole Christian world...'

The Archbishop smiled.

'That is right,' he said, 'not another like him,' and with this he turned to the Rural Dean and said:

'Just go into the vestry and get the book that Savva has prepared, bring it in and read the place where it is open.'

And he sat down.

The Dean brought the book and started to read: 'Moreover, brethren, I would not that ye should be ignorant, how that all our fathers were under the cloud, and all passed through the sea; and were all baptized unto Moses in the cloud and in the sea; and did all eat the same spiritual meat; and did all drink the same spiritual drink: for they drank of that spiritual Rock that followed them: and that Rock was Christ.'

At this point the Archbishop interrupted him, asking:

'Do you understand what you have just read?'

The Dean replied:

'Yes, I understand.'

'And is it just now that you understood it for the first time?'

The Dean did not know what to say, and answered at random:

'I have read it before.'

'But if you have read it, why did you raise such a hue and cry and upset these good people, to whom he was such a good pastor?'

The Dean replied:

'By the rules of the saints, the Father...'

But the Archbishop interrupted:

'Stop,' he said, 'and go to Savva again, he'll give you the rule.'

The Rural Dean went, and returned again with another book.

'Read it,' said the Archbishop.

'We read,' began the Dean, 'that St Gregory the Theologian wrote of Vasily the Great that "he was a priest for the Christians before his consecration."'

'So what is all this fuss about?' said the Archbishop.

And the Dean replied:

'I simply felt it was my duty as a priest to point out that he was not baptized while holding the position he did...'

But at this point the Archbishop stamped his foot.

'Again,' he said, 'you repeat the same thing again. I suppose you think that having been under the cloud and having passed through the sea you can be baptized unto Moses but not unto Christ? Surely you were told that these people, seeking baptism, both passed through a cloud in the fear of death and made the sign of the cross with the melted water from that same cloud in the name of the Holy Trinity. What else do you need? You are a shallow man and not fit for your office. I shall put Father Savva in your place: and you good fellows need have no doubt that your Savva, who is so dear to you, is good in my eyes and pleasing in the sight of God. You can go home assured of that.'

They fell at his feet.

'Are you content?'

'Doubly content,' said the men.

'You're not going to join the Turks?'

'Pooh! Of course we shan't, we shan't at all!'

'And you won't drink off all the liquor at once?'

'We shan't drink it all at once, we shan't drink it at all!'

'Go with God's blessing and live good Christian lives.'

They were ready to depart, when one of them, seeking more reassurance, gestured to the Archbishop with his finger and said:

'Would your holiness be so good as to come over here into the corner where no-one can hear us?'

The Archbishop smiled and said:

'Very well, let's do so: what is it you want to know?'

When they had stepped aside, the Cossack asked:

'Please, your holiness, tell us how you knew everything before we told you?'

'And why does that matter to you?'

'Was it Savva who explained it all to you?'

The Archbishop, to whom the whole matter had been recounted by his laybrother Savva, looked at the Cossack and said:

'You have guessed; it was Savva who told me it all.'

And with that he left the room.

Well, these simple fellows interpreted all these events as best they could. And from that time forth, the tale was told how the not very powerful Savva quietly and thoroughly managed the business so that the Muscovite Nikola with all his strength was outflanked and left standing.

'That Savva of ours,' people would say, 'is a joker; he took on strength and reasoned it out so that they were all dumbfounded: it was shown in Scripture, then the Holy Fathers pushed it under their nose, so cleverly that you couldn't understand a thing. The Lord God knows either that he baptized the priest Savva truly in Kerasivna's bosom or that the matter was so truly muddled that even an archbishop couldn't sort it out. Anyway, it all turned out well in the end. Thanks to him for that.'

Father Savva, I am told, is still alive today, and all around his village the Shtunda prospers, but his little church is still full of people...And although we do not know if St Savva still 'upholds' the flock today as he did once, people do say that, as before, there are no Mikhalkas and Potapkas going around showing their bare midriffs.

Rebellion Among the Gentry in the Parish of Dobryn

'As the priest is, so is his flock'
Proverb

I

THIS is a local story, which might even be termed domestic, which originated in memories of my childhood, when we lived on our estate in the village of Panino in the district of Kromy, Province of Orel. This locality was of the type which have long been known as 'nests of gentlefolk'. Around us there lived a numerous assemblage of large and minor landowners. In the village of Raznovilya Prince Trubetskoy had his country seat, in Krivtsovo lived the Krivtsov family, a whole colony of them, and the Adadurovs to boot; in Kosarevo lived old Ilya Ivanovich Krivtsov, and in Zinovievo the large and moreover extremely well-educated family of the Ivanovs.

Prince Trubetskoy represented the genuine long-established family aristocracy of the region, while the Ivanovs were the intellectual ones. The Adadurovs were great drinkers, and my father and Ilya Krivtsov were regarded as eccentrics. They were both very intelligent men, who lived like anchorites and were bored to death. Ilya Ivanovich did, however, drink from time to time, but always 'solo', while my father spent his time reading books and becoming depressed.

The centre of our intellectual life was the Ivanov family. The most highly educated of them was their mother, an old lady called Nastasya Sergeevna, née Masalskaya, and her son, Nikolai Alekseevich, who served as our Marshal of the Nobility. The four young Misses Ivanova, the youngest of whom was just a fraction older than me, were all very well read, and were not lacking in talents of various sorts. I am indebted to them for my first acquaintance with literature, which to my great misfortune soon turned into an overwhelming passion. This passion was supported and nourished by the rather large library of old Mr Masalsky, which had been transferred to Zinovievo.

The parish to which all this community of noblemen belonged had as its place of worship the little wooden church in the village of Dobryn, which was attended by all except Nastasya Sergeevna and Ilya Ivanovich Krivtsov; but even they did not stay away by reason of free-thinking, but because the old lady suffered greatly from the cold, and because Ilya Ivanovich, having reached middle life, considered himself sexless, and on this pretext dispensed with his trousers, and henceforth refused ever to put them on. By reason of this inveterate characteristic, the landowner Krivtsov was always known among the peasants in his last years as 'the trouserless gent'. Needless to say, he could not attend church in this state, but he saw no reason to change his uninhibited behaviour.

All the other gentry attended the church in Dobryn and made their confession there despite the fierce cold. The parish had two junior deacons, but the only 'confessor of the nobility' was Father Vasily B—in, during whose tenure of office the whole of his noble congregation was in good standing, but when he left, they were said to have 'rebelled' to such an extent that it nearly became a hanging matter, as the rest of this tale will recount in some detail.

The affair of the rebellion of the gentry had a very strong political character, and although it all took place 'secretly—extremely secretly', the secret is much more amusing than significant, and the story can now be told.

Our rebellion is very interesting in many respects, not forgetting that it was broad in conception and highly secret in its operation.

But as the affair was not only political, but religious, in that the rebellion was discovered and established by a priest, before I write of the rebellion itself I consider it necessary to say a few things about our spiritual fathers in Dobryn. First I shall write of those, under whose tutelage we gentry lived in peace and harmony, and later of the one we appointed to the parish with great care and foresight, but once we had him there—we 'rebelled'. It relates to an epoch when there appeared in our nation a dangerous type of man, malevolent towards authority and striving towards the overthrow of the monarchy in Russia. But, as I have said, the country was saved by a priest.

II

I remember three priests in Dobryn: the first was Father Vasily B—in, who was the most senior in years and in education. He was of the very best and had many excellent qualities, for which people forgave him his failings, which amounted to one particular 'weakness'.

During my childhood Father Vasily was aged around fifty; he was short in stature, he had a shock of thick chestnut hair which was totally unkempt, like an Old Believer; he trimmed his moustache in the normal way; his eyes were small, grey, wise and very sincere. His whole face was miniature, and his entire nature exuded the rather crude good nature of a seminarist. He was very kind, honest through and through, without having to set himself any rules, and lacking in any troublesome attitudes. He was respected and liked by all the gentry, and enjoyed the reputation among the ordinary people as 'a decent priest'. As a farmer he had his limitations—so work in the fields went badly; he left the running of the house and the farmyard to his 'good woman Marfa Tikhonovna'; but Father Vasily was an excellent gardener, fruit-grower and bee-keeper, and he kept this department in the very best order. We were fed with the best apples from his orchard, served with first-rate honey; once a year, at the 'festival of the Saviour of the honey harvest' he entertained the entire 'laity' (that is, the peasants)—during the whole of the rest of the year they used to steal his produce, either straight from the orchard or the apiary, or from his larder. Father Vasily for some reason found this thieving entirely natural and never complained. He would simply say, 'They've been pilfering again', and did not expatiate further. The place where we live, along the River Gostomlya, is a burglarious part of the world.

In contrast with all common beliefs about the 'enviousness' of the priesthood, Father Vasily was entirely unselfish, and, as people said, 'a generous host of the very, very best'. At every major festival he held a 'gentry' luncheon in his front room and a 'lay' one in the 'labourers' premises'.

As for himself, he made no claims to status, but he observed 'distinctions' for their good selves, the gentry. To do otherwise would have been impossible. To bring the quality together with their serfs would have been to spoil the party. And, of course, the serfs themselves would not have been able to put up with it, for the very good reason that our wise ordinary person has had a profound sense of genuine dignity instilled in him by his Russian nature.

The only outsiders allowed into the gentry section were the 'farmsteader', a free peasant from Opalkovo, who could carry on a conversation not without interest for the gentry about strangers passing through the district and about prices of produce, and 'Zinovievo Dunyasha', the Ivanovs' serf chambermaid. This warm-hearted unmarried woman was allowed in because she was 'always recognized by the gentry when they met her', and while she never sought such a distinction, she was fully worthy of it.

She therefore came 'close to the gentry' during her life and was not separated from them even in death. In the aristocratic cemetery of the Alexander Nevsky Monastery (to the left of the church) there is a recently dug grave marked by a white cross, on which may be read the short, but warm words: 'a faithful servant, Dunyasha'. This is she, and the resting place of the body of the blameless Dunyasha, among the good and great of St Petersburg, was established for her by the grateful love of a lady whose children Dunyasha had nursed; it was this lady who composed the very appropriate epitaph.

While entertaining the gentry and the non-gentry, Father Vasily never sat down at the table himself and never drank a drop. He simply 'blessed the eats and drinks', and then 'helped his good woman Marfa Tikhonovna to entertain the guests.'

The entertainment was never very refined, but it was plentiful, and certainly delicious, especially at Christmas, at Easter, at the Patronal Festival of St Nicholas, at New Year, and on the Day of Vasily the Great, when all Orthodox Christians in the diocese of Orel feast in honour of this noble philosopher of Caesarea on a 'Caesarean sucking pig'—stewed with a horse-radish in its mouth, and then roasted with onion and buckwheat porridge.

Nature herself fostered this feast: the sows of Father Vasily always seemed to litter so that their offspring might achieve their certificates of maturity just at the right time to become 'caesars'. Then they had their great moment: they were slaughtered, and, as the peasants assured us, this gave the piglets great pleasure, since any animal slaughtered for a Christian festival 'goes gladly to receive the knife'.

And in fact, when the sucking pigs had been prepared, having been dipped in water, and were laid out on a mound of earth outside a peasant's hut in order to freeze, they did look somehow childishly reverential: as they froze all in a row with their severed trotters raised to heaven, they seemed to be offering themselves as a full, perfect and sufficient sacrifice.

The peasants would say: 'The Father's piglets aren't half praying! We'll eat that lot on Vasily's Day.'

Everyone thought that was very funny.

The drinks Father Vasily served were not all the same. On the gentry table there was plum liqueur and dark red wine, while the peasants got home-made vodka and home-brewed ale sweetened with honey, which gave it an extremely pleasant taste.

According to peasant preferences, they spoilt it considerably by adding vodka, which meant that the beer was stronger, or, as the people said, 'had more of a kick', but without this addition it was a very good drink, which we children liked better than fruit syrup.

Father Vasily never drank in the presence of his guests: he drank 'after'. That is what he would say when anyone asked him: 'Why aren't you drinking, Father?'. He'd say: 'I will, after.'

And he kept this promise of 'after' with the most unfortunate punctiliousness, which caused very great trouble indeed to his household and to the whole parish.

Yes; along with Father Vasily's household, the whole parish suffered. Father Vasily did not know how, or simply was not physically able to confine himself to one glass, or two, or three. He could only drink himself senseless, and once he had taken a sip of wine he felt the need to drink deep, long, tirelessly, until he reached the point where had no strength left, and in fact more than once came within an inch of his life. And then, when this point of anguish was reached, the news of it spread around the village in a flash, and sympathy arose, briefly expressed in peasant homes, but at great length among the gentry.

This news got around usually through the house-serfs, who, being restrained by the sense of delicacy derived from their masters, used to report, in a quiet and sad tone of voice:

'Father Vasily is ill.'

No-one ever asked about the nature of the illness, but everyone knew what it meant. Everyone sincerely and totally without hypocrisy felt very sorry for the patient and his 'good woman Marfa Tikhonovna'. And the way this sympathy and tactfulness was expressed is truly a cause of touching recollection.

The first rule of the Gospel: 'Visit the sick', immediately came into everyone's mind, but how could they do it tactfully?..No one would enter the house of the inebriated Father Vasily, so as not to embarrass him in any way, so they simply asked after him. Either that, or they sent servants to Mistress Marfa Tikhonovna, or, better, they 'took a ride' in his direction. This meant they would order a charabanc or a waggon to be harnessed in summer, or in winter a one-horse sleigh, and without a coachman, 'self-driven', they would slip over to Dobryn in the twilight to the gate of the priest's house. Here they would call Marfa Tikhonovna to the door, commiserate with her, show sympathy through whispered remarks, and surreptitiously put into her hand a small sum of money and a bottle of Orel 'Varentsov' madeira. Vorontsov (more correctly) madeira contained in a 'pot-bellied bottle', as Gogol called it, was at that time a great favourite of the quality, and they gave it to Marfa Tikhonovna so that she could try to pass this useful wine off to the sick man as vodka. There was a notion current that madeira was supposed to 'relieve the weakness' of all serious drinkers. And when Father Vasily's 'illness' was past, that is when he stopped drinking intoxicating liquor and simply lay ill in bed, sometimes in a totally shattered state, little gifts started to arrive for him of an eatable or medicinal nature, adapted to 'the taste of a drinker'. Mainly it was the highly-born granddaughter of Mr Masalsky who saw to this—Nastasya Sergeevna Ivanova. Her gifted chef, Kondraty (who is still alive and active)—a pupil of the once-famous restaurateur Yard—himself suffered from the same 'weakness' as Father Vasily and well knew how to prepare particular 'salted dishes' which would assist his recovery.

As I remember, one of these was something in the style of a light meat hash in chicken stock, which smelt deliciously of gherkins and olives and with a glaze of chicken fat. This tempting delicacy, 'adapted to the taste of a drinker' was prepared in Zinovievo, three miles from Dobryn—where Father Vasily languished, having shot his bolt—and was immediately transported to the presbytery.

It was always the faithful servant Dunyasha who brought the 'medicinal eatables'. The provisions would always be contained in a small pan, and there would also be a bowl of stewed apples, cranberry jam and a small number of olives, of which Father Vasily was very fond 'when he was recuperating'. Usually even the first words he uttered were 'oliverives, give me some oliverives'. And so they would give him some 'oliverives'. And the old woman, Nastasya Sergeevna, Russian through and through, but who was happier speaking French, would know about this, order some, look them over herself, select the best, wrap them up and give firm instructions to the 'faithful servant':

'Be quick, Dunyasha, you go along there, and make sure you warm them up over a fire of small sticks so you don't make them taste too smoky for the poor little priest. Everything turns his stomach as it is.'

It was only the 'trouserless gent' Ilya Ivanovich Krivtsov who did not visit Father Vasily, and that was only because he did not want to change his policy and put his trousers on. However, he too enquired kindly about Father Vasily through his serf maid (an old woman already by this time) Aksinya Matveevna, and sent him some 'homeopathy', as well as some rhyming prayers of his own composition, an activity for which he had plenty of time. Ilya Ivanovich composed prayers 'for the three crises in life': what he referred to as 'inebriation, rowdy agitation and nocturnal peregrination'. These prayers may have been rather blasphemous, but, anyway, they were funny, and Father Vasily would always read them when in his 'fog' and would smile, but then burn them afterwards.

The tact of the parishioners went even further than this. The people knew that the priest, 'after he sobered up', would be upset,—'He'd be ashamed to show his face', and so the 'bearers of spikenard', in the persons of Aksinya Matveevna and the 'faithful servant Dunyasha' had not only to assist Father Vasily's recovery by taking him everything his aristocratic circle of soft-hearted spiritual children saw fit to send him, but also to 'keep an eye on his condition and report as soon as he was fit again.' Usually they did not admit of Father Vasily's 'complete recovery', because then, he would be 'very ashamed', but they awaited the moment when he 'came back into his element'; it was then, without any delay, that an ambassador from Nastasya Sergeevna would rush to his house in Dobryn, bearing a letter in which Nastasya Sergeevna herself, in her amazingly clear and handsome French style of handwriting would say that her heart was indeed sad to have been deprived of the joy of praying with him, and that she therefore earnestly begged him to come to her home with the other clergy and celebrate Vespers.

The salutation at the opening of the letter was always the same: 'Honourable priest and greatly respected friend, Father Vasily', and at the end, equally invariably, she would sign it: 'Ever in the greatest respect, your spiritual daughter, Anastasia Ivanovna'.

This was usually the final *coup de main* which restored Father Vasily's health. He must have realized the reason for the desire to 'pray with him', and would immediately set about saying his own prayers in private.

III

A full day before the appointed service Father Vasily would eat nothing at all and would drink nothing but cold spring water as an apéritif to a lump of sugar. He enjoyed this. While so doing, he would weep and pray, in Marfa Tikhonovna's phrase, 'till you thought he would meet his dreadstiny', but on the other hand, during these twenty-four hours he would become radiant to the point of rapture, which I always found inexpressibly and indescribably wonderful. He was transfigured, and his red face recalled pictures of a fiery seraph. To attend worship with Father Vasily was a very great pleasure for many, though he was not showy in the way he sang the service, but simply prayed like the most ordinary sinner. I remember how often during the conduct of the service such abundant tears would flow down his face that he could scarcely sing the final acclamations of the prayers. But when Father Vasily led the prayers after his 'sobering up', there was something about it which took you right down to hell and then brought you up again to the highest heaven, just as this peasant-like seraph had himself fallen to the depths and risen again to the heights...

These services of vespers in the tiny village of Zinovievo were attended by as many as possible of the gentry, so as all at once to relieve Father Vasily of the embarrassment of meeting people again. It cannot be that he failed to understand this purpose, but the matter was never discussed, and moreover the whole occasion was managed so that he had no time to feel awkward. At the same time as the priest was sent for, a table was set in the hall, covered with a fair white cloth and the icon of the Saviour with a lamp burning before it, and when Father Vasily arrived, wax candles set in everyday candlesticks were lit, and the service began. At the words 'Worship the Lord in fear and be glad in him with reverence' everyone joined in the prayer in tears, especially Nastasya Sergeevna and Father Vasily himself. He led the prayers on his knees, fastening his gaze on the heavens, and he knelt there with his head inclined downwards, as though turned to stone, but the tears ran silently down his cheeks.

When the service ended Father Vasily hurried off home, and no-one tried to detain him, but they all kissed his hand as he left. Neither the Marshal of the Nobility, nor the highly educated old lady with the Parisian education, nor the elegant young ladies tried to escape this ritual...But Father Vasily's hands, as one expects of all passionate gardeners, smelt not of the roses he cultivated, but of the manure with which he fed his roses and cuttings. And this smell of the stable was in his case always blended with the smell of the strong plug tobacco, which Father Vasily smoked in an ordinary peasant pipe along with his farm labourers.

A day or two after the vespers in Zinovievo, Father Vasily would be summoned to Kosarevo by the 'trouserless' Ilya Ivanovich, the composer of prayers, who had been on occasion a victim to the same tendency from which Father Vasily had been recalled. Ilya Ivanovich very much enjoyed singing along with the deacons, particularly 'In the days of my youth my passions did rage', but when this coincided with one of his drinking bouts, he would sing: 'From the daysh of my youth Chrisht shave me at the lasht', and after that you could hear nothing but a sound something like 'zib-zib-zib', and then a thundering outburst of 'Alleluia, praisèd be His name', and finally there would be something quite disconnected which was most likely to be totally incomprehensible.

The Heavenly Father of All that is Spirit and Flesh was being praised in language which no human creature could understand.

Tact was observed in this respect too: the priest left, seeing that there was no reason for him to be embarrassed—he could see we were all men, all human beings, and, thank God, that we being mired in the depths of our sinful nature, were still able, however uncertainly, to call upon the unfathomable depths of the Father's mercy. (And may this capability ever be possessed by every living soul!)

In short: as the priest was, so was his flock, and our priest, Father Vasily, was simply a peasant who had passed a training course in his theological seminary, and I paint his portrait here in detail, not just for idle entertainment, but to show with what sort of spiritual leader the noble denizens of our parish had to deal, while they not only respected him, but actually came sincerely to love him. There was only one thing wrong: Father Vasily twenty years previously had been widowed in the first month after his ordination, and his good woman Marfa Tikhonovna was not his wife...

People looked upon this as the Old Believers do: 'Behold, but do not see, and do not reason'. Maybe that is a worse attitude, or maybe it is better than a rationally worked-out religious heartlessness, which strives to correct others rather than correct oneself.

Father Vasily's career ended when, during one of his attacks, he injured his temple and received a wound that would not heal. In this he saw 'the finger of God' and became a monk in the monastery at P—, where he led a very austere life and finished up in the *schema*, the strictest of all monastic rules. His good woman Marfa Tikhonovna died as a nursing orderly in a home for the incurably sick. Everyone loved her in the village and in the hospital, and—this was not my doing—referred to her as a 'righteous woman'.

The shortest, but best description of Father Vasily was what the peasants said about him:

'He was highly worthy of his calling: he never hemmed you in.'

He was buried with honour and greatly missed.

Of such an event as the 'rebellion of the gentry', which later stained the annals of the parish of Dobryn, there would have been not the slightest thought in the days of Father Vasily, and I ask the reader to remember this personality so as better to compare him with others, whose turn it now is to figure in this story.

IV

THE next of our priests was Father Parmen, whom some of our peasants referred to as the 'tearaway' and others the 'joker'. However, they said nothing other than that he was 'sharp and prickly'. He was years younger than Father Vasily, was of very tall stature and handsome appearance: shapely, slim and with an aquiline nose. Like Father Vasily, he was a widower 'from the start', but he kept no female companion, simply living 'to suit himself'. Father Parmen was no regular hard drinker either, and would drink occasionally when the fancy took him, but when he did so he became very disorderly and 'turbulent', which is to say he readily got mixed up in arguments and fought like a trooper. There were many whom Father Parmen had thrashed, and several who had thrashed him, but that never harmed his reputation. When he was sober, according to the other clergy, he was 'susceptible to the female sex' and in this mood he would take to various notable fantastic practices: sometimes he would ride off to the town of Kromy to see a certain 'little woman' who was well-known at that time, Maria Savrasievna (or, more correctly, Gervasievna) and her daughter Piashka, and he would stay with these ladies with scant concealment, so that everyone knew about it and would say, 'The priest's gone off to stay with the Savrasievna woman.'

Nor did anyone hold it to his discredit that he was sometimes referred to by the rather undignified diminutive 'Parmeshka'. In our villages, we call Timothy 'Uncle Timoshka', Pelageia 'Aunty Palashka', Aksinia 'Godmother Aksyusha', so why not call the priest Parmeshka? It expressed a certain warmth and friendly familiarity.

When he was short of money Father Parmen would not go to Kromy, but would go into the wood with the peasant lasses and the more 'experienced' younger women, gathering mushrooms and berries. People did not hold this against Father Parmen either, but would simply say to him: 'Don't get up to anything, Father!' and he respected the request, would go around looking for berries quite honourably and nobly, simply to relieve the solitary boredom of his lonely widower's existence.

A time of year when Father Parmen's temperament was particularly disturbed was the autumn, when the geese and flocks of grey ducks and drakes would be chased from the ponds, and in Zinovievo and our village Panino they would be used for soaking the hemp harvest in water and mud and for crushing it. Peasant women from all over the area would descend on us in countless numbers with the hemp they had harvested and would patiently wait their turn; the only place provided for their living accommodation was a wattle shed, in which the atmosphere was cold, but stuffy. From year to year a thick layer of white hemp dust accumulated here, covering the walls, so they seemed to be made of porous stone; while swathes of this age-old dust covered the rotting laths which had come half-loose and hung down from the wattle ceiling. In fact, this shed looked rather like a mysterious grotto with stalactites, which my childish imagination loved to people with nymphs and satyrs. And these creatures really were here once a year at least—in the autumn, when the hemp-crushing was in operation. At this time it turned into nothing less than Sodom and Gomorrah. Heaps of hemp lay around on the floor, some of it made up into bales, other of it wound into hoops, and amidst all this dusty clobber there sat or lay, yawning and stretching, juicy young peasant women, eager for a mug of wine as they rested from their labour in the open air. Finding themselves free and having every impulse to sin, like savages they gave in to it without any reserve, more or less whoever came along. This was not organized in any way. Sometimes they would have to wait their turn to crush their hemp for up to a week, and during all that time considered themselves to be in the position of the priestesses of some voluptuous cult. In consequence the very devils in hell must have been sickened by the need to keep a record of so much human transgression.

With the arrival of these women transporting their crop, which began as the crushing of the hemp was set in motion, control of the young males in the gentry's households got completely out of hand. Coachmen, footmen, cooks and kitchen-boys—they all went around during the day in a highly somnolent state, and at night not one of them could be found in his bed. 'The hemp-crushing is on,' the older men would say, and, to be sure, they did not seem to expect the decencies to be observed until Sodom and Gomorrah closed down.

This custom was observed with such great openness that when my parents first moved to the country, more than once young girls would come to my father to complain of our young lads, on such grounds as: 'He promised me a spice cake if I gave him what he wanted, but he never handed it over.' Once I remember two peasant girls bringing the offender, a man from another village, who had 'bribed' them with a piece of soap and had then given them a block of wood wrapped in paper. My father, a very serious and bookish man, repulsed all attempts to get him to adjudicate in such affairs, but Mr Adadurov was both willing and expert—a connoisseur of peasant customs and a real past-master in dealing with them.

His accounts of the stories he had had to listen to relieved our rural boredom every bit as well as the Sunday papers.

The main saturnalia began in the above-mentioned dusty and cold shed, the gloom of which was barely pierced by one little oil lamp in a shaded lantern, after which the participants would cool off on the 'hot snow'. This was the joking name given to the area of tall tussocky weeds surrounding the pond, under a canopy of huge old brittle-willows, in the hoar-frost-covered branches of which countless flocks of noisy crows roosted...They had plenty to be noisy about, since they saw everything and knew more about what went on than anyone.

At times, the sleeping birds would be scared witless and then they would raise a riot of squawking which went on for some time, and which in any case signified that the hot snow was either the scene of passionate love or that the 'chase' was afoot. This was not mere fervour, but rather a shameless hunt, or, as the peasants used to call it, the 'chase'. Never mind the name they gave it—it was a matter of passion, and at one time a special nocturnal police operation was set up around the weeds in the person of Mishka, the miller, who, although he was not obliged to prevent love-making, since that would have offended against the very spirit of the hemp-crushing season, he was supposed to prevent fighting. He liked to present himself as a very alert fellow, and one morning his alertness led to the discovery in the weeds of a seriously wounded Father Parmen.

There was blood all over his beard and moustache, and around him on the snow too there was blood, which was pouring out of his mouth almost in a stream.

They lifted him out, laid him on a sledge and took him home. There, by a near miracle he rallied somewhat, and though he never recovered completely, he did manage to last until the spring thaw, when he died.

There was no evidence about the circumstances of his death, and it was nobody's job to discover any, since around that time our village policeman had been eaten by wolves. Father Parmen himself never laid any complaint against anyone, and older people in the village concluded that, probably, when he was driving his sledge alone, somehow 'his mare must have caught him with her hind legs.'

This phrase survived long as a joking way of describing events when people wanted to conceal something which could not be concealed; it lasted longest on the lips of the next priest, the one who took Parmen's place, and whose name was very rarely mentioned: people simply called him 'Ginger'.

V

THE rebellion, though, occurred not in Ginger's time and not in consequence of anything he did, but under his successor, whose tenure of office we now come to. 'Ginger' was so enormous and broad-shouldered that not a single set of vestments could be found to fit him. The biggest cassock there was, made to measure for Father Vasily, rode up on Ginger like a hussar's tunic,—only up to his shoulders, and as a result his standing among the gentry declined from the very start of his ministry. 'People are treated according to their dress.' Ginger in his hussar tunic was not majestic and not 'worthy of his holy office', but simply ludicrous. Into the bargain he had a very strange and unusual speech impediment,—he could not pronounce the sound represented by the letter k, and therefore some words sounded extremely odd on his lips.

I really do not know how anyone with such a defect could have been ordained priest; but that was not our business.

The gentry looked Ginger over in church and received him in their homes when he called, but did not seek him out and felt no spiritual affinity with him.

They could not go to confession with him for three reasons: the first was that, according to the very exact judgement of the peasants, he was 'a bit of a buffoon', in particular he liked to play at knucklebones, and during the spring thaw he would ride his horse in his cassock in front of the peasants; in the second place he could not pronounce the sound k and would ask at confession, 'Have you pi'ed anyone's po'et?' or 'Have you been 'ursing and swearing?' or 'Have you been forni'ating?' And although it might have been possible to get used to this, from the first week of fasting the rumour went around that the coachman Tikhon, who had intended to marry the maid Parasha, after he had gone to confession with Ginger, refused to do so, and started telling Parasha all the sins she had committed, which no-one could have known about, since they happened in Moscow, and the only person to whom they had been revealed was Ginger. Maybe it was not his fault, but 'Caesar's wife must be above suspicion',—and the same applies to a spiritual leader.

His reputation was already in tatters, and he was absolutely no use to our gentry as a spiritual father, but he continued to hear confession from the peasants, because they did not particularly care: all their sins were out in the open anyway. And by the time

Ginger had demoted himself in effect, the question of a new priest for the gentry became crucial, since it was at this time that Father Vasily entered the monastery, so there was no suitable confessor for the gentry in Dobryn.

The parish gentry, who had the Marshal of the Nobility among their number, requested the Archbishop of Orel to give them a priest who was 'not too simple'. The Archbishop replied:

'Very well, very well, we'll look around for someone with a bit more imagination.'

The Marshal passed this on, and the Christian ladies of our landowning classes were delighted, and they even wondered what this man would be like if he was going to be imaginative.

The priest awaited in Father Vasily's place had the ground excellently prepared for him: it was obvious that the one who came would be just right as a confessor for the gentry. But the archbishop took his time rather over the choice: clearly he was seeking, but 'did not find, but wanted his choice to match his promise'. So much the better that the archbishop did not act in haste; finally the order of appointment for the new priest was received and made a very pleasant impression: the pleasantness of the impression was due solely to the name of the new priest: Illarion Obolensky.

A sonorous name, even perhaps an aristocratic one. It was clear that the archbishop had tried, and what is more had succeeded in choosing just the man to suit the noble taste of our gentry. Nevertheless, it was Obolensky who was responsible for the rebellion of the gentry in the parish of Dobryn, which tore the landowning community apart.

VI

THE newly arrived priest Illarion Obolensky was immediately nicknamed 'priest Varivon' by the peasants. The reason for this, of course, was that they found the name Illarion difficult. Obolensky was a man in middle years, of medium height, and maybe even of average sex. At least, he looked very much like a woman with no hat on. Neither tall, nor thin, nor fat, he was merely what they call 'smooth-faced'; his countenance was of the most effeminate in appearance. The very growth of his facial hair was like that of a woman: he had none 'sprouting' on his face, as the peasants would say, but he had luxuriant hair on his head which fell in a pigtail down to his waist and below. When he sallied forth in an extremely greasy grey under-cassock—you might have thought you were looking at a woman selling pies; when he put on his broad, deep blue over-cassock—you would think you were seeing a country merchant's wife, and it was only when he put on his proper priest's hat that you would exclaim: who the devil can that be!

In the history of the clergy of our parish Varivon was remarkable for one more fact: he was the first priest ever who very rarely touched a drop of wine. This factor, as it had never previously been experienced or even heard of, seemed quite unbelievable, and consequently our uneducated village people must be forgiven if they did not believe it. The peasants used to say: 'That one waits till midnight and creeps under the chest of drawers where you can see him supping.' The gentry too were accustomed to doubt the genuineness of the abstinence of Father Illarion, and they too, like the peasants, assumed that he was a 'soloist'. But maybe this was all very unfair and was based on nothing more than Father Illarion's practice, when he was out and about in the parish, of not drinking any wine he was offered, but of pouring it into a little flask which he kept on his person or in his trap. The peasants did not like this, finding it a bit too austere for their taste.

'Why go on like that?' they argued. 'If you're offered a drink, go on and drink it, as good Orthodox Christians ought; don't go saving it for later.'

But Father Illarion had a large family and was very poor, and I am ready to believe that he never drank his wine, but kept it for some future domestic emergency. I am even more ready to believe that he actually sold these 'outpourings', because, as I repeat, he was very poor. And the reason for his extreme poverty was that he was always being moved about from place to place; and the reason they moved him around was, as it turned out later, that he was 'inclined to procriminations', or, in the words of our sharp-tongued deacon, he was a 'holy tell-tale'.

Which of these led to the other: poverty to the holy tale-telling or tale-telling to poverty, it is difficult to see. It may be that it was like looking at a squirrel on a treadmill in a cage, when you don't know if the squirrel is turning the wheel or the wheel is making the squirrel run along. But he was a poor man and a most unpleasant one, malevolent into the bargain, and that was the impression he made on me the first time I met him. This impression was intensified when he reached his apotheosis, having tried to see that the harmless gentry of our parish should be condemned to penal servitude.

VII

THE first important 'cause for complaint' against Father Illarion was raised by the peasants, and the cause was that he was 'leaning on' them, that is, in their opinion he was too demanding, and sought a very great deal from them. This may mean simply that he tried to extract more than half a copeck for hearing confession and more than a copeck for saying prayers for the dead, and as a result of such greed he acquired the reputation of an extortioner.

'He leans on us mighty hard.'

It was not only the unworldly Vasily that people began to recall; they missed the brawling Parmen and even Ginger,— because even if he acted the fool, at least he placed no 'pressure' on the parishioners. And what is more, Ginger, like all good Orthodox folk, would call in at the inn when he was in Zinovievo and buy the odd drink for one person, while accepting a glass from others, all in a 'very friendly fashion', while as for Father Varivon, if he was seen in Zinovievo at all, you never saw his horse tethered outside the tavern; it would be sure to be standing outside the policeman's house, or as people used to call him, 'the Pole's'. (The police officer appointed to replace the one eaten by wolves was a Pole, Albert Osipovich Witowski.) But it had to be said Varivon's horse stood not at the front gate of the Polish establishment, as horses belonging to people who had legitimate business with the Pole did, but Varivon invariably tethered his horse to the shed at the rear entrance, the side of the house where a crop of long luxuriant hemp grew.

'Why does he call in secret? When a priest has to call at a policeman's back door, there's dirty tricks in the air, and one day we'll find out what they are.'

The gentry were not put out at all by this, but the peasants were already saying: 'Sneaking up to an official's back door means there's some tale-telling going on. And who can he be telling tales on in a village if not on some peasant? What can he be telling tales about? Can't be about anything. So he thinks, at least, but that doesn't make things any easier—more difficult, if anything.'

They would say: 'Perhaps it's something too dreadful to think about.'

It was horrifying! Dreadful!

So they started to avoid him. Little by little everyone dropped away from him and from the church: even on festival days people would hide from him. They would leave a cottage loaf and a copeck outside their hut, but the occupants would be nowhere to be seen.

There began what looked like a re-enactment in miniature of the struggle under Ivan the Terrible between the populace in the boyar domains and the newly constituted administrative élite, as represented by the Pole and the village priest.

Varivon, who had begun by 'leaning on' the peasant parishioners, and then 'toadying up to the Pole', by these very actions antagonized the gentry too, who could happily do without the delights of taking their spiritual needs to such a pastor. While visiting each other at Shrovetide, amidst all the joking and jollity, the ladies conspired over a table laden with delicacies not to prepare for communion in the village church, but to 'travel in a cavalcade to Orel', and this is exactly what they did. They compiled a communal shopping list of things they needed, and 'by the way, we'll worship in a warm church', and so they set off in 'cavalcade' to Orel.

It was a merry company. A number of vehicles assembled. They met at one household which was situated opposite the end of the narrow street leading to the church of Michael the Archangel and set off in horse-drawn procession. And where *didn't* we go? We went to church, we went shopping, we ate Lenten food—fish pie in a tavern, and spent the evenings telling each other stories, and indulging in constructive criticism of our nearest and dearest. This Lenten self-denial became a feast in itself. But our local clergy took great offence. In all ways this was very hard for them, as all the gentry paid a rouble each for confession, and Nastasya Sergeevna Ivanova always gave one gold piece, which was at that time worth two roubles sixty copecks, and an extra rouble for heating the church. All that now went to Michael the Archangel in Orel, and was lost to Dobryn. They could not remain indifferent to this, but it was difficult to do anything about it. But if you can't flog the horse you can at least take it out on the cart. The peasants began to think the Pole was starting to oppress them a great deal—he was very strict in raising taxes from them, and exasperated them in the name of the Governor, and so on, and so on.

'He's persecuting us,' said our homespun politicians, as they came to the conclusion that it all 'came from Varivon'.

'He's eggurging the Pole on,' they said with one voice, and everyone was dissatisfied with everyone else, priest and parishioners.

But just at that time came the 'cholera year' and there was a great thinning out of the gentry of the parish, 'among the quality the whole male sex extincted itself.' The first to die was my late father, and then Marshal Ivanov and 'trouserless' Ilya Ivanovich followed him into eternity. The manor houses were left without men, and a 'regiment of women' took over, in the course of which my mother (who, thank God, flourishes to this day) was once elected 'churchwardeness' by the parishioners, that is, she acted as organizer and treasurer in the affairs of our Dobryn church.

To elect a woman to such a post was quite out of order, but that's what people wanted, so that's what they did. Not having any very good knowledge of the rules, they said:

'Either let the Leskovess run it, or we'll not have anyone. The sparrows can fly in at the church windows and sit on the priests' heads for all we care.'

The shortage of male persons had indeed reached this point. My mother led the work of the church and oversaw it along with Deacon Vasily Ivanovich, and a peasant from the village of Khvastovka, Vasily Moskin; but in the course of a restoration of the church building, as a result of their indifference to the preservation of antiquities, certain interesting artefacts were allowed to decay, among which I remember a fascinating icon which had hung below the church's icon of the Virgin. It was called 'The Vast Womb of the Heavens', and pregnant women used to light candles before it. There was no trust in the priests, neither in Ginger nor in Varivon. They avoided Varivon particularly, but he 'ritualiated'. The first to complain of this was Moskin, who was a craftsman of all trades; he was a joiner, a turner, a painter and a locksmith. He was valued because he knew his way around any sort of skilled work, but all of a sudden the Pole met him somewhere, swore at him this way and that, and placed him under arrest, God knows why. Everyone said it was Varivon's doing. Moskin took fright and refused to have anything more to do with the church. Then the deacon left, and finally my mother too removed to Kiev. The other gentryfolk, all women, closed their doors to Varivon, and broke with the clergy; they got along somehow as a sort of priestless sect. After this the Pole began holding services at home on the first of every month. Again, this caused puzzlement: what was the Pole doing, singing services himself? Was it right that he should? Perhaps he's hoping to spite us, and our priest is holding services for him? After all, he's not Orthodox, like us, he's got his own foreign faith.

And it was indeed true that the police official's sole aim was to further the interests of Varivon and restore some of his lost prestige as a worthy pastor. He indeed made a recommendation to this effect somewhere, and he also went off to Orel to speak for him to the archbishop, by which it was suspected that he was blackening the characters both of the peasants and the gentry,—not sparing even Nastasya Sergeevna.

The peasants gave credence to all this, because 'after all, the gentry have gone to the dogs—they're all women. They'll never be able to deal with the Pole.' Varivon could hold up his head again, and as a result of his arrogant attitude the rumour got around that the Pole was trying to get him the 'insignifia of an order'. Orders and civil honours were not held by anyone in the parish at that time; one had not even been conferred on the deceased Marshal himself. It is quite clear, then, what impression must have been made by the rumour that Varivon was going to receive his 'insignifia'. The way the peasants saw it, it amounted to the notion that Father Illarion, once he had received his insignifia, would be so far 'above everybody' that he could 'write letters to the Tsar about anybody'.

What these letters might be, and about whom—they of course had no idea, but actually they thought it would be 'about high treason'; only there could not possibly be any high treason in our area, because there were only women around, about whom there might be only one possible misunderstanding: why did they go around to each others' houses carrying red boxes with the requisites for harmless games like 'musical lotto'? In those days women never came into it when politics were discussed, so the full weight of extra significance which Varivon acquired thanks to the rumours about his order fell upon the peasants themselves and increased their feeling of insecurity. Since they were very poor attenders at church, the Pole and Varivon tried to seek out some heresy among them, just to scare them. The heresy they fixed upon consisted in making the sign of the cross with two fingers, a practice observed by a good half of the Orthodox peasantry in the Province of Orel, for no other reason than that 'our grandfathers did it that way'.

Varivon established himself firmly, and whether or not he applied for the 'insignifia' of an order, everyone was afraid of him, and years passed, as they do, and we young people fled the nest and finished up in distant places as we came to years of discretion. And so, in the parish of Dobryn, a masculine spirit again came to the fore, and what was more, it was younger men full of ridiculous ideas about truth and justice and of the notion that if anyone set about oppressing the peasants it was your duty to stand up for them.

In those days such men were a novelty, and it has to be said this was so unexpected, that people did not know how to cope with them in out-of-the-way places like ours. Again and again scenes of misunderstanding like those in Turgenev's *Fathers and Sons* were replayed in one way and another. And it was the very time in which the novel was set; clerical figures play no part in the book, although they were not inactive here!

When Father Varivon first perceived a 'new man', he sensed that there was a game here to play for, and he pricked up his ears.

VIII

THE man concerned was Petr Nikolaevich Antsyferov. He was the same age as me, and he had been my classmate ever since the first form in the Orel Grammar School. When I left Orel for Kiev, Antsyferov went off to Yaroslavl, passed successfully through the Demidov Lycée there, worked for a while in the Ministry of Justice, and when he returned to the Province of Orel, he married one of the Ivanov girls. After that he settled in Zinovievo on his estate.

Antsyferov was still young at that time, but he knew quite a bit about the world, and in character he was what is known as a practical man.[1] In all other matters he conformed to the

---

[1]Petr Nikolaevich Antsyferov even now is not an old man. He flourishes to this day and he and I have long maintained friendly relations. He served as assistant

conventions of his years and his time: he was ardent, he loved the good, he harboured dissatisfaction with injustice and was ever willing to take the side of the oppressed. There were plenty of oppressed people around,—the uneducated of the whole parish, who were suffering under the yoke imposed by the Pole and Varivon.

Father Illarion recognized the young landowner as his implacable enemy, who had to be fought to the death, and he made no mistake. Antsyferov took the part of the peasants and would not allow them to be downtrodden, and if there was any hint of oppression over funerals or marriages, he would boil over and gallop off either to Kromy to take it up with Rural Dean Ptitsyn, or to Orel to see Archbishop Polikarp (Radkevich), and every time he won his case. It seemed impossible even to continue the struggle. Varivon was tied up, bound hand and foot, and disparaged to the extent that reconciliation was quite impossible. There was no point any more in even thinking of 'insignifia'. Even the peasants, sensing they had a protector, would say: 'Oh, no, Father Varivon, Petr Mikolaich'll stop you getting your insignifia.' But then, in the words of a German lady living in the parish, 'The goat was led to the sacrificial altar': Father Illarion was no less determined than Mr Antsyferov, and in response to the direct and open opposition of the young landowner he carried on a low-down intrigue, which, I am sorry to say, in later years attracted many imitators of every rank and status in society.

Father Illarion had picked up from somewhere the notion that there were rumblings of dissent against the authorities, and that educated people were held responsible.

This factor seemed to him to be a good enough pretext, and conditions in the Province were conducive to success. Following the term of office of the calm and very intelligent and highly educated civilian Governor Valerian Safonovich, a military man, Count Levashov took over as Governor, a man of very different

---

to the Procurator in the Province of Moscow, then as Justice of the Peace in St Petersburg, and now works the abundant seams of iron ore in that same parish of Dobryn where he was once accused of fomenting a revolt among the gentry against the Tsar. [Author's note.]

stamp.[2] The Count ran the province energetically and autocratically (our story will show the lengths to which he went to maintain his authority single-mindedly). News reached the village of the measures Count Levashov took, which established his reputation as 'more fearsome than Trubetskoy himself'. The climax of Trubetskoy's governorship was the occasion when he 'flogged six men in Ilminka with thick rods' (this was in connection with suspicion of arson), while under Levashov things were more serious: he 'put a man up before a firing squad'. Trubetskoy had sworn in foul language at any petty officials and merchants that came his way, but Count Levashov 'didn't even hobnob with real gentryfolk'. He went in for reorganization and raised the status of the police to such an extent that everyone really began to fear them. In this last respect particularly instructive was the case of the elected chairman of the criminal court, Lukyan Ilich Konstantinov, a man of the greatest integrity, who was 'dragged before the courts' for having shown impatience at the arrogance of a certain policeman. Thieving and obstruction were rife.

In the air one somehow smelt that specific tang which you get when administrative concerns and arbitrary action predominate, and when restraint is to be expected in no quarter. We no longer had with us figures such as A. P. Yermolov, nor the old Burnashovs, the Saburovs, Bolotov, Afrosimov and Abaz, real 'martinets of the nobility', who punched their weight and knew how to give others their due. People said of the new marshals that they were 'bowers and scrapers' and they did not rely on getting any protection from them, and they themselves were not interested in offering such help. Tale-bearers and petty police officials could hold their heads high, and they did...

---

[2]As an interesting sidelight on the manners and the atmosphere of these years of reaction, it is worthy of mention that Governor Safonov eventually left his post in circumstances quite unconnected with politics; but he too was a man of education, and education and intelligence were highly prized and respected in his family. In this respect the household of Safonov was a positively pleasant exception. But, then, what difference did it make? When ugly reactionary policies came in, this was remembered and everyone tried to make an open issue of it.

'It's all Valerian Ivanovich's fault,' they said,. 'He was all on the side of the papers and his daughters were for the journals...They were even in favour of schooling for all,—and now look how it's turned out.'

And no-one was concerned that it not only 'turned out': it turned sour. [Author's note.]

In order to deprive his enemy the landowner of the right to speak in defence of the oppressed peasants of Dobryn parish, Father Varivon had the idea of accusing Antsyferov of the most serious state crime. And we shall see that, despite the lack of any real grounds for a charge of this sort, the accusation raised a rumpus and general alarm, and the fact that it had no fateful consequences for the man accused was only due to the great energy and skilful daring of my school friend.

IX

FATHER Illarion intended to tame and to ruin Antsyferov by a direct accusation of rebellion, which this man, who always stood firmly on the ground of legality, was supposed to have instigated 'along with all the gentry' against his Majesty the Emperor. Rumours suddenly started going around Dobryn, Zinovievo, Kosarevo, and Khvostovka that the whole rebellious affair was being pursued here in our homeland, on the banks of the River Gostomlya. All the gentry were supposed to have assembled at night by the makeshift bridge at Yarushki, to have been 'drinking Jamaica drum' and sweet French vodka, and to have conspired with godless malice against the sovereign to free the peasants, and to 'turn everything back'. It was said that they were intending to assemble again in Panino in an empty threshing-barn, and then again in the Lomovetsk forest, or at night in the open, when, after 'supping Jamaica drum' again they would rebel good and proper and enlist 'to the banner of treason' all the peasants, whom they would then lead far from home 'against the imperial forces of Bibich-Zapalkansky'.

It goes without saying that the peasants are all devoted to the Tsar and genuinely appreciate his 'benevlivance', and they had not the slightest desire to leave their homes to fight either for or against Bibich-Zapalkansky. They became uneasy, first 'improportionately' and then rather more than at first.

A 'confidential and highly confidential' file on this rebellion, which only now begins to figure in our story, is held in secret in the Orel archives (that is, if it has not been burned) and I am unable to report in exact detail how the trouble-making and the machinations were carried out, but I do possess documents which show conclusively that Father Illarion was in this matter up to his neck.

The reader will soon see what grounds give me the right to state with such certainty that this is so, but meanwhile, before we reach the documentary evidence, I shall relate what I remember of what I was told about the way people came across the first traces of the work which our spiritual father was doing on the sly.

This discovery was made by chance, as are the discoveries of most conspiracies. Father Illarion was betrayed by the 'Bawdy-o Wine Cellar'. People who had been visiting the market in the town of Kromy once claimed to have spotted Father Illarion coming out of the only grocery shop and wine merchant's, which was known as the 'Bordeau Wine Cellar'. In his company were the village elder Averkin and two peasants from Zinovievo, Tishkin and Kashcheev; a little later Grigory Kotov was seen leaving.

They caught up with Kotov and asked him why he had been to the Bawdy-o Wine Cellar, and got the answer: 'On business'.

'And who paid for the drinks?'

Kotov is supposed to have replied: 'The priest.'

The conversation did not continue; the affair was related in the brief but ominous laconic style of the inquisitions of the eighteenth century.

It was enough that they had been in the Bawdy-o Wine Cellar and that the priest had paid for the drinks, a man who was neither rich nor generous. He must therefore have had good reasons. The Bawdy-o Wine Cellar was frequented only by court officials bent on cooking up their dirty tricks.

Circumstances soon proved that there were dirty tricks in this affair too.

The rebellion began when some Zinovievo gentryfolk instructed the coachman to harness the carriage, and he refused; when a reason was demanded, he replied shortly: 'You're not going anywhere.'

When the servant who had conveyed the masters' instruction and the reply was sent to summon the coachman to their presence, he said: 'I'll come in a minute', but instead locked up the stable, the carriage shed, and the store-room where the harness was kept; he took the key and went off to the inn for a drink.

There, in the presence of three other men, he felt free to do exactly as he liked, and he gave those sent to him answers which were even more explicit. The general sense of these answers was that he had no intention of fetching the horses or harnessing them, and he wasn't afraid of anybody, because *he* was faithful to his Emperor, he wasn't a traitor, and he wasn't intending to take up arms against him, and he was intending to sit till midnight in the Tsar's own tavern. Let Bibich march his army wherever he saw fit.[3]

The coachman would not budge from this policy in the slightest, and indeed all the other folk shared his mood and were prepared to support him. It was only the female sex, who were more kindly disposed to the masters and who stood somewhat aside from the political movement, which did not threaten them with the necessity of enrolling in the force against Bibich, that did not break off friendly relations with the gentry. The women passed on news at hourly intervals, but the news was not reassuring; on the contrary, it rather increased the feeling of alarm. One moonlight night, which followed the day of the rebellious coachman's disobedience, the chambermaids say they saw a small group of peasants hiding in the ruins of the old Zinovievo church, which for many a long year the peasants had pilfered of its bricks for building stoves, and these peasants were supposed to have been standing with cudgels in their hands, smoking their pipes, and, never letting their eyes leave the manor

---

[3]I have never been able to understand, and I still cannot, why the name of Diebitsch-Zabalkansky enjoyed such firm and resounding fame among our local peasants. It would seem on the face of it that Yermolov and Field Marshal Count Kamensky, who were both from Orel, should have been much closer to them; but their names were not known, while 'Bibich' is; to the present day it is fresh in their minds and enjoys great repute. If the news is received that our troops have won a victory, the response is: 'Bibich has done a good job there,' and if they are beaten: 'Bibich betrayed us.' He is a military genius, but his conscience is not entirely clear: he has 'betrayed' us more than once, and has himself been swindled: once, instead of a crock of gold which he was to have been given as a spoil of victory, they gave him a crock of sand. He had beaten the retreat and withdrawn his troops, but when he saw that it was sand, he turned the army around, and thrashed the enemy decisively. He was therefore forgiven and not dismissed the service. In more recent times there were stories about Skobelev, that he was really only second in hand to Bibich, and Bibich had given him a winning talisman, which could only be taken along on a white horse. Probably the stories of Bibich had reached our villages quite by chance, but for some reason appealed to our people and became rooted in their minds. [Author's note.]

house, and repeating over and over again, 'Come out, come out!' Apart from this, which they actually saw with their own eyes, the girls also heard from others, supposedly from Panino, that there was also a 'pickelt' by the makeshift bridge on the Yarushki, and a bonfire was burning all night. Peasants from Krivtsovo and Khvostovka flocked there as if they were pasturing their horses for the night, and they stayed awake all night; they sat by the fire uttering really terrifying threats, 'watching out for the gentry' and finally, as morning approached, they took a delivery-man on his way to market with honey-cakes for an enemy, inspected his cargo, and lightening his load significantly, released him to sell what remained.

What 'gentry' was it they were looking out for? I repeat once more, there were no gentryfolk around, except the women and Petr Ivanovich Antsyferov, in the whole neighbourhood, and the only conspiratorial assembly Petr Ivanovich could have joined would have consisted of himself alone. And the good Christians in the village had no excuse for not knowing this, only they had been deceived into believing that 'he turned all the masters against the Tsar, and here they all are, coming from Orel, from Fatezh and Dmitrovka.' This whole spacious locality, wider than anything the peasants' short-sighted imagination could encompass, was 'from end to end' seething with revolution. The peasants were alarmed, they alarmed the gentry too, who for several days had been hearing pieces of news, each one more worrying than the last. In one place the ladies driving to visit their friends with the box of 'musical lotto' met a peasant on a cart, and when the coachman shouted to him, 'Get out of the way, you blockhead!', he replied:

'Where can I go? Can't you see I'm driving the cart?'

This was taken as an insolent and provocative remark.

One visitor came from Kromy and remarked:

'What a funny lot of peasants you have round here!'

He had felt like a drink of milk, and had asked a peasant woman somewhere along the road: 'Give me a mug of milk and I'll give you ten copecks.'

The woman just looked at him, said nothing, and shut the door in his face.

The spirit of disobedience was typified by many other similar examples which I only vaguely remember, but there were open threats too, which filled the ladies' hearts with terrible fear.

A steward was sent from Krivtsovo to Zinovievo in a fast drozhky to fetch some wine. It was towards sunset; he was to get the wine home by nightfall, but instead of doing so, he arrived back much earlier with an empty barrel and only three wheels on his vehicle. The fourth had been broken, and he was unable to pick it up and put it back on the drozhky.

All out of breath from fright, the steward explained that he had galloped through the 'ryes' (that is, across a field planted with rye) when all of a sudden he saw by the side of the Panino pond Vasily Moskin emerging from the rye, all wet in a straw cap, in his shirt sleeves, and with two wild duck hanging from the belt around his waist, a gun over his shoulders, with bare feet and no trousers on. He came out and stood in the very middle of the road along which the steward had to drive, and was laughing... And his teeth, said the steward, were ever so white. The steward reined in the horse and, as he approached, asked, 'What are you doing standing there, Uncle Vasily?' And the other grinned again and said very shortly, 'Come closer and I'll tell you.' Well now, at this point the steward realized that all was not well, so he abruptly turned the horse round in a very short space, so that he had to cling firmly to the vehicle, and galloped back home at full speed. 'I whipped the horse as hard as if my life depended on it,' but all the time had the feeling that he was slipping out of the drozhky, and it was only when he approached the village that he saw the left-hand rear wheel had gone.

A fiasco like this could not be kept secret, all the more so since one consequence of this occurrence was that all the supper guests from Kromy had no vodka with their meal, and when the guests got home they were able to tell everyone that there was some strange and terrible unrest in the villages, and that the upper classes could get nothing from the peasants as a result of this insolence, neither vodka nor milk, and that they even had to fear their own servants. They were saying, 'Nothing for it but to get out!' and one or two did flee their homes: some to Kromy, others to Orel, and others to distant places where their relations lived, where no rumour of rebellion had yet penetrated.

There were also some insulting jokes played: so, for example, the wheel from the fast drozhky which the steward from Krivtsovo had lost did not disappear completely, but reappeared the same night in the cattle yard where the drozhky was always kept; no-one had brought it there, but it had obviously been hurled over the top of a shed, smashing three large earthenware pots full of washing, which all had to be laundered again for a second time. Many other stories were told, not all of which I remember. All the fears, needless to say, were vain, but considering the state of mind people were in, they had a powerful effect, and the gentry of Dobryn should not be too severely censured for this if they felt that they were suffering from slanderous misconceptions to the effect that the peasant would no longer step aside and bow, and that in general they felt they were 'at the mercy of the peasants'. Just remember the newspaper stories of 1880, when the wives of officers in the Petersburg Guard panicked for no real reason and tried to flee their married quarters, which were protected by army guards, and then if you compare this with the fears and the flight of the Dobryn gentry, who were not normally defended by military patrols, then you might be more prepared to understand what they did. A coachman who will not harness the horses in town, and one who shows the same insolence in the country make two quite different impressions.

It was forgivable to be afraid and forgivable to accept uncritically as alarming certain news which on calm reflection could not be at all alarming. The reason why it is forgivable is clear when you ask yourself about the unquestioned bravery of those who have ever taken part in military manoeuvres and who know how false alarms can be caused by so-called 'drumbeat fever'. The drummer is ordered to watch carefully for the signal and then sound the alarm. He pays such close attention and his concentration reaches such a point, that he may sometimes take any firework set off by children in the next-door garden for a signal, or the same if, as soldiers say, 'someone farts'. The drummer sounds the alarm, the moustachioed soldiers saddle their horses, all is prepared, but there is nowhere to go and no reason for going. According to military men, this is repeated on army manoeuvres with fateful regularity at least three times every ten years. It is bound to.

But now, at this point in the history of the Dobryn rebellion, we reach a new stage, which all at once gave the whole thing official status: the authorities started to interfere, and everything had to proceed 'according to the book'. Clearly they knew all about it.

Averkin, the elder of Dobryn, and the Zinovievo peasants Yakov Tishkin, Nikolai Kashcheev, Khristofor Azorov, Lavrenty Kuznetsov and Grigory Kotov were all 'hauled up' to Kromy.

These were the very ones who, it was said, had met Varivon in the 'Bawdy-o Wine Cellar' in Kromy on that memorable day. They were the ones, of course, who knew about the rebellion and they had to name the conspirators to the government. At first they were 'hauled up' just to Kromy, and then later 'to the Clownt himself'. But of course every peasant has a wife at home, and these womenfolk set up such lamentation that, no doubt, 'in Rama was there a voice heard, lamentation and weeping and great mourning'. The women sobbed and could not be comforted, because 'the Clownt was going to shoot them', and what good is a peasant after he's been shot? You can only bury him in the ground, whereas what you need him for is to work that ground in the sweat of his brow. The women were right to lament, but none the less, through their weeping and wailing, the morale in the locality, which has always been so backward and obscure, fell to a miserable degree and became 'rife with politics', something no-one knew anything about. Who it was who was in rebellion—the landowners or the peasants who were now being 'hauled up'—you could not now make out, sitting at home in the country; but the only thing was that the picture was extremely alarming, unpleasant, and, for anyone who was in the slightest degree good-hearted, worrying and insufferable. But then the second act took place: P. N. Antsyferov was 'hauled up'. Actually, he rode into Kromy of his own accord to face the rising political storm, but people said he had been 'hauled up'.

The peasants were glad, not out of any feeling of ill-will, but because they saw in this a 'turn for the better'. Petr Nikolaevich was firmly regarded as a man of good judgement and experience, 'shrewd', and people started saying: 'He'll see it through, he'll see something's done about it.' He did indeed see it through and get something done about it.

The scene of action now passes from the rural locality, where backward yokels had been struggling with it, to the towns, where it was taken over by the educated representatives of secular and ecclesiastical authority, which, as I shall have the opportunity to demonstrate, did everything they could to implant in the memory an impression of their seriousness, thoroughness and ability to assess the character of events, and to settle them in a manner concomitant with reason and good conscience. Here our story begins to take on redoubled interest and, if I may say so, redoubled shame.

X

AMONG the certified copies of documents held by me relating to this matter, which interests me so much in connection with my native parish, one may discover that 'Collegiate Assessor Petr Antsyferov, resident in the hamlet of Zinovievo in the region of Kromy, brought to the attention of His Grace (the Right Reverend Polikarp Radkevich, Archbishop of Orel and Sevsk) that the priest of the parish of Dobryn, Illarion Obolensky, had roused the peasants to rebellion, and, having bribed one of the said peasants to level against him, Antsyferov, charges of unspeakable and terrible crimes, to the effect that he, Antsyferov, knew a criminal who had made an attempt on the life of the Tsar, and had taken part in illegal assemblages. In so doing, the same Illarion Obolensky was falsely persuading the peasantry that the entire landowning class was involved in the crime, and that a huge number of them had been arrested and imprisoned in the fortress.'

His Grace Polikarp had the priest Obolensky summoned to the Orel Spiritual Consistory, where he demanded a response to Antsyferov's complaint.

Father Illarion was summoned to Orel and interrogated. He admitted nothing, saying that 'he had merely heard of these matters from the Zinovievo peasant Tishkin, and that on a basis of this "he had informed the other peasants'.

Obolensky was released, and His Lordship the Governor was supplied with a copy of the explanation Father Illarion had given and from which it was obvious that it was not Father Illarion who was the informer, but that there was none the less some political intrigue going on in the parish of Dobryn, and that it was led by Antsyferov who was inciting all the other landowners to rebel. It was only the source of the revelation which had changed: it turned out that the actual information about the gentry rebellion had come from Tishkin, the peasant from Zinovievo.

Marking his letter 'most important and highly secret', the Governor wrote to the Chief of Police in Kromy, who immediately 'hauled up' Tishkin, who had been named by the priest, and then all the others who had taken part in the discussions at the Bawdy-o Wine Cellar, and who should therefore all possess detailed information about the gentry rebellion which had originated in the region of Kromy and spread to all quarters of the Russian Empire.

We can level no complaint at Archbishop Polikarp: in this case he could not have acted otherwise, but it must be said that, as we shall see, he occupied his episcopal throne in a spirit of irresponsibility. He was not a bad man, one may even say he was good-natured, if only something could show him the path to righteousness; but unfortunately for himself and for others, he was

'At heart a decent ignoramus'.

In addition he was constantly unwell, and, to use another poetic assessment:

'It all depended how he slept
And on the state of his digestion'.

He had two main states of mind, the first when he was 'strong' and the second when he was 'weak', and in both these states His Grace was not up to running his diocese, but the archbishop's weak and disordered organism 'did not recognize' any half-way condition between these two extremes. According to this frame of mind, Archbishop Polikarp found the old government bureaucratic system of 'formal reply' unquestionably the most suitable and the best: 'sign it and be done with it'.

The consequences of such 'formal replies' for the human beings concerned are a matter of indifference for the enthusiasts for such replies, and the Archbishop was no exception.

The 'colonel of gendarmes', that is the local corps commandant of gendarmes, had, as many sharp-eyed people had noted, made several trips to St Petersburg 'to pull strings and undertake some crossings-out'. He even used to receive communications in code. In short, the rebellion had developed exactly as one might expect, and it all fitted with encoded messages and written reports, which must lie in the archives of the Third Section, until the earnest hand of some historian 'shakes off the dust of time from all the reports' and demonstrates the sound reasoning of certain guardians of our era.

In general it must be said that the leaders of society, left to themselves, were totally unable to come to terms with this affair and with the persons involved. Their attitude to Antsyferov wavered: should they take him in, put him in prison and interrogate him, or not take him in and not interrogate him, or simply arrest him and lock him up wherever they saw fit as a most pernicious enemy of public order? In discussions with him and in connection with his affairs there was a powerful sense of falsity, as if those talking to him could not come to terms and choose the right pitch, and, not being able to find the right note to sing, they constantly sounded one that was too high or too low, too hoarse or too nasal; finding the right key in which to discuss this affair was quite beyond them. But in the end that key was found, and as a result the affair immediately received different and genuine illumination. It is worth noting that this beneficial standpoint was not alighted on by Count Levashov in any way, nor was it due to the politician in charge of the secret department of his chancellory, nor to the corps commandant of gendarmes, nor to Archbishop Polikarp, but to one of the minions of the last named personage.

Meanwhile, as all this political alarm which had stretched from Dobryn to Orel flared up and became the subject of 'string-pulling' by the 'big pots' in the capital,—the rural dean of Kromy, Archpriest of the Cathedral of the Assumption Vasily Ptitsyn, on 27 May 1866 sent the Right Reverend Polikarp a report in which it is impossible not to discern the intelligence and courage with which he sought to act in order to assist the authorities to understand what this affair was all about.

Archpriest Ptitsyn, concealing nothing, emphasized that in his deanery an unsavoury story had certainly been played out, but in understanding it, the most important issue was to recognize the personality of the priest Obolensky, who 'has long been known for his tendency to utter slander and inform falsely against others in all sorts of ways, and that the latest events confirm the opinion held of him by many religious and secular persons who know him well, namely that Obolensky's passion for incrimination and counter-incrimination have turned into mental disturbance and lunacy'.

In consequence the Rural dean of Kromy 'proposed that Obolensky should without any delay be barred from exercising his priestly function'.

Written on this report the decision of his Grace appears as follows: 'Remove priest Obolensky from his church, forbid him to celebrate the Liturgy, to wear a cassock or to perform the laying-on of hands, and until his presence is required by the secular authorities, to confine him to the city of Orel, and bearing in mind the letter from Mr Antsyferov, Obolensky's own statement, and the report of the Rural Dean, and all things considered, send him to the Provincial Government for investigation of his mental condition'. Whether Archbishop Polikarp believed the Dean Ptitsyn's statement about Obolensky's madness or not, he obviously appreciated the rational nature of the new approach to the problem and was not prepared to indulge the 'holy stool-pigeon' of Dobryn. On the other hand, from this time the non-sensical situation arose whereby Father Illarion was spoken of first as a madman, and then as no longer a madman, from which there ensued a most decided absurdity.

XI

THE Orel Spiritual Consistory 'having considered the above, decides: according to the decision of his Grace to demand (sic) from the Governor of Orel information as to exactly what the priest Obolensky is guilty of and to what extent'.

The Consistory's first decision was: Obolensky is guilty.

The Governor, Count Levashov, did not reply to the 'demand' from the Consistory, but wrote direct to the Archbishop that he had much earlier 'received an intimation from the Kromy regional police chief on the subject of the matter in question, and that he had himself personally interrogated the elder of the village of Dobryn, Averkin, and the peasants of the village of Zinovievo, Yakov Tishkin, Nikolai Kashcheev, and Grigory Kotov, who were all temporarily detained for the purpose of making inquiries, and they all confirmed that the complaint made by the landowner Antsyferov was justified. For that reason, considering it harmful to allow the priest Obolensky to remain in his present place of residence in the region of Kromy, the Governor requests His Grace to move the priest Obolensky to a similar living in another region. 'Otherwise,' wrote Count Levashov, 'he could not accept the responsibility for any disorder which might result from leaving the priest Obolensky in his present position.'

The Governor and the Archbishop matched each other in their mutual respect for the limits of the power they each exercised. The Orel Spiritual Consistory, as we saw, 'demanded' from the Count information as to the nature of Obolensky's guilt, since, according to the statement of the rural dean, he had moved 'from a passion for incrimination and counter-incrimination to mental disturbance and lunacy'. Count Levashov did not reply to this directly and clearly: he did not wish to say that Obolensky was guilty of serious political slander. The Governor confined himself to the statement that 'the complaint of the landowner Antsyferov is justified', that is, that Father Illarion had made up the story of the rebellion among the gentry led by Antsyferov, and had stirred up the peasants against the gentry, but he did not refer to the notion that Father Illarion, who had cooked up all this porridge, had gone off his head. It was as if he did not believe it, or did not consider it important, and in answer to the Consistory's 'demand' wrote to the Archbishop without a moment's hesitation to ask him to allow the disturbed criminal to remain a priest, but only see to it that he should be 'removed to a similar living in another area.' He has been wreaking havoc here; now let him go and wreak some more somewhere else.

But this was not enough: in the paper in which the Governor informed the Archbishop of Orel and Sevsk of how he should act in regard to Obolensky there was something even more autocratic, illegal, and one might almost be justified in saying arrogant, in the sense that the General had disgracefully intervened in a purely ecclesiastical matter. In this message, which the Governor sent to the Archbishop telling him he should assign the priest who had gone mad as a result of his passion for tale-telling to another parish, Count Levashov added 'that he did not wish Obolensky to be deprived of his priestly orders, but asked that he should be moved elsewhere and the Governor should be informed appropriately'...

He, Count Levashov, did not *wish* a man who had besmirched his own mind or his good name to be prevented from being a priest,—a man whose standing as a priest was after this affair to become a scandal and a profanation of religion,—as the Archbishop understood correctly...What significance could this wish of the Count's have for His Grace the Archbishop? Needless to say, it was the significance of the groundless wish of a layman and a Governor who did not have a clear idea of the limitations of his authority.

But what did Archbishop Polikarp do? Did he feel the insult and injury which had quite improperly been offered to him by the autocratic Governor to a highly-placed office-bearer in the Church? Did he show the Governor firm resistance worthy of his position and did he remain immovable in his correct conviction that neither an exposed political slanderer nor a lunatic could hold priestly office in the region of Kromy or in any other? Did he point out that if the Governor was concerned for civic order in the region of Kromy, it was the anointed of the Church who was responsible for something much greater—to rid the consciences of men of temptation and the priestly office from censure?

Such a reaction might well have been expected, all the more so, because all of this was required by the vital interests of the Church and had nothing to do with any supposed obstinacy or discourtesy on the part of the Archbishop. And if he had done it, the Archbishop needed have no very great fear of the Governor. Polikarp was after all no Filipp Kolachev and Count Levashov was no Ivan the Terrible, but merely 'caliph for the day', like many others. But the facts show that the Archbishop thought quite differently.

His Grace did not raise his voice as loud as would have been appropriate to defend the integrity of his sacred pastoral right to oversee his flock; he meekly accepted the instruction of the Governor...Only, ashamed of openly submitting to the arrogance shown towards him by the layman, His Grace Polikarp handed over the paper which insulted the honour of his holy office to the Orel Spiritual Consistory for them to deal with. And that was no worse a thing to do, since the Consistory conceived a surprising measure to satisfy Count Levashov, by which one strange thing countered another.

XII

INQUIRING in true bureaucratic fashion about all that was known of the lunatic criminal and counter-criminal Illarion Obolensky, the Orel Consistory listened respectfully to the paper written by the Governor in autocratic tone to the Archbishop and 'gave instructions: to remove the priest Obolensky from the parish of Dobryn this day, having sent there according to the decision of His Grace the priest Nekrasov, in relation to whom an order for transfer should be prepared and sent to the Rural Dean for the area for delivery to him, and in place of Nekrasov in the village of Studenets Obolensky should be appointed. But' (and here the difficulties begin) 'prior to permission being given to him to exercise his priestly office and the handing over of this instruction, he should be transferred into the Archbishop's Palace in Orel for observation, and then, following a decision by His Grace, he should be transferred to the Provincial Administration of Orel for assessment of his mental condition, for which he shall be summoned to the Consistory by the Rural Dean'.

This was set out in its entirety, without any concealment of the impertinent demands of the Governor which were so degrading for the Archbishop, in instruction No. 4990 which was handed to Archpriest Ptitsyn on 21 June 1866, with the addition that Rural Dean Ptitsyn 'should send Obolensky to the Consistory, and at the same time oblige him to provide an undertaking that he would remove his property and his household to the village of Studenets'.

How much absurdity, contradiction and cruelty there is in this, and how obvious it is that it all results from the pusillanimity and subservience with which the Right Reverend Polikarp allowed his high holy office to be stained.

We shall briefly recount the results of these dispensations, which concluded the preposterous, but comical and disreputable story of the rebellion 'of all the gentry', which had been thought up in the presbytery at Dobryn.

Whether or not Illarion Obolensky had gone mad as a result of his obsessive enthusiasm for incrimination and counter-incrimination, let us assume that either is true, as if the issue is of total indifference to us. Let us even give credence to what the whole parish of Dobryn and 'the whole rural deanery' said, that is that Illarion Obolensky was certainly not mad, but was simply a congenital and incorrigible stool-pigeon. Let us assume also that Rural Dean Ptitsyn, seeing that Father Illarion 'had attained the realm of theological politics', demonstrated his resourcefulness in order to free himself and all the authorities from the problem, by subjecting Obolensky to a clever device in making out that he had done everything through madness...The 'perspicacity' of the Kromy archpriest, which in this instance became a matter for general approval, did in any case represent the only happy outcome for the political affair which had arisen in his deanery. Moreover, this clever device was beneficial: it discredited the originator of the rebellion and also made him not responsible for his frightful calumnies. It was no great hardship for him to be kept in an asylum for an offence of this nature, and then, when he recovered, he would have the right to exercise his office again, to wear a cassock and to lay on hands. And in all this Obolensky's family would not be 'hauled up' from Dobryn, and he himself would be investigated a little and then subjected to assessment. This assessment would doubtless be fairly educative for Father Illarion, but on the other hand it really would clarify for the Archbishop the moral and mental state of the maniac.

But the Governor managed to mix the whole thing up, as only he could, and administrative confusion resulted which was far worse than anything the peasants could cause.

The Governor satisfied himself completely that Antsyferov's complaint was justified, that Obolensky had stirred up the peasants against the landowners by assuring them that the whole landowning class was guilty of rebellion and that Antsyferov was even acquainted with a man who had designs on the life of the Tsar.

It is a fearful accusation. If it had been correct, it could have cost Antsyferov his life; but since it turned out to be unjust, without any doubt at all, the slanderer was surely liable to the heaviest penalty. The one means to mitigate his fate was the rural dean's 'clever trick': to present Obolensky to the world as being not responsible for his actions by reason of madness.

Simple common sense and justice, it seemed, would have obliged the Governor, had he not believed in Obolensky's madness, to report on the political slanderer to the Procurator's office, and if he had believed the Rural Dean's opinion about his madness, he should not have prevented the Archbishop from carrying out his plan of having him declared a maniac. But Count Levashov wanted neither one thing nor the other; he somehow did not want to admit that such things as political slanderers could possibly exist. It was not his business that neither a proven slanderer nor a madman should be serving as a priest; his *wish* was law, or even above the law, not just the secular law but the spiritual one as well, and the venerable Polikarp, Archbishop of Orel and Sevsk, would not oppose the fantasies of the Count: he 'appointed the madman Obolensky priest in the village of Studenets'.

I say 'madman', because with the appointment of Obolensky as priest in Studenets at the desire of the Governor, the Consistory continued to believe him to be damaged in his mind and liable to be sent off for examination. The consistory therefore cannot be blamed for this senseless situation,—it was in a difficult position and was forced to improvise all sorts of variations and fugues in order somehow to reconcile the need for the Archbishop to satisfy the illegal wishes of the Governor with the protection of the unfortunate parishioners of Studenets from a lunatic priest. Such was the first priority of the Consistory in view of the inability of the Archbishop to explain to the Governor that the wish of His Excellency to keep a lunatic as a priest in holy orders could not be granted in accordance with propriety. And the Orel Consistory, by indulging in its bureaucratic capers, solved the problem as best it could.

The lunatic priest was transferred to Studenets, and as priest, but the instruction was to 'oblige' the madman to give an undertaking to 'move all his property and household'; the rural dean summoned the madman, he appeared, and listened to the ruling that he was 'instructed' to move his property and household', then to go to Orel, live in the Archbishop's dwelling, and finally to present himself to the Provincial Administration for assessment of his mental condition...And the madman fulfilled all this: he travelled the length and breadth of the Province of Orel by the route prescribed for him, transported his beggarly goods and chattels and his family, and delivered his very self up to the doors of the collective presence of the Provincial Administration, in order to pass through them to the madhouse or the prison camp...And this was all done 'to the letter', like Yakushkin's peasants who transported each other across the whole of the Province of Orel in order to be flogged.

It would seem, purely on account of the exactitude with which Obolensky, 'darkened by incriminations', laboured and fell ill while moving his family and property and presenting himself for investigation, that the Provincial Administration had reason to declare Father Illarion to be in full possession of his senses, and to reflect on the mental state of those who had got the whole affair into such a mess.

Fate itself laughed at the Archbishop's fear: on 21 June 1866 the Consistory issued its remarkable order, in which it denounced the 'wish' of the Governor and the meekness of its own archbishop, and exactly a month later, on 22 July 1866, Count Levashov was removed from the position of Governor of Orel...

It would have taken very little to stand up to his illegal desires regarding a matter which was purely ecclesiastical.

XIII

THE events I have recounted here took place a mere fifteen years ago, when there was still much discussion in the press about church affairs, and, most prominently of all, the question was raised 'of the need to free hierarchs from the oppressive power of lay persons in positions of authority, exercising power in the central institution of the church'. By this obscure and tortuous circumlocution was meant the Holy Synod and its 'layman in a position of authority', the Chief Procurator. 'If only we could get rid of him, if only we could remove this strange ordinance, our church would thrive.' This was the general opinion among the more timid 'traditionalists', who expressed their view in a near-inaudible whisper in a manner of 'nervous concealment', until not long before his death Archbishop Agafangel of Volyn plucked up courage to speak out openly. The journal *The Citizen* managed to pick up his message, and gave it currency to some extent in other parts of Russia: 'The Procurator is damaging the Church'. (The success of the Rt Rev. Agafangel was greatly enhanced by the fact that it was directed against the present Metropolitan of Moscow Makary Bulgakov and the 'layman in a position of authority' in the Holy Synod at the time, Count D. A. Tolstoy, who had a gift for bringing down upon himself the general displeasure of the whole country, but who, in his work in the Synod, came close to doing a lot of good among a whole series of mistakes.)

This seemed to most people ever so true, and was received with approval, and it is easy to see why it was approved of then and why it still is. It was a protest, and incidentally a protest of the most fruitless nature, against something we cannot change. What can be more congenial to Russian minds and hearts than such a complaint? A single voice among the swarm of pundits, all expressing their misgivings on the matter, spoke up and said that this was not the principal issue; that the main issue lay in the morale and attitude of the bishops themselves, who can lose nothing of the high significance of their office in the presence of a 'layman', unless they act as though in the spirit of Judas: 'What will ye give me, and I will deliver him unto you?' The single voice was right, and in that voice more than in any other, was heard a real understanding of the matter and a real love for the nation's church; but it was drowned by the empty bleating of the multifarious 'misgivings'. They vainly repeated, and are still desirous of repeating, their complaints about a 'layman' having so much say in ecclesiastical affairs, whereas a whole mass of instances similar to those we have been discussing here bears witness to the willing submission of bishops even to such laymen as have no right at all to give them any instructions in an ecclesiastical matter.

Who can defend the bearers of high sacred office from their own feebleness?

The answer would appear to be no-one but themselves. At least the well-known classical phrase runs: 'No-one will be saved who within himself, in the feebleness of his soul, carries his own enemy.'

The talk and counter-talk about the 'layman with authority' may be no more than to divert attention from the real reason for the troubles of the Church. Complaints of procuratorial interference,—to use the metaphor of a certain ecclesiastical writer—are no more than figleaves with which to cover the nakedness of those who are ashamed to stand before God when he calls and says unto them: 'Where art thou?'

XIV

AND what of the parish of Dobryn after the departure of the instigator of the universal rebellion of the gentry, whose calumny inevitably, as it would seem, became a problem for the whole Province?

The dispersal of the parish landowners, who, as the peasants said, 'trickled away' was final: they never reassembled. The parish was taken over by the peasant class. From the 'landowning class' there remained only one, namely Mr Antsyferov himself, and he did not visit very often, confining himself to flying visits 'for the exploitation of ore'. The little houses which had been part of the landowners' properties were now inhabited by what one might call the new middle classes: mainly tradespeople and smallholders.

In their diaspora the refugee landowners could never understand how it was that Father Illarion was both designated 'mad' and at the same time sane, but not convicted of any offence. Who indeed could understand such a thing? They reasoned that it was all due to the fact that the Right Reverend Polikarp was hoping to be awarded another star on his chest, and therefore gave in to the Governor's wish to leave the calumniator in holy orders. So they thought and continued to think; but maybe it was not true at all. It seems much more likely that Archbishop Polikarp was not a rich man, and he knew that even an Archbishop can expect little protection if his hands are empty.

He knew it and he submitted, and I think this is the reason. The fact could not be confirmed, because Polikarp died in 1867 and no new insignia appeared on his breast.

The gentry neither as an assembly, nor as represented by their permanent spokesmen, responded to the calumnious charges which had been made against them. The simply rejoiced that God had taken away Count Levashov, and imagined that they had been responsible for his 'moving on'. Their joy continued for almost a year, until Prince Lobanov-Rostovsky took over as Governor, after which God sent them Mikhail Nikolaevich Longinov. This conservative aristocrat, by some strange play of extremes, fell into agreement with Herzen, and considered that there was nothing more laughable on God's earth than any opposition mounted by the Russian nobility—in which belief he was probably right. Incidentally, Longinov's true way of thinking is very little known, because among all Russian men of letters he was the only one of whom no organ of the press published an obituary.

Longinov's arbitrary behaviour in Orel is even more interesting and of quite a different nature, but of that we may read elsewhere.

How did the peasants react to the rebellion, and how did they take the comical dispensations of the Provincial high-ups towards Varivon?

No reaction at all. They received the new priest 'with one voice', and argued like this:

'As for us, whoever the priest is, he's our Father in Christ. We couldn't have wanted better than the likes of Father Vasily—*he* didn't make up stories about rebellions, *he* didn't cause trouble in the Province, and—drunk or sober—*he* didn't lean on us peasants and *he* was the worthy man we wanted.'

And this parish of Dobryn is in my view a microcosm of the whole of rural Russia:—don't alarm us or 'lean on' us; don't talk to us about rebellions; just go and live as you ought—then you'll be 'the worthy man we want'.

Selivan, the Bogeyman

Fear has big eyes
Proverb

Chapter I

I SPENT my childhood in Orel. We lived in the Nemchinov House, which was not far from the 'little cathedral'. These days I cannot make out exactly where our tall wooden building stood, but I remember that from its garden we had an expansive view onto a broad and deep gully with precipitous sides, which were marked with layers of red clay. Beyond the gully stretched a large area of common land on which there stood some state-owned shops, and, at the side of these, soldiers would be drilled in the summer months. Every day I used to watch them being drilled—and beaten. In those days beatings were customary, but I could never get used to the sight and would always cry when I saw it. To prevent this happening too often, my nurse, the very elderly widow of a Moscow soldier, Marina Borisovna, would take me out for a walk in the town park. Here we would sit above the shallow waters of the Oka and watch little children bathing and playing in it. I greatly envied their freedom.

The main advantage of their free and easy position in my eyes was that they were wearing neither shoes nor linen, as their shirts had been taken off and the sleeves tied up to the collar. The shirts therefore took on the appearance of a large sack, and the children would hold them in the water against the current and catch tiny little silvery fish. These fish were so small that they could not be gutted, and this was held to be sufficient reason for cooking and eating them whole.

I never had the courage to taste them, but to catch them, as the diminutive fishermen did, seemed to me to be the highest degree of rapture which freedom could have granted a boy of my age.

My nurse, however, knew all sorts of reasons why such freedom would have been quite improper for me. These reasons came down to it that I was the son of noble parents, and everybody in town knew my father.

'It would be quite different if we were in the country,' Nurse used to say. There, among simple uneducated peasants, maybe I too would have been allowed to enjoy this sort of freedom now and then.

Somehow, this feeling that I was unreasonably constrained began to beckon me strongly and insistently towards the country, and my rapture knew no bounds when my parents bought a small estate in the District of Kromy. That same summer we moved from our large town house to a very comfortable, but small country house with a balcony and a thatched roof. Woodland in the Kromy District even then was hard to come by and sparse when you found it. It is an area of steppe and arable land, and in addition it is well watered by little brooks full of pure water.

Chapter II

AS soon as I settled in the country I made extensive and curious acquaintance with the peasants. While my parents were fully occupied in setting up their farm, I lost no time in forming close friendships with the older boys and the young children who took the horses out to graze 'on the clearings'.[1] My strongest attachment, however, was to an old miller, Granddad Ilya—an old man, all grey, and with a huge black moustache. He was more accessible for conversation than all the others, because he did not go away from me to work, but would either walk up and down along the dam carrying a manure fork, or else sit below the vibrating mill race and listen in meditative mood to whether the mill-wheels were rumbling away regularly, or whether the water was seeping out somewhere under the race. When he got tired of doing nothing, he would sit making cogs of chestnut wood or spools for the pinion. But whichever of these he was engaged in, he was easily distracted from whatever he was doing and would

[1] *kuliga*—a place where trees have been chopped down and burned off, a clearing. [Author's note]. The word is local to Orel.

willingly start to chat; his talk was conducted in disconnected bursts, without any relationship to what went before, but he liked to use a system of hints, which gave him the chance to make gentle fun to some extent of himself, but also of his listeners.

By reason of his craft, Granddad Ilya had a pretty close relationship with the water-sprite which reigned over our ponds, the upper and the lower, and the two marshes. This demon had his main headquarters under the disused race at our mill.

Granddad Ilya knew all about this, and would say:

'*He* likes me, *he*, if he comes home angry because there's been some trouble,—he won't do me any harm. If someone else was lying here on the sacks in my place,—he'd just tear him off his sack and chuck him out, but me he wouldn't dream of touching.'

All the younger folk assured me that between Granddad Ilya and the 'water-sprite granddad' the relationship he had described really did exist, only it depended not on the fact that the water-sprite liked Granddad Ilya, but that Ilya, as a real miller through and through, knew the special word that only a real miller would know, and which the water-sprite and all his little demons would obey without question, as did the adders and toads which lived under the races and on the dam.

With the other children I fished for gudgeon and loach, of which there were very many in our narrow, but pure river Gostomlya; but, being a serious little boy by nature, I spent more time with Granddad Ilya, whose experienced mind was quite new and unfamiliar to a town boy like me. From Ilya I also learned about the house-demon, which slept by the stove, and about the water-sprite which had a marvellous and important position under the mill-wheels, and about the witch who was so shy and unreliable, that she hid herself from any immodest glance in various piles of dust—perhaps in the threshing-barn, or the drying-barn, or the mill where they ground hemp stalks in autumn. What Granddad knew least about was the wood-demon, because he lived a long way away, near Selivan's household, and only sometimes came to us and hid in the broom plantation in order to make himself a new set of pipes of brittle willow, which he would play under the trees near the reservoir where the hemp was dampened. Moreover, Granddad Ilya, in the whole of his adventurous life, had seen the wood-demon face to face only once, and that was on St Nicholas's Day, when we had a festive service in church. The wood-demon came up to Ilya, having disguised himself as a perfectly normal peasant, and asked for a pinch of snuff. And when Granddad said to him. 'The devil take you—here you are!' and opened his snuff-box,—at this point the demon simply could not maintain his good behaviour and started fooling about like a schoolboy: he slapped the snuffbox from below with the palm of his hand and sent snuff straight into the honest miller's eyes.

All these lively and entertaining stories I found totally convincing, and their rich and picturesque content so filled my imagination, that I became something of a seer. At least, once when at great personal risk I looked into the granary by the mill, my eye took on such sharpness and sensitivity, that I perceived, sitting there in the flour-dust, a witch! She was unwashed, wearing a dusty married peasant's headdress, and she had scrofulous eyes. And when, scared by this vision, I fled mindlessly from the place, then my other sense—that of hearing—perceived the presence of the wood-demon. I cannot swear to where he was actually sitting, probably on some tall willow-tree, but I know that when I was running away from the witch, the wood-demon whistled as loudly as anything on his green pipe, and grabbed me so firmly by the foot that he tore off the heel of my shoe.

I scarcely drew breath before I had told all this to the people at home, and my honesty was rewarded by being shut in a room to read a book of sacred history, while a barefoot serf boy was sent to a soldier's wife in the next village to get her to repair the damage done by the demon to my shoe. But even reading sacred history did not keep me from believing in the supernatural beings to whom I had been introduced through the mediation of Granddad Ilya. I knew and loved sacred history—even now I enjoy dipping into it again—but all the same, I could not have renounced the attractive children's world of those mythical creatures Granddad Ilya told me about. The woodland streams would have been all the poorer if they had been deprived of the genii which folk fantasies had endowed them with.

Among the unpleasant consequences of the affair with the wood-demon's pipe was that Granddad Ilya received a good telling-off from my mother for teaching me a course in demonology, and for a while he avoided me and did not seem to wish to continue my education. He even pretended to chase me away when I approached.

'Run away to nurse!' he would say, turning me round and applying his calloused hand to my backside.

But I was highly conscious of my age and considered such treatment inappropriate. I was eight, and had no need to go off to my nurse. I conveyed this feeling to Granddad Ilya by bringing him a slop-basin full of the cherries from which they were making cherry brandy.

Ilya loved this fruit. He accepted the gift, relented, and laid his gnarled hand on my head, and the closest and most friendly relations were re-established between us.

'Now, look you here,' he said. 'Always pay close attention to what a peasant like me tells you, but don't go telling it to everyone. If you do, I'll send you away.'

From that time I kept everything the miller told me a secret, and in return I learned so much that was of interest, that I began to be afraid not only at night when all the household spirits, wood-demons and witches became very daring and malevolent, but I even began feeling scared in the daytime. This fear overcame me because our house and all the area where we lived was in the power of one enormously fearsome brigand and bloodsucking sorcerer, whose name was Selivan. He lived a mere four miles from us 'at the fork in the road', that is, at the point where the main post road divided into to two: one way, the new road, went in the direction of Kiev, and the other, the old one, led to Fatezh through a plantation of hollow willows dating from Empress Catherine's time. This road was disused now and had gone to rack and ruin.

Less than a mile beyond this fork in the road there was a wood of sturdy oak trees, and by the wood there was the most forlorn, broken-down, and half-ruined inn, in which people said no-one ever spent the night. Now, this was not hard to believe, since the inn offered no conveniences for an overnight stay, and also because it was too close to the town of Kromy, where even in that half-savage age travellers might hope to find a warm room, a samovar and a left-over loaf of bread. And it was here, in this dread household that Selivan, the 'empty innkeeper', lived: a fearful fellow, whom nobody wished to meet.

Chapter III

THE story of the 'empty innkeeper', Selivan, was told to me by Granddad Ilya. Selivan had come from a small tradesman's family in Kromy; his parents had died young, and as a boy he lived in the home of a baker, and sold white wheatmeal loaves near the inn by the gate on the Orel road. He was a good boy in those days, good-natured and obedient, but people were constantly telling the baker that he should be careful with Selivan, because he had a fiery red birthmark on his face,—and you never get that for nothing. There were people too who claimed to know a proverb: 'God marks a scoundrel'. Selivan's baker employer was forever praising him for his hard work and loyalty, but everybody else, by reason of their sincere good will, held that genuine good sense nevertheless obliges people to watch out and not trust him too far,—since 'God marks a scoundrel.' If he had a birthmark on his face, it was there for the very reason that all over-trustful people should be warned. The baker did not wish to shun these wise people, but Selivan was an excellent worker. He sold loaves honestly and every evening meticulously handed over to his employer all the small coins from his big leather purse, exactly as he had received them from his peasant customers. However, the birthmark was there for a reason, as would one day be clear (and so it always is). There arrived in Kromy from Orel a 'retired hangman', Borka by name, and people said, 'Borka, you've lived by the knout, we'll now keep you out,' and everyone tried to make sure that this crude rhyme came true for the retired executioner. And when Borka arrived in Kromy on foot from Orel, he had his daughter with him, a girl of about fifteen who had been born in the prison where Borka worked—though there were many who thought it would have been better had she never been born.

They arrived in Kromy to live there by official registration. No-one now understands what this means, but in those days the situation was that retired executioners were designated residents in certain little towns, and this was done at random, without asking what anyone wanted or seeking their agreement. And so it was with Borka: some governor instructed that he should be registered in Kromy, and registered he was, and he arrived here with his daughter to live. The only thing was that in Kromy it went without saying that he was not a welcome guest to anyone, rather the reverse: everyone disregarded him, honest folk that they were, and no-one would allow him or his daughter into their household. And at the time they arrived it was very cold indeed.

The hangman asked to be allowed first into one house, then another, but then gave up troubling people. He could see that he aroused not the slightest sympathy in anyone, and he knew that this was no more than he deserved.

'But the child!' he thought. 'The child isn't responsible for my sins, someone will take pity on her.'

And Borka again went knocking on door after door, asking people to take in if not him, then his daughter...He swore he would never come to visit his child.

But this plea was as much in vain as the other.

Who wants to have anything to do with a hangman?

So, having gone round the whole village, the ill-starred newcomers asked to be let into the prison. There at least they might get warmed up after enduring the autumn damp and cold. But the prison would not let them in, since the period of their service had expired, and they were now free people. They were free, in fact, to die in the lee of any fence or in any ditch.

The hangman and his daughter were sometimes given alms, not for their sakes, of course, but for Christ's sake, but no-one would let them into their house. The old man and his daughter had no refuge and spent the night sheltering sometimes under a cliff, sometimes in the hollows in a clay quarry, sometimes in deserted guard huts in vegetable gardens in the valley. Their severe fate was shared by a scraggy hound which had come with them from Orel.

This was a large once-shaggy dog, whose hair had all been smoothed down into the appearance of felt. What it fed on in the company of its beggarly owners no-one had the faintest idea, but, of course, they guessed that it didn't need feeding, because it was 'innardless', as the saying was, in other words it was no more than skin and bone and a pair of exhausted yellow eyes, but there was nothing 'in its inside', and so it needed no food.

Ilya used to tell me how this effect could be achieved 'in the simplest possible manner.' Any dog, when it was a puppy, needed to be fed thinly diluted molten tin or lead, and it would become 'innardless' and could get away without food. But, of course, you also needed to know a 'special magic word'. And on account of the fact that the executioner obviously knew this word,—people of strict moral principles killed his dog. That's just as it ought to be, of course, so as not to give any quarter to sorcery; but it was a terrible misfortune for the beggars, since the girl slept close to the dog, which imparted to her something of the warmth in its coat. However, such trivial considerations, needless to say, were no reason to pander to magic, and everyone was unanimous that it was absolutely right to destroy the dog. Let there be no notion that sorcerers may lead right-thinking people astray!

Chapter IV

AFTER the killing of the dog, the girl was warmed in the shacks where they spent the night by the hangman himself, but he was old, and it was his good fortune that he did not have to experience this worry, which was unendurable for him, for long. One frosty night the girl realized that her father had become colder than she herself, and she was so afraid that she moved away from him in horror and lost consciousness. Until morning she continued in the embrace of death. When dawn broke and people on the way to morning service in the church looked into the hut out of curiosity, they saw father and daughter frozen stiff. They managed to revive the girl, and when she saw her father's strangely staring eyes and wildly bared teeth, she understood the truth and burst into sobs.

The old man was buried outside the cemetery, because he had lived an evil life and died without repentance, but they rather forgot about his daughter...It's true, it wasn't for long, only a month or so, but when they did remember—she was nowhere to be found.

Perhaps the orphan had run away to some other town or was begging around the villages. Much more curious was the fact that the disappearance of the orphan was accompanied by another strange occurrence: before the girl was missed, it had been noticed that the bread-seller Selivan had disappeared without trace.

He disappeared completely unexpectedly, and without any apparent reason, quite unlike any previous runaway. Selivan took absolutely nothing belonging to anyone else, and even the loaves he was to have sold were all left lying on his tray along with the entire takings from his sales; but he himself never returned home.

For three whole years the two orphans were considered to be missing without trace.

Then unexpectedly one day a merchant came home from market. This was the owner of the empty inn 'at the fork', and he said he had had an accident: he was driving along, and he drove his horse carelessly onto an embankment and was trapped under his overturned cart, but he was saved by an unknown tramp.

Then he recognized the tramp, and it was none other than Selivan.

The merchant rescued by Selivan was not one of those people who are indifferent to those who do them a good turn; so as not to stand accused at the Last Judgement of ingratitude, he sought to do some good to the tramp.

'I must reward you,' he said to Selivan, 'I have an empty inn at the fork, you can go and live there and look after it for me and sell oats and hay and pay me no more than a hundred roubles a year rent.'

Selivan knew that there was no point in an inn on a deserted road four miles from a town, and he had no hope of having any patrons; but on the other hand it was the first time in his life he had been offered a place of his own, so he agreed.

The merchant took him on.

Chapter V

SELIVAN arrived at the inn pushing a little one-wheeled manure cart bearing all his possessions, and on top of them lay a sick woman with her head right back, dressed in wretched rags.

People asked, 'Who's that?'

He replied, 'It's my wife.'

'Where is she from?'

Selivan meekly replied:

'She's a child of God.'

'What is she suffering from?'

'Her legs are weak.'

'And what caused that?'

Knitting his brows, Selivan growled:

'The cold ground.'

He would say no more than that. He took his feeble cripple into his arms and carried her into the hut.

Selivan lacked any willingness to talk and any pleasant social graces; he avoided other people and indeed even seemed to fear them. He never showed his face in town, and his wife was never seen again from the time he brought her in the handcart. But many years had passed since that time,—those who were young in those days grew old, and the inn at the fork became ever more decrepit and dilapidated; but Selivan and his wretched crippled wife went on living there, and to everyone's surprise, he was able to make some payments in rent to the heirs of the merchant.

Now how did this strange fellow manage to raise enough for his personal needs as well as what he had to pay to rent a completely broken-down inn? Everyone knew that *not a single* traveller *ever* looked in here and that *not a single* carter ever fed his horses here, yet Selivan, though he lived in poverty, did not actually die of hunger.

That was the question which, however, did not worry the local peasantry for very long. Soon they all realized that Selivan must be acquainted with an impure power. That impure power managed to set him up with benefits that would be quite impossible for normal people.

It is well known that the Devil and his forces love to do evil to people; but they particularly enjoy snatching away their souls so suddenly and unexpectedly that they are unable to cleanse themselves by repentance. If any human being helps such intrigues, the whole world of impure spirits, that is wood-demons, water-sprites and witches, gladly grant that person various favours, though, one must admit, on very tough conditions. He who helps the devils must himself follow them down to Hell,—sooner or later, but inescapably. This was the fateful position in which Selivan found himself. So as to survive somehow in his dilapidated little house, he had long since sold his soul to several devils at the same time, and these devils had set about driving travellers onto his premises by the most forceful measures. No-one ever left Selivan's inn. This was managed by the wood-demons, in league with the witches, who would suddenly just before nightfall raise snowstorms and blizzards, in which any traveller would despair and rush to take refuge from the wild elements anywhere he could. This was the point at which Selivan would try his tricks: he would put a light in his window, and this light would attract merchants with fat body-wallets, gentry with secret hidden cashboxes, and priests with three-flapped fur caps absolutely stuffed with banknotes. It was a snare. None of those who entered Selivan's gates ever came back through them. What Selivan did with them no-one had any idea.

Granddad Ilya, when he got to this point in his tale, waved his hand in the air and said significantly:

'The owl flies, the harrier soars—everything is black: storm, snow and...dead of night covers a multitude of sins.'

So as not to lose Ilya's good opinion, I pretended I understood what 'The owl flies, the harrier soars' meant, but all I really understood was that Selivan was a bogeyman in the eyes of all and sundry, and it was extremely dangerous to meet him...God preserve anyone in the world from such a fate.

However, I tried to check the fearful stories about Selivan against the accounts of other people, and everybody agreed in every respect. Everyone saw Selivan as a fearful bogey, and they all, just as Ilya had done, sternly warned me never to 'tell anyone at home in the fine mansion about Selivan.' On the advice of the miller I kept this peasant commandment until one particular terrible occasion when I myself fell into Selivan's clutches.

Chapter VI

IN winter, at the time they fixed the double frames in the windows, I could not see Granddad Ilya and the other peasants as often as I usually did. The grown-ups kept me inside out of the frost, and the peasants went on working in the cold, while one of them had an unpleasant experience, which again brought Selivan onto the scene.

At the very beginning of the winter a nephew of Ilya's called Nikolai went to visit people in Kromy to celebrate his saint's day, and never returned. A fortnight later he was discovered in the fringe of Selivan's wood. Nikolai was sitting on a tree-stump with his beard resting on a walking stick, apparently in a state of such severe exhaustion that he had never noticed that the blizzard had covered him with snow above his knees, and the foxes had bitten off his nose and his cheeks.

Obviously Nikolai had missed the road, tired himself out and frozen to death, but everybody knew that it hadn't happened just like that and that Selivan had some responsibility for it. I discovered this from the maids, of whom there were very many working in our house, most of whom seemed to be called Annushka. There was Big Annushka, Little Annushka, Plump Annushka, Pock-marked Annushka, and then yet another Annushka, known as 'the Hucksterette'. This last girl was something of a satirist and raconteur in her own way. It was due to her vivacious, irrepressible character that she had been given this lively nickname.

There were only two maids not called Annushka—Neonila and Nastya, who both enjoyed a rather special position, since they had received special training in Madame Morozova's shop in Orel, which was a very fashionable establishment at that time. There were also three little girls who ran errands and did odd jobs—Oska, Moska and Roska. The baptismal name of one of them was Matrena, another was Raisa, but what Oska's real name was I have no idea. Moska, Oska and Roska were all still children, and therefore everyone treated them somewhat disparagingly. They ran about barefoot and were not allowed to sit on chairs: they had to use low benches. It was their job to perform various demeaning tasks, such as cleaning washbowls, emptying washtubs, taking the house-dogs for walks, running errands for the people in the kitchen, and taking messages to the village. In manor houses today there is no longer such a superfluity of servants, but in those days they seemed quite indispensable.

All our maids and the girls, of course, knew a lot about that frightful fellow Selivan, near whose house Nikolai the peasant had died. The incident was cause to recall all Selivan's old evil deeds, including some I had known nothing about. It now emerged that Konstantin the coachman had once been driving past to fetch some beef from town, when he heard pitiful groans and cries coming from Selivan's window, among which he made out the words: 'Ouch, my hand's painful! Ouch, my finger hurts terribly!'

Big Annushka's explanation of this was that Selivan had during a blizzard (she used the old Orel word *kury*) lured a coach containing a whole family of gentryfolk to his inn and was slowly cutting off the children's fingers one by one. I was greatly horrified by this fearsome barbarity. Then Ivan the cobbler had an even more dreadful and even less explicable experience. Once, when he had been sent to town to collect some equipment for shoemaking, he was delayed and had to return home in the dark, when a small snowstorm blew up,—and this was the first thing that delighted Selivan. He got up and went out into the open in order to prance about in the gloom with Yaga, the evil sister, and with the wood-demons and other witches. Now Ivan knew he would do this, so kept an eye open to avoid him, but he didn't manage it. Selivan arose right in front of him and barred his way...The horse stopped. But the cobbler, fortunately for him, was naturally bold and resourceful. He went up to Selivan, pretending to be friendly, and said, 'Greetings, friend,' but in the same instant drew the longest and sharpest awl he had out of his sleeve and stabbed Selivan with it straight in the stomach. That is the only place you can mortally wound a sorcerer, but Selivan saved himself by instantly turning himself into a solid mile-post, in which the cobbler's sharp tool stuck so firmly that he couldn't get it out however hard he tried, and was obliged to part company with his awl, even though could not possibly do without it.

This last incident was no less than an offensive insult to all honest people and it convinced everyone that Selivan was not only a great evildoer and cunning sorcerer, but an impudent fellow who should be given no quarter. It was decided to teach him a very firm lesson; but Selivan was no fool and learned a new trick: he started 'changing himself', that is, at the slightest sign of danger, even simply when he met other people in the normal course of events, he would change his human form and, before your very eyes, would change into various animate and inanimate objects. It's true that, thanks to the general awareness of what he was up to, even when he did this he still suffered to some extent, but nevertheless, you could never flush him out; rather did the struggle against him take on a slightly amusing character, and this further provoked and infuriated people. So, for example, after the cobbler had stabbed him with an awl and Selivan saved himself purely by managing to turn himself into a milepost, some men saw the awl sticking in a real milepost. They even tried to extract it, but the awl snapped, and they were able to return to the cobbler nothing more than a useless wooden handle.

Even after this Selivan used to walk around the wood as if he had never been stabbed, and he would change himself into a wild boar so realistically that he enjoyed eating acorns, as though such fruit were very much to his taste. Most often of all, however, he would emerge in the shape of a red cockerel onto his decrepit black roof and sit there calling: 'Cock-a-doodle-do!' Of course, everyone knew that he wasn't just singing 'Cock-a-doodle-do', but looking to see if there was anyone passing by for whose downfall it might be worth inciting the wood-demon and the witch to whip up a fine old storm and plague them to death. In short, the people hereabouts knew all his dodges so well that they never fell into his toils, but rather were able to frustrate Selivan's crafty manoeuvres. Once, while disguised as a boar, he met Savely the blacksmith, who was walking back from Kromy after a wedding party, and a real skirmish occurred between them, but the smith was the winner thanks to his fortunately having in his hands at the time an extremely heavy wooden club. The werewolf pretended he had no desire to have anything to do with the smith, and, snuffling loudly, went on champing acorns; but the smith, being an intelligent chap, saw through this ruse, which was to let him walk past and then set upon him from behind, throw him to the ground and eat him instead of an acorn. The smith decided to avert the danger by raising the club high above his head and hitting the boar so hard on the snout that it yelped piteously, fell to the ground and did not rise again. And when the smith made off at high speed after this, Selivan took on again his human aspect and watched him for a long time from his front steps—obviously harbouring some malevolent intent against him.

After this frightful encounter the smith fell ill of a fever, from which he recovered only because he let the quinine powder he had been sent to take blow away out of the window.

The smith had a reputation as a very sensible man, and he knew that quinine and all other pharmaceutical remedies were powerless against magic. He patiently tied up a bundle with coarse string and buried it in the dunghill to rot. And that was the end of the matter, for as soon as the bundle and the string had rotted, Selivan's power over him should have waned. And so it indeed came about. Selivan never again after that turned himself into a swine of any sort, or at least after that no-one ever met him in such an unseemly guise.

As for Selivan's tricks in the shape of a red cockerel, things went more successfully: the one-eyed miller Savka took up arms against him; he was a very dashing young lad, whose deeds were always more imaginative and daring than anyone else's.

Having one day been sent to town the day before the market, he was riding along on a very lazy and obstinate horse. Knowing the character of his mount, Savka had surreptitiously taken with him a stout birch staff, in case he needed it, to imprint a souvenir on the flanks of his melancholic Bucephalus. He managed one or two incidents of this sort and succeeded in so arousing the ire of his horse that it lost patience and started prancing along.

Selivan, not expecting Savka to be so well armed, as soon as he saw him passing, leapt in the guise of the cockerel up onto the eaves and started twirling around, staring in all directions and crying, 'Cock-a-doodle-do!' Savka wasn't afraid of the sorcerer, and, on the contrary called out to him: 'Here, mate, you're talking nonsense, and you won't get away from me', and with this and with little further thought, he hurled his staff so accurately at the rooster that he didn't even get to the end of his call of 'Cock-a-doodle-do', but fell dead instantly. Unfortunately, he did not fall into the road, but into the yard, where all he had to do was assume again his natural human form. He turned back into Selivan, ran out into the road, chased after Savka, carrying in his hand the very staff that Savka had treated him with when he was impersonating a cockerel on the roof.

According to Savka, Selivan this time was so enraged that Savka might have come out of the encounter very badly; but Savka was a lad with many good ideas, and he knew one further trick. He knew that his idle horse would forget its lethargy if he turned for home—to the manger. And that is what he did. As soon as Selivan, armed with the staff, hurled himself on Savka,—Savka immediately turned the horse around and beat it. He galloped home, scared out of his wits, and didn't tell his fearful story until the next day. Thank God he told the story, or people feared he might have been dumb for good.

Chapter VII

IN place of Savka, who had thoroughly taken fright, another more bold ambassador was appointed, who actually reached Kromy and got back home safely. However, this man said, on returning home again, that he would rather be swallowed up in the ground than ride past Selivan's inn. There were others who felt the same: fear became universal; but on the other hand everyone in general intensified the watch they kept on Selivan. Wherever and into whatever he transformed himself, he was invariably detected, and in whatever shape he appeared people strove to cut short his baleful existence. If Selivan appeared outside his inn as a sheep or a calf,—he was immediately recognized and beaten up, and he could not go unrecognized whatever form he chose. Even when he took on the shape of a newly-oiled cartwheel and lay out in the sun to dry, even this cunning device was recognized for what it was and people who knew smashed the wheel into little bits so that the hub and the spokes flew in all directions.

All these events comprised an heroic epic of my childhood, and in due course I received immediate information of the most reliable nature. The speed at which news spread was fostered by the constant presence at the mill of a first-rate collection of passing customers who had come to grind their grain. While the millstones were grinding the grain people had brought, these same people were chewing over and grinding out all sorts of rubbish, and from this centre of information all the strange stories found their way to the maids' room by means of Moska and Roska, and then the polished version was passed on to me, and I started spending whole nights compiling highly entertaining notions relating to myself and to Selivan, towards whom, despite everything I had heard, I harboured in the depths of my heart a sincere attraction. I firmly believed that a time would come when Selivan and I would somehow meet in odd circumstances, and that we would be much fonder of each other even than I liked Granddad Ilya, who had one thing about him I didn't like: one of his eyes seemed always to be laughing, and the left one at that.

I could never maintain my belief for long that Selivan could perform all his supernatural tricks with evil intent towards other people, and I used to like thinking about him; and usually, just as I was dropping off to sleep, I would dream of him as a man who was calm, good natured and even gravely misunderstood. So far I had never seen him and could not imagine what he looked like, having heard merely the distorted accounts of those with a tale to tell, but I dreamed of his eyes just as my own were closing. They were large eyes, all blue, and very kind. And while I slept, Selivan and I were in the most perfect communion: we discovered all sorts of secret hiding places where we secreted lots of bread, butter and warm children's coats, which we would fetch, take around to various peasant houses that we knew, push them through the skylight, knock on the door to attract attention, and then run away.

These were, I feel, the most pleasant dreams I have ever had, and I always regretted that, when I woke up, I again started to regard Selivan as a scoundrel, against whom all decent folks should take every possible protective measure. I have to confess that I did not want to be different from the others, and although in my dreams I experienced the warmest feelings of friendship towards Selivan, in real life I thought it essential to protect myself from him, even at a distance.

With this in mind and by descending to no small amount of flattery and other ways of abasing myself, I extracted from the housekeeper my Father's old Caucasian dagger, which was kept in her store-room. I attached it to a length of braid which I took from my uncle's old hussar shako, and cunningly hid this weapon under the mattress at the head of my bed. If Selivan were to appear in our house at night, I should certainly show him some resistance.

Neither Father nor Mother knew of the existence of this secret armoury, and it was essential they did not, since otherwise the dagger would certainly have been taken off me, and then Selivan would have been free to disturb my sleep, because I was dreadfully afraid of him. While all this was going on, he was already running a campaign against us, but our lively maids always immediately recognized him. He dared to appear in our house disguised as a huge light-brown rat. At first he did no more than make a noise in the store-room, but then once he got down into the deep hollow pit, where sausage and other delicacies were placed on a shelf at the bottom, covered with a grille, for consumption when we had guests. Selivan's aim here was clearly to cause us serious domestic unpleasantness, doubtless in revenge for what he had suffered from our peasants. Turning into a brown rat, he leapt down to the shelf, shifted the stone weight which had been placed on the grille, and ate all the sausage, but then failed utterly to leap out of the tall barrel. Here Selivan, to all appearances, would simply not have been able to escape just punishment, which the quick-thinking Annushka the Hucksterette volunteered to administer. She arrived with a cast-iron kettle full of boiling water and an old fork. Annushka's idea was first to scald the werewolf with the boiling water and then transfix it with the fork and throw the dead body into the undergrowth to be scavenged by the crows. But while the execution was taking place, some clumsiness on the part of Plump Annushka caused the water to splash on Annushka the Hucksterette's arm; she dropped the fork in pain, and at that moment the rat bit her finger and with astonishing dexterity ran up her arm and got out. Having caused general panic among all present, it then became invisible.

My parents, looking on the event with prosaic eyes, attributed the ridiculous outcome of the rat-hunt to the clumsiness of our Annushkas; but those of us who knew the secret springs of the affair also knew that they could not have done any better than they did, because it wasn't any normal rat, but Selivan the werewolf. However, we didn't dare tell the adults this. As simple-hearted people, we were afraid of criticism and mockery over matters that we regarded as unquestionable and obvious.

Selivan never ventured in any disguise across the threshold of our living quarters, as it seemed to me, because he knew one or two things about my dagger. I found this both flattering and disappointing, because, actually, I was beginning to get fed up with nothing but talk and rumours, and I conceived a passionate desire to meet Selivan face to face.

This feeling of mine turned into a constant sense of vexation, in which I spent one whole winter with its endless dark evenings, and when the first torrents of spring flowed from the hills, an event occurred which upset the whole order of our life and gave rein to dangerous bursts of unrestrained passion.

Chapter VIII

THE occurrence was unexpected and sad. As the spring thaw began, when, according to the folk saying, 'an ox can drown in a puddle', a mounted messenger arrived from the distant estate of my aunt with the fateful news that my grandfather was dangerously ill.

The long journey at a time of year when the roads were virtually impassable was fraught with great danger: but this did not prevent Father and Mother from travelling, and they set off immediately. It was over sixty miles, and it had to be done in nothing other than a primitive cart, because it would have been completely impossible for any other vehicle to get through. The cart was accompanied by two men on horseback carrying long poles. They rode ahead and prodded the floods to detect hidden ruts and potholes. I and the rest of the household were left under the supervision of a special provisional committee, comprising various persons with different duties. Big Annushka was entrusted with all persons of the female sex down to Oska and Roska; but the highest moral oversight was placed in the hands of the village elder's wife, Dementievna. The intellectual leadership of our community—in the sense of the observance of religious festivals and Sundays—was the responsibility of Apollinary Ivanovich, the deacon's son, who, by reason of his religious qualifications (he had been expelled from theological seminary, where he had enjoyed the grand title of 'rhetorician') was appointed my moral tutor. He was teaching me Latin conjugations and in general preparing me for entry to the Orel grammar school the following year so I should not be a total ignorant savage and be astounded by Bellyustin's Latin and Lomonde's French Grammar.

Apollinary was a young man of secular instincts and was preparing to enter the ranks of minor officials, or, as we say today, clerks, in the Orel provincial administration, where his uncle was also employed, a man who had a very entertaining job. If some district police officer or senior policeman failed to carry out some instruction, Apollinary's uncle was sent out on horseback as a 'courier' to attend to the recalcitrant official. He rode without having to pay for the expense of his horse, and in addition used to receive gifts and presents from the guilty person, while seeing various towns and getting to know people of all ranks and walks of life. My friend Apollinary also intended in due course to achieve happiness on this level and had every hope of doing much better than his uncle, because he was blessed with two great talents which had every likelihood of being very advantageous in enhancing his social accomplishments: Apollinary could play two songs on the guitar: 'A maiden went a-cutting of the nettles' and another which was more difficult—'One rainy autumn evening', and, something which was even less often encountered in the provinces in those days,—he was good at writing beautiful poems addressed to ladies, which was actually the reason why he was thrown out of the seminary.

Apollinary and I, despite the difference in our ages, maintained good friendly relations, and, as loyal friends should certainly do, we kept each other's secrets. In this respect he had fewer to guard than I had: all my secrets were related to the dagger under my mattress, but I was obliged to keep two deadly secrets which he entrusted to me: the first concerned a pipe which Apollinary kept hidden in a cupboard and which he used every evening to smoke bitter-sweet white inferior imitation tobacco, blowing the smoke into the stove to conceal the smell, and the second was even more important—this was the matter of the verses Apollinary wrote in honour of a certain 'fleet-footed Pulkheria'.

I believe the lines were very badly written, but Apollinary insisted that they could only be appreciated properly when you saw the impression they made if recited elegantly and with feeling to a tender and sensitive woman.

This presented a great difficulty; it might even be said in our situation an insuperable one, because there were no refined little ladies in our house, and as for any visiting grown-up aristocratic misses who happened to call, Apollinary never dared to suggest they should listen to him, since he was very shy, and the young ladies in our circle of acquaintance included many who greatly enjoyed making fun of such things.

Necessity obliged Apollinary to think up a compromise,—and this was: to declaim his ode addressed to 'fleet-footed Pulkheria' before our maid Neonila, the one who had assumed certain refined manners in the fashionable shop in Orel, and, as Apollinary imagined, must have acquired a subtle sensibility, such as was necessary in order to appreciate the value of poetry.

Being so young, I was reluctant to offer my tutor any advice about his poetic ventures, but I considered the idea of declaiming the poem before the seamstress to be a risky undertaking. Of course, I was judging by my own ideas, but it did seem to me that while young Neonila was familiar with some aspects of urban society, she was scarcely likely to understand the language of high poesy in the way that Apollinary addressed Pulkheria, the object of his creation. Moreover, in the ode to the 'slender' one there were expressions like: 'O thou, cruel one!' and 'Depart from mine eyes!' and things like that. Neonila was a shy and retiring character, and I was afraid that she would take this personally and burst into tears and run away.

But the worst thing of all was that, by reason of the strict régime by which our house was run, the poetic rehearsal planned by our 'rhetorician' was completely impossible. There was neither time nor place nor any other of the necessary conditions which must obtain in order that Neonila could listen to Apollinary's poem and be its first critic. But on the other hand, the lack of supervision which came into being when my parents departed changed everything, and the rhetorician wanted to take advantage of this. Now we all, oblivious of any difference in our social position, spent the evenings playing cards, and Apollinary even smoked his wretched imitation tobacco inside the house and sat in my father's chair in the dining room, which I found slightly objectionable. Apart from that, on his insistence, we actually played blind man's buff a few times, in the course of which my brother and I acquired some bruises. Then we played hide and seek, and once we even had a formal feast with lots of good things to eat. I think all this was done 'at Sheremetiev's expense', as many incautious revellers did in those days, living the high life and leading us down the primrose path to perdition, in this case under the leadership of the 'rhetorician'. To this day I do not know whose idea it was to collect a whole sackful of wild nuts, retrieved from the lairs of fieldmice (where usually only nuts of the highest quality are to be found). Apart from the nuts there were three parcels of grey paper containing soft, moist yellow mushrooms, sunflower seeds, and pears stewed together with figs. This last delicacy was very sticky and hard to wash off our hands.

Since this last fruit was particularly sought after, pears were only given as prizes in the game of forfeits. Moska, Oska and Roska, by reason of their total insignificance, got no figs at all. The game of forfeits was played by Annushka, me and my tutor Apollinary, who turned out to be a very inventive player. This all happened in the drawing room, where normally only the most honoured guests were entertained. And it was here, where, carried away by all the merriment, an almost desperate spirit entered Apollinary, and he thought of an even more daring undertaking. He got the idea he would like to declaim his ode in a grandiose and even fearsome setting, such as would cause even the strongest nerves to be strained to the limit. He began to try to persuade us all that we should go off together the next Sunday to gather lilies of the valley in Selivan's wood. And later in the evening when we were going to bed, he confided in me that the lilies of the valley were merely a pretext, and that the main purpose of our visit was for him to recite his poem in the most dread surroundings.

On the one hand, there would be fear of Selivan, on the other fear of his dreadful poetry...What would come of this, and could we survive?

Just imagine: we really *did* decide to dare all.

In the lively mood which swept us all up on that memorable spring evening we imagined we were all really brave and would be able to do this desperate deed quite safely. Indeed there would be a good lot of us, and into the bargain I would of course take along my huge Caucasian dagger.

I confess that I very much hoped everyone else would arm themselves according to their strength and opportunity, but I did not detect in any of them the necessary attention and preparedness. Apollinary took nothing but his chibouk and his guitar, and the girls set out with kettle-stands, frying-pans, pans full of eggs and a little cast-iron cooking stove. The idea was to use this to cook gruel with lard, and to make an omelette in the frying pan; in this sense it was a splendid idea to take these goods with us, but as for defending ourselves against Selivan's knavish tricks, they would be no good at all.

Moreover, to be honest, I was just a little displeased with my companions in some ways,—in particular I did not sense in them the same degree of respect for Selivan as I myself was imbued with. They were afraid of him, as I was, but somehow irresponsibly, and they even risked making malicious jokes about him. One of the Annushkas said she would take a rolling pin and kill him with it, and the Hucksterette laughed, saying she would bite him to death and showing her ever-so-white teeth, with which she bit off a piece of wire. All of this was somehow not very substantial; it was capped by the rhetorician. He completely denied the existence of Selivan, even going so far as to say that he had never existed and was simply an invention of fantasy, just as were Python, Cerberus, and the like.

It was at this point that I appreciated for the first time how easily human beings can be led into contradictions! What was the point of rhetoric if it allowed these two things to be placed on the same level: the fabulous Python, and Selivan, whose real existence was confirmed by a multiplicity of obvious events?

I did not succumb to this temptation and preserved my belief in Selivan. I even went further than this, and believed that the rhetorician would be soundly punished for his lack of faith.

However, for those who did not take these cunning arguments too seriously, the proposed excursion into the forest promised to be a great deal of fun, and no-one wished to, or else could not make themselves prepare for manifestations of another sort. But nevertheless good sense made us all highly cautious in that accursed forest, where we would, so to speak, be putting ourselves into the jaws of the beast.

Everyone was thinking only of how jolly it would be to wander about the forest where everybody else was afraid to go, but *they* weren't afraid. We dreamed of making our way through the whole dangerous forest, hallooing, shouting to each other, jumping over little holes and the cracks in the ground where the last snow was still melting, but no-one gave a thought as to whether all this would be approved of when higher authority returned from their journey. In relation to that we had the idea of preparing for Mother's dressing table two large bunches of the best lilies of the valley, and of distilling the rest into a fragrant essence which would be an excellent lotion for sunburn and should last the whole summer.

Chapter IX

WHEN the impatiently awaited Sunday came, we left the elder's wife Dementievna in charge of the house and set off to Selivan's wood. The main party was on foot, and we kept to the high ridges which had for the most part dried out after the thaw, and where the first emerald green shoots of grass were appearing, while the baggage train, consisting of a cart harnessed to our old dun mare, followed us on the road. This cart bore Apollinary's guitar and the girls' cloaks, taken along in case of wet weather. I was in charge of the mare, and behind me my passengers were Roska and some other little girls, one of whom was carefully holding a bag full of eggs on her knees, and another was generally looking after various articles, but her main duty was to hold on to my huge dagger, which I had slung over my shoulder attached to a length of braid filched from my uncle's old hussar uniform, and which was significantly impeding my movements by swinging from side to side and distracting my attention from the task of driving the horse.

The girls who were walking along the ridge were singing: 'When I plough the fields or sow the flax', and the rhetorician was supplying a bass line. Any peasants they happened to meet saluted them and asked:

'Where are you making for?'

Annushka would answer:

'We're going to take Selivan prisoner.'

The peasants shook their heads and said:

'They're out of their minds!'

Actually, we were somehow bewitched, we were in thrall to an irresistible half-childish need to run, sing, laugh and generally act in an over-excited manner.

And meanwhile the hour's journey along an appalling bad road was beginning to have a bad effect on me—I was fed up with the old mare, and my enthusiasm for holding the reins had cooled; but not far away on the horizon Selivan's wood hove into view and I brightened up again. My heart began to beat faster and then sank, like Quintilius Varus's as he entered the Teutoburg Forest. And just then a hare ran out from a half-melted strip of uncultivated ground, crossed the road and ran off over the field.

'Pooh! Run away and rot!' cried the Annushkas after him.

They all knew that to meet a hare boded nothing but ill. I too lost courage and felt for my dagger, but I got so distracted with worries about how to extract it from its rusty sheath, that I didn't notice I had let the reins drop, and to my total surprise found myself under the overturned cart, which our dun mare had tried to drag up onto the ridge when searching for some grass to eat; she had succeeded in upturning the cart so successfully that all four wheels were pointing upwards, and Roska and I and all our provisions were trapped underneath...

The accident had happened in a flash, but the consequences were numberless: Apollinary's guitar was smashed to bits and the broken eggs had made a right mess over our faces. And into the bargain, Roska was yelling her head off.

I was crushed beyond measure, and ashamed, and so lost heart that I no longer had any desire to be rescued from my predicament; but I could already hear the Annushkas' voices. As they laboured for our rescue they were explaining the reason for our misfortune, and this worked strongly to my advantage. It wasn't the mare and I who were responsible: the whole thing was Selivan's fault.

This was his first trick to stop us getting into his wood; however, it didn't frighten anyone very greatly, on the contrary, it only made us all the more disgruntled, and it strengthened our determination at all costs to fulfil the entire programme we had in mind.

We only needed to right the cart, get on our feet again, wash off the horrid eggy slime from our faces in some woodland stream, and look to see what had survived the crash from among the things we had brought to provision the numerous party.

And this was all soon done. Roska and I washed in the stream which flowed right by Selivan's wood, but when I opened my eyes the light seemed anything but transparent. The girls' pink dresses and my new quilted blue cashmere coat were good for nothing: the mud and the eggs which covered them had ruined them and they could not be cleaned without soap, which was one thing we had not brought. The stove and the frying-pan were broken, the kettle-stand was reduced to its legs alone, and the only bit of Apollinary's guitar to remain was the finger-board and some tangled strings. The bread and the rest of the dry provisions were covered in mud. The least we could expect was to be hungry all day, not counting any other terrors which we could sense in all the surroundings. A wind was blowing in the valley above the stream, and the dark forest, not yet showing any signs of green, was rustling and malevolently waving its branches above our heads.

Our spirits fell significantly,—especially Roska's; she was feeling chilled and was crying. Nevertheless we decided to enter Selivan's kingdom, come hell and high water.

Anyway, there was no chance of the very same mishap occurring again, whatever happened.

Chapter X

WE all crossed ourselves and began our incursion into the forest. We went among the trees timidly and uncertainly, but we all concealed our nervousness from each other. The only thing was: we agreed to call to each other as often as possible. But anyway there turned out to be little need for calling out, because no-one went very far into the depths, somehow we constantly happened to stick together in the edge of the wood and spread out in a long line on the outskirts. It was only Apollinary who appeared more daring than the rest of us and penetrated a little farther into the thicket: he was seeking the most remote and spine-chilling spot where his declamation might produce the most terrible impression on the audience; but, on the other hand, as soon as Apollinary disappeared from sight, the wood rang with his penetrating, frenzied cries. No-one could imagine what danger Apollinary had encountered, but everyone abandoned him to his fate and charged out of the wood into a clearing, from where, without a glance behind them, they made for the road home. All the Annushkas ran, so did the Moskas, pursued by the pedagogue, still yelling with alarm, leaving me and my little brother alone.

Not one remained of our company: it wasn't just the people who ran away from us, but the inhuman example of these persons was followed even by the horse. Frightened by their cries, the animal tossed its head and, turning away from the trees, galloped homewards, scattering into the potholes and ruts the few things that remained in the cart.

It was not a retreat, but a complete and utterly shameful rout, because it was accompanied not just by the loss of the baggage train, but also by the lapse of all common sense, as a result of which we children were left to the whim of fate.

Heaven knows what we might have had to endure in our helpless orphaned state, which was made even more dangerous by the fact that we did not know the way home on our own, and our shoes, which were simply light goatskin bootees with thin, unsubstantial soles, were not adequate for a walk of two and a half miles over soggy tracks on which many icy puddles still remained. To cap it all, by the time my brother and I had fully taken in the horror of our plight, a roaring sound was heard in the trees, and then from the opposite side from the stream a breeze was blowing which became a cold, damp, persistent wind.

We looked beyond the hollow and saw that from the direction in which our way home lay, and in which our suite of companions was shamelessly fleeing, a huge storm-cloud was blowing up laden with spring rain and threatening the sort of early spring thunder which young girls took advantage of in order to wash themselves with a silver spoon, superstitiously believing it would make them whiter than silver.

Seeing ourselves in this desperate position, I was on the point of bursting into tears, and my little brother was already crying. He had turned all blue with fear and cold, and with his head stuck under a bush was earnestly praying to God.

God, it would seem, heard his childish prayer, and we were sent salvation from a totally unexpected quarter. At the very moment when the first thunderclap came and we lost the last vestige of our courage, we heard a twig break behind some bushes, and out of the dense branches of a mature hazel there appeared the broad face of a peasant we did not know. This face seemed so terrifying to us, that we cried out and hurled ourselves full tilt towards the stream.

Out of our minds, we crossed the hollow, tumbled head first down the damp and unstable bank and directly found ourselves up to our waists in the muddy water, with our legs knee deep in mud.

There was no chance of running any further. The stream was too deep for boys as small as we were, and we could not hope to cross it, and what was more, reflected in the swift-flowing water we could see flashes of lightning—they shook and twisted like snakes of fire and seemed to be hiding in the remains of last year's water-weed.

Once in the water we seized each other's arms and stood there totally bemused, while heavy raindrops fell on us from the branches above. Fortunately, this bemusement saved us from the great danger which would have threatened us if we had gone one step further into the water.

We could easily have fallen into a deep pool, but, happily, two sinewy arms caught hold of us, and the very same peasant who had stared at us so frighteningly from the hazel tree said kindly,

'You stupid children, how have you got into this mess?'

So saying, he picked us up and carried us across the stream.

When we reached the other bank, he set us down on the ground, took off his short jacket which was buttoned at the collar by a round copper button, and wiped our wet legs with the jacket.

As this was going on we looked at him in utter dismay and felt that we were completely in his power, but—strange to say—his features quickly changed before our eyes. In his face we not only saw nothing fearful, but on the contrary it seemed very kind and likeable.

He was a sturdy man, stocky, with streaks of grey in his hair and moustache, his beard was a clump of hair, he had lively, darting eyes that looked very serious, but on his lips there was something akin to a smile.

After he removed as far as he could the mud and slime from our legs using the hem of his jacket, he even went so far as to smile openly and spoke once more;

'You...you have nothing...you mustn't be afraid.'

He looked around and went on:

'It's nothing, but it's going to start raining heavily.' (He was walking by this time.) 'You children can't go home on foot.'

We said nothing, but went on crying.

'Don't worry, don't worry! Don't cry. I'll take you home,' he said as he wiped my brother's tear-stained face, leaving stripes of dirt on it.

'Oops! What dirty hands I've got,' said our saviour, wiping my brother's face with his hand in the opposite direction, which did nothing to remove the dirt, but simply adjusted the shading in the opposite direction.

'You won't get home on your own...I'll take you...You'll lose your shoes, they'll get stuck in the mud.'

'Can you ride a horse?' the peasant asked.

I plucked up the courage to say something, and replied:

'Yes.'

'If you can, that's good!' he said, and in a flash he lifted me onto one shoulder and my brother onto the other, told us to kept a firm hold of his neck, put his jacket over us both, firmly gripped out knees and carried us, with swift, long strides over the mud, which was quickly melting and squelching as he stepped along firmly in his huge bast-shoes.

We sat on his shoulders under his jacket. This must have made us look like a gigantic figure, but we were comfortable: the jacket got wet through from the rain, and became so stiff that we were dry and warm beneath it. We bounced along on the shoulders of our carrier, as if on a camel's back, and soon fell into a sort of cataleptic state until we revived when we reached the spring by our own home. For me personally, this was really a profound dream, from which I did not wake up immediately. I remember that the peasant unwound the jacket from us; by now we were surrounded by all our Annushkas, who tore us from his arms and, as they did so, berated him mercilessly and threw the jacket, which had protected us so well from the element, contemptuously at his feet. In addition, they threatened him with the return of our father and said they would go running immediately to the village and fetch a crowd of women with flails and men too, and that they would set the dogs on him.

I could not understand the reason for this cruel injustice, and this was not surprising, since, under the régime obtaining in our house at that time, there was a conspiracy to conceal from us the identity of the man to whom we owed our salvation.

'You don't owe him any thanks,' said the girls who were supposed to have been looking after us. 'On the contrary, he was the one who did it all.'

By this remark I immediately guessed that the man who saved us had been none other than *Selivan* himself!

Chapter XI

AND so it was. The next day, in view of the imminent return of our parents, the fact was revealed, and an oath was exacted from us to the effect that we would not say a word to Father or Mother about what had happened.

In those bygone days, when there were such people as serfs, it sometimes happened that the children of the squires harboured the most tender fondness for servants from the ranks of the serfs and would keep their secrets religiously. So it was with us. We would even conceal from our parents, as well as we could, the sins and transgressions of 'our people'. Such relationships are referred to in many works of literature in which the rural life of those days is portrayed. As for me, I can say that our friendships with our serfs, as they then were, are the subject of the most pleasant and warmest memories of my childhood. Through these friendships we learned of the needs and worries in the life of the poor on our estate and of their friends in the village, and we learned to *sympathize with the ordinary folk.* But these good-natured ordinary folk were unfortunately not always just and sometimes were capable of casting a dark shadow on their neighbour for the most trivial of reasons, giving no thought to the harmful effect this could have. This was how the 'ordinary folk' acted towards Selivan, not wishing to know anything important about his real character or what moved him. Not fearing to offend against the spirit of justice, they brazenly spread rumours which made him into a *bogeyman* in everyone's eyes. And, surprisingly, everything anyone said about him not only appeared to be true, but even gave certain clear signs that led people to imagine that Selivan was in truth a bad man and that in the neighbourhood of his lonely habitation frightful acts of evil took place.

The same happened in this case, when we were scolded by those who should have been looking after us: not only did they cast all the blame on Selivan, who had saved us from the storm, but even contrived another misfortune for him. Apollinary and all the Annushkas told us that when Apollinary had noticed a suitable hillock from which he thought he could declaim his ode very conveniently, he had run towards this hillock along a hollow in the ground which was deep in dead leaves from last autumn, but then he had stumbled on something soft. This 'soft' thing moved under Apollinary's feet and caused him to fall, and when he tried to stand up he saw that it was the dead body of a young peasant woman. He realized that the corpse was in a clean white dress with red embroidery and...had its throat cut, from which blood was pouring.

When unexpectedly faced with such a frightful apparition, of course you would expect him to be shocked and to cry out,—as he did: but here was the strange thing—Apollinary, as I said, was far away from everyone else and was the only one to stumble over the dead body, yet all the Annushkas and Roskas swore before God that they had *seen* the murdered woman...

'If we hadn't, why should we have been so frightened?' they said.

And I was quite convinced at the time that they were not lying, that they were firmly convinced that they had seen a murdered peasant woman in Selivan's wood in white peasant apparel with red stitching, her throat cut, and blood coming from it...How could this have happened?

Since what I am writing is not fiction, but really happened, I must pause here and say that this incident remained for ever unexplained in our household. The dead woman lying among the leaves according to Apollinary could not have been seen by anyone but him, because no-one but Apollinary was there to see it. Yet they all swore they had seen it, as if the dead woman had appeared in the same instant in several different places and been seen by all. And apart from that, had Apollinary really seen this woman? It was scarcely possible, because the whole thing had taken place at the beginning of the thaw, when the snow had not melted everywhere. The dead leaves had lain under the snow *since the previous autumn*, yet Apollinary had seen it dressed in an embroidered white dress, with the blood still flowing...The whole thing was utter nonsense, yet everyone crossed themselves and swore blind that they had seen the woman just as they described it. And they all were afraid to sleep at night, and they were all fearful, as if we had all committed a crime. It was not long before even I became convinced that my brother and I had seen the murdered woman too. And so we all became very frightened, so much so that the whole matter was related to my parents, and Father wrote a letter to the local official–who came riding to see us with an immensely long sword and interrogated us all one by one in Father's study. Apollinary was twice called in to the official, who on the second occasion gave him such a talking-to that when he came out, both ears were bright red and one of them even was bleeding.

That was something else *we all saw!*

However all that may be, we caused Selivan much grief with our silly talk: his property was inspected, his whole wood was searched and he was arrested and held for a long time, but nothing suspicious was found, and there was no trace at all of any murdered woman. Selivan returned home again, but this did him no good as far as public opinion was concerned: from this time forth, everyone knew that he was an undoubted if undetected criminal, and no-one wanted to have anything to do with him. And, so as not to be subject to any intensified influence of the element of poetic fantasy, I was removed to a 'gentleman's school', where I began to imbibe what educational science had to teach me; I stayed there in total submission until the approach of the Christmas holidays, when I should have to drive past Selivan's inn and see fearful sights there with my own eyes.

Chapter XII

SELIVAN'S bad reputation lent me great prestige among my boarding-school friends, with whom I shared my information about this dread man. Of all my fellow-pupils not one had yet experienced such fearsome experiences as I was able to boast of, and now that I was anticipating having to drive past Selivan's place again,—no-one could contemplate the forthcoming exploit calmly and indifferently. On the contrary, most of my friends were sorry for me and admitted straight out that they would not wish to take my place, but two or three of the more courageous ones envied me, and flattered themselves that they would very much like to come face to face with Selivan. But two of them were inveterate braggarts: one because, as he expressed it, his grandmother had *a 'Tausin' stone in a very old Vennition ring*, and anyone wearing the ring was 'immune to all misfortune'.[2] In our family we had no such valuable articles, and what was more, I had to undertake my Christmas journey not with my own horses, but in the company of my aunt, who had sold her house in Orel just before the Christmas festival, and bearing the thirty thousand roubles she had been paid for it, was travelling to our house in order to pay for an estate which my father had long since negotiated on her behalf to buy.

To my annoyance, my aunt's preparations were held up for two whole days by some important business considerations, and we set off from Orel on the morning of Christmas Eve.

We were travelling in a spacious carriage with a cover made of bast and drawn by three horses, with Spiridon, the coachman, and a young footman called Boriska. Inside were my aunt, I myself, my boy cousin, a baby girl cousin, and the nurse, Lyubov Timofeevna.

With decent horses in good road conditions it should have been possible to get from Orel to our village in five or six hours. We arrived in Kromy by two o'clock and stopped off at the house of a merchant of our acquaintance to drink tea and feed the

---

[2] A Tausin stone, or tausen, is a bright sapphire with a suggestion of the colours of peacock's feathers, and in the old days was considered to be a protective talisman. Ivan the Terrible had such a talisman, also contained in a ring or, as they used to say in a 'fingerlet'. A 'fingerlet' is a golden finger-ring enshrining a *tausin* stone, in which may be descried sediment and what appears to be a tiny bubble. [Author's note]

horses. It was our custom to make this stop, and it was necessary to change my little cousin who was still in napkins.

The weather was good, almost on the point of a thaw; but while we were feeding the horses it began to freeze slightly, and then 'started smoking', that is, fine snow began to blow around close to the ground.

Aunty was in a quandary: should we wait, or should we rather put on a spurt and try to reach home quickly before a real storm set in?

There were only thirteen or fourteen miles to go. The coachman and the footman, who were anxious to spend Christmas with their families and friends, were insistent that we would make it all right—so long as we did not delay and got a move on.

My wishes and those of my aunt were fully in accord with those of Spiridon and Boriska. No-one wanted to spend Christmas morning in a strange house in Kromy. At the same time, Aunty was doubtful and anxious, and she had this significant sum of money with her in a red wooden cashbox wrapped in thick green baize.

To spend a night in a strange house with such financial riches seemed far from safe to Aunty, and she decided to follow the advice of our two faithful servants.

By just after three o'clock our carriage was harnessed and we left Kromy in the direction of the Old Believers' village of Kolchevo; but scarcely had we crossed the River Kroma on the ice than we felt somehow short of air, and unable to breathe very deeply. The horses were going along uncertainly, snorting and shaking their heads—a sure sign that they too felt a lack of air. All this time the carriage was moving forward easily, as if something were pushing it from behind. The wind was behind us and seemed to be driving us with doubled speed to some predetermined spot. Soon, however, the clear signposts along the road 'hiccoughed'—some of them seemed to be missing; soft snowdrifts lined the road,—we saw more and more of them, and finally, in place of the previous clear waymarks not a thing could be seen.

Aunty looked out of the carriage in alarm to ask the driver if we were still on the road, and immediately fell back covered in fine, icy snow, and, before we could call the men on the box to speak to us, the snow was drifting in heavy flakes, the sky very quickly darkened and we were at the mercy of a real blizzard.

Chapter XIII

IT would have been just as dangerous to turn back to Kromy as to go on forward. The road behind us was scarcely any less dangerous, since we had already crossed the river, in which near the town there had been several gaps in the ice, and in a snowstorm we could easily have failed to notice them and fallen through the ice, while ahead all the way to our little village there was open steppe, and only at the seventh mile-post was there any noticeable feature—Selivan's wood, which did not signify any greater danger in a snowstorm, since it might even afford some protection. Moreover the road did not run through the centre of the wood, but kept to the edge of it. The wood might be no more than a useful indicator that we had covered half the distance to our destination, so therefore Spiridon drove the horses a little harder.

The way became ever more difficult and snowy: whereas formerly the runners had sounded a cheerful rattle beneath our carriage, now nothing was to be heard, rather did the vehicle crawl over shifting snowdrifts and soon began to yaw first to one side and then the other.

Our calm frame of mind deserted us, and we started asking the footman and the driver for ever more frequent reports on our position; we received vague and uncertain replies. They tried to assure us that we were quite safe, but it was obvious that they did not share this confidence themselves.

After half an hour of swift travel, during which we heard Spiridon's whip cracking over the horses' backs ever more often, we were glad to hear the cry:

'Selivan's wood ahead!'

'Is it far?' asked Aunty.

'No, we're almost there.'

And so we ought to have been—we had been driving about an hour from Kromy, but another good half-hour passed—we were still driving, the whip was cracking over the horses more and more, and there still was no wood.

'What's going on? Where's Selivan's wood?'

There was no answer from the box.

'Where's the wood?' insisted my aunt. 'Have we passed it, or what?'

'No, we aren't there yet,' said Spiridon in a muffled voice, sounding as if he had a pillow over his face.

'Well, what does this mean?'

Silence.

'Come here, the pair of you! Stop the coach, stop!'

Aunty looked out from under the cover and let out a desperate yell of 'Stop!' She then fell back into the carriage, enveloped in a whole cloud of snowflakes, which, blown by the wind, did not settle immediately, but hovered like swarming flies.

The coachman stopped the horses, and it was as well he did, because they were having difficulty supporting themselves and were tottering with fatigue. If he had not given them a moment's breather the poor creatures would have collapsed.

'Where are you?' my aunt asked Boriska when he got down from the box.

He was transformed. Before us there stood not a man, but a pillar of snow. The collar of his wolfskin coat was up and tied with a scrap of material. It was all covered with fluffy snow which had stuck together in a solid lump.

Boris was no expert on the road, and he timidly replied that, *as it seemed*, we were lost.

'Tell Spiridon to come here.'

It was impossible to call him: the blizzard stopped our mouths and was the only thing that could be heard, roaring and howling all around with venomous menace.

Boriska climbed back onto the box so as to grab Spiridon by the arm and fetch him to us, but...he spent a very long time doing so before he appeared beside the carriage again, and said:

'Spiridon's not on the box!'

'What do you mean? Where is he, then?'

'I don't know. I suppose he's gone to try to find the way. If you'll allow me, I'll go too.'

'Heaven preserve us! No, don't. Don't go; or you'll both get lost and we'll all freeze to death.'

When we heard this, my cousin and I both started to cry, but at this very moment another pillar of snow, even bigger and more terrible, appeared beside Boriska.

This was Spiridon. He had put over his head for protection a spare bag made of bast, stuffed full of snow, which had frozen solid.

'Where's this wood you saw, Spiridon?'

'I did see it, Madam.'

'Well, where is it now?'

'You can see it now.'

Aunty tried to look, but could see nothing, it was quite dark. Spiridon insisted that this was because 'she wasn't looking hard enough'; he had seen the dark outline of the wood a long time ago, but...the trouble was that as we approached it, it was retreating from us.

'With the greatest of respect to your ladyship, it's all Selivan's doing. He's leading us on somewhere.'

Hearing that we had fallen at such a fearful moment into the hands of the evil man Selivan, my cousin and I cried even more loudly, but Aunty, who was a country squire's wife by birth and later an army officer's wife, was not so easily dismayed as are town ladies, who have far less experience of misfortune. My aunt had both experience and skill, and these qualities came to our rescue in a situation which was indeed very dangerous.

Chapter XIV

I DO not know whether or not my aunt believed in Selivan's evil power of sorcery, but she understood perfectly that the most important thing for our salvation was not to run our horses into the ground. If the horses became exhausted and stopped moving and the frost intensified, we would certainly all perish. The storm would suffocate us and the frost freeze us to death. But if the horses could conserve their strength in order to move in some way, pace by pace, we could nurture the hope that, sensing the direction of the wind, the horses would somehow find their way out of the trees back onto the road and take us to some habitation or other. Even if it was no more than an unheated hut on hen's legs in a ravine, at least the blizzard would not lash us so angrily, and we should not feel the jerking as the horses strained to stay on their feet...We should be able to get some sleep...My cousin and I were desperately tired. In this respect the only fortunate person was the little girl, who was sleeping in her nurse's arms covered by a warm little hareskin coat, but they would not let the two of us fall asleep. Aunty knew that to do so would be disastrous, since a sleeping person quickly freezes to death. Our plight got worse with every minute that passed, as the horses were by now scarcely moving, and the coachman and footman sitting on the exposed box were beginning to suffer from the extreme cold and speak in inaudible tones, while my aunt ceased to pay much attention to me and my cousin; meanwhile we, huddled close together, both fell asleep at the same time. We even had pleasant dreams: it was summer, we were in our orchard with our family. Apollinary was there, and suddenly everything switched to the excursion to gather lilies of the valley and to look for Selivan, of whom sometimes I heard things said, and at other times actually recalled—everything was mixed up...so that I could not make out how much was the dream and what was really happening. I felt the cold, could hear the moaning of the wind and the heavy knocking of the bast covering on the roof of the vehicle, then right before my eyes stood Selivan, with his jacket over one shoulder and a lantern held out with his other hand towards us...was it an apparition, a dream, or an invention of fantasy?

But it was not a dream and not a fantasy. It had suited fate to lead us on that awful night straight to Selivan's dread inn, and we could not find safety in any other place, because there was no other dwelling anywhere else around. Into the bargain Aunty had her cashbox with thirty thousand roubles in it, comprising her entire fortune. How could we stay in the home of such a suspicious man as Selivan with such a tempting treasure in our possession?

It stood to reason: we were lost! The choice was simply whether we would do better to freeze to death in the blizzard or fall under the knife of Selivan and his evil allies.

Chapter XV

JUST as in the instant when lightning flashes, the eye which has been in total darkness distinguishes all at once a whole range of objects, so then, when Selivan's lantern illuminated our hapless carriage, did I see the horror written on everyone's face. The coachman and the footman all but collapsed onto their knees in front of him and stood stock still on the sloping ground, while my aunt started back as if she wanted to disappear through the back of the carriage. The nurse bent over with her face towards the baby and all at once screwed herself up until she seemed no bigger than the baby herself.

Selivan stood in silence, but...in his ugly face I could see no trace of ill-will. Only this time he seemed more concerned than when he had carried me on his back.

'Would you like to get warm or anything?'

Aunty recovered before the others and replied:

'Yes, we're freezing...Save our lives!'

'God be your Saviour! Drive up, there's a fire inside.'

And he came down from the doorstep and held up the lantern inside the carriage.

Between the servants, my aunt and Selivan some brief words were exchanged, betraying mistrust and fear on our part towards our host, and on Selivan's side a certain deeply concealed peasant irony and, maybe, mistrust too of a different sort.

The coachman asked if there was fodder for the horses.

Selivan replied;

'We'll go and see.'

Boris the footman asked if there were any other travellers inside.

'Come up and you'll see.'

The nurse said:

'But is it dangerous to stay with you?'

'If it's dangerous, don't come in.'

My aunt stopped them, saying as quietly as possible to them all:

'Leave it, don't argue,—there's no point anyway. We can't go any further. We'll stay here and trust to God.'

Meanwhile, as this exchange took place, we found ourselves in a section panelled with wooden boards and partitioned off from the rest of the large hut. Aunty led the way followed by Boris who was carrying the cashbox. Then my cousin and I followed with the nurse.

The cashbox was placed on the table, and on top of it was a tin candlestick covered in tallow with a small candle-end in it which might last an hour, no more.

My aunt's practical sense was now directed to this object, namely the candle.

'First of all, Sir,' she said to Selivan, 'just bring us a new candle.'

'There's one there already.'

'No, you give us a new one, a whole candle!'

'A whole new candle?' asked Selivan insistently, with one hand on the table and the other on the cashbox.

'Bring a whole new candle at once.'

'Why do you want a whole one?'

'That's no business of yours—I'm not going to lie down to sleep straight away. The storm may pass, and we'll leave.'

'The storm won't pass.'

'That's no matter—I'll pay you for the candle.'

'I'm sure you'd pay, but I just don't have a candle.'

'Go and look for one, Sir!'

'There's no point in searching for something you don't have!'

A very, very feeble voice unexpectedly joined in the conversation from behind the partition.

'We don't have a candle, ma'am.'

'Who's voice is that?' asked my aunt.

'It's my wife.'

The faces of my aunt and the nurse lightened somewhat. The proximity of another woman seemed to be an encouraging sign.

'What's the matter with her, is she sick, or something?'

'Yes.'

'What's the matter with her?'

'She's just ill. You lie down, I need the candle end for the lantern. I have to see to the horses.'

However much they urged Selivan, he simply insisted: he needed the candle-end, that was that. He promised to bring it back—but for the moment he took it and left.

Whether Selivan kept his promise to bring back the candle I never saw, because my cousin and I went back to sleep; something, however, was troubling me. In my sleep I could hear my aunt and the nurse whispering, and the most frequent word I could make out was 'cashbox'.

It was obvious that the nurse and the other servants knew that this casket contained great wealth, and all had noticed that from the very first moment this box had been the object of avid attention on the part of our unreliable host.

Being possessed of great experience of life, my aunt perceived the necessity of submitting to circumstances, but on the other hand she made certain dispensations contingent upon the dangerous situation.

To prevent Selivan from cutting our throats it was decided that no-one would go to sleep. Instructions were given that the horses should be unharnessed, but their collars not taken off, and both the coachman and the footman were to stay in the vehicle: they were not to separate for a moment, because if they were on their own, Selivan could strike them down one by one, which would leave the rest of us helpless. Then, of course he would kill us and bury us all under the floor, where already rested many victims of his savagery. The coachman and the footman could not stay with us in the house, because if they did Selivan would cut the tugs from the horse-collars, so it would be impossible to harness the horses; either that, or he would simply give away all three animals to his friends who were assumed to be hiding somewhere for the moment. If that happened, we should have no way of escape, while it might very well happen that the storm would abate, in which case the coachman would harness up and Boris would knock three times on the wall, and we should all rush outside, get in, and drive away. So that we could be ready at any time, none of us got undressed.

I do not know how the passage of time seemed to the others, whether it felt long or short, but to us two sleeping boys it flew by as if in a moment—which suddenly culminated in a frightful awakening.

Chapter XVI

I AWOKE because I was finding it very difficult to breathe. When I opened my eyes I could see absolutely nothing, because it was dark in my immediate vicinity, and only in the distance could I discern a grey light: the window. By the light of Selivan's lantern I could make out in that fearsome scene the faces of all the people present, and in the same moment I recalled everything—who I was, where I was, why I was there, I remembered that my nearest and dearest were still at home,—and I felt very sorry about it all and for them all; I felt hurt and afraid, and I wanted to cry out, but it was impossible. My mouth was firmly closed by a human hand, and a trembling voice whispered in my ear:

'Not a sound, keep quiet, not a sound! We're lost—someone's trying to break in.'

I recognized my aunt's voice and pressed her hand to show I understood her demand.

At the other side of the door which led out into the porch I could hear a rustling sound...Someone was quietly moving from one foot to the other and feeling the wall with his hands... Obviously this evil person was trying to find the door, but could not do so...

My aunt held us firmly in her arms and whispered that God might yet help us, because she had built a barricade against the door. But at that very moment, maybe because we had given ourselves away by our whispering and trembling, behind the wooden partition where the main part of the hut was, and from whence we had heard Selivan's wife make her comment about the candle, someone ran out and grappled with the person who was quietly creeping up to our door, and the pair of them started to hammer against the door; the door shook, and the table, a bench and our cases, with all of which my aunt had built her barrier, collapsed in a heap, and Boriska's face appeared in the opening, while Selivan's powerful hands had him by the neck...

When she saw this, my aunt screamed at Selivan and dashed towards Boris.

'Ma'am! Thank God,' said Boris in a hoarse voice.

Selivan removed his hands and just stood there.

'Come on, quickly, we're getting away from here,' said my aunt. 'Where are our horses?'

'At the front door, ma'am, I was just going to call you...Then this brigand...I was saved in the nick of time, ma'am!' stammered Boris, grabbing me and my brother and sweeping away everything in his path. Everyone rushed to the door, leaped into the carriage, which set off at the gallop, as fast as the horses could carry us. Selivan looked immensely embarrassed as he watched us leave. It was obvious he knew that there were bound to be consequences to all this.

By now it was growing light, and the frosty red Christmas dawn appeared in the East.

Chapter XVII

It took a mere half hour to reach home, and we spent the time ceaselessly talking about the terrors we had experienced. Aunty, the nurse, the coachman, and Boris kept interrupting each other; they crossed themselves constantly, thanking God for our amazing escape. Aunty insisted that she had not slept a wink all night, because she could hear someone several times approaching our door and trying to open it. This had obliged her to bar the entry using anything she could find. She could also hear some suspicious whispering from Selivan's room behind the partition, and she thought that he had more than once opened his door, gone out into the porch and stealthily tried the handle of our door. The nurse had heard this too, although she said she had dropped off briefly from time to time. The coachman and Boris had seen more than anybody. Anxious about the horses, the coachman had not left them for a moment, but Boriska had more than once approached our door, and every time he did so Selivan immediately appeared at his door. When the storm abated towards dawn, the coachman and Boris quietly harnessed the horses and just as quietly drove out, opening the gates themselves; but when Boris, quietly again, returned to our door to lead us out, Selivan saw that his prey was going to escape, hurled himself on Boris and tried to strangle him. Thank goodness he failed, of course, but now no longer could he get away with mere suspicion as so far he had done: now his evil intentions were clear for all to see, and it had all happened not merely to one person, but in the presence of six witnesses, of whom my aunt alone was worth several by reason of her standing in society, because she had the reputation in the whole town of being an intelligent woman, and—despite her modest fortune—the provincial Governor used to visit her, and the chief of police was obliged to her for his family happiness. One word from her, and it went without saying he would investigate the matter before the trail had gone cold, and Selivan would not escape the noose he had wanted to place round our necks.

Circumstances were conspiring, as it seemed, to ensure immediate vengeance on our part against Selivan, and to see that he would be punished for his bestial attempt to end our lives and steal our property.

As we drove up to our house, which was built on a hill behind a spring, we were met by a lad on horseback, who was highly delighted when he saw us; he dug his heels into his horse's flanks, took off his cap while still a good distance away, galloped up to us, beaming all the while, and began telling Aunty how much anxiety our absence had caused.

It emerged that my father, mother and all the servants had not slept any more than we had. We had been expected at any time the previous day, and since the blizzard blew up in the afternoon, everyone was very alarmed, wondering if we had missed the track or if some other misfortune had struck us: maybe we had fallen into a pothole and broken the shaft,—maybe we had been attacked by wolves...Father had sent out several riders to meet us with lanterns, but the storm had torn the lamps out of their hands and blown them out, and neither men nor horses could get far from the house. They would step out for a very long time, and when they stopped, discover that the horse was no farther forward. The rider would urge the beast on, even though he himself could scarcely breathe in the suffocating atmosphere, but the horse would not move...The rider would dismount and take the nervous animal by the bridle to lead it on; and then to his surprise would discover that the horse was standing with its head up against the wall of a stable or a shed...Only one of the scouts succeeded in riding any distance, and he actually had an encounter on the road: this was Prokhor, the saddler. They had given him the trace-mare, which had the bit so firmly between her teeth that the metal never touched her lips, and she was unresponsive to any restraint on the part of the rider. She carried Prokhor into the hellish blizzard and galloped a good distance, kicking with her hind-legs and bending her head down almost to her knees, until finally at one such jerk, the saddler flew over her head and landed face first in the middle of a strange heap of living persons, who, moreover, showed him little sympathy at first. On the contrary, one of them clouted his head, another hit him in the back, and a third trampled on him and struck him with something cold, metallic and very unpleasant to the senses.

Prokhor knew what was what,—he realized he was dealing with creatures of a particular sort, and he let out a desperate yell.

The horror he experienced apparently lent his voice particular strength, and he was quickly heard. For his rescue there appeared just three paces from him a 'fiery illumination'. This was the light which had been placed in our kitchen window, beneath the walls of which certain people were taking refuge: the Chief of Police, his clerk, a soldier deputed to accompany them, and a driver with a troika of horses which had got stuck in a snowdrift.

They too had missed the road, and on reaching our kitchen, imagined they were still out somewhere in the open fields behind a bale of straw.

They were dug out and invited in—some into the kitchen, and some into the house, where the Chief of Police was by now drinking tea and preparing to hasten on to his family in town before they awoke and had time to be alarmed about his absence after such a severe night.

'That's excellent,' said Aunty, 'the Police Chief is just the man we want.'

'Yes, he's a dashing fellow,—he'll show Selivan a thing or two!' the servants chimed in, and we set off at the gallop and arrived home while the Police Chief's troika was still standing at the front door.

We would now tell the Chief of Police everything, and within half an hour that rascal Selivan would be firmly in his hands.

Chapter XVIII

MY father and the Chief of Police were impressed by what we had experienced on our journey and particularly in the rascal Selivan's house, Selivan who had intended to kill us and take all our property and money...

By the way—the money. When this was mentioned Aunty at once exclaimed:

'Good heavens! Where is my cashbox and the money?'

Where indeed was the box and the thousands in it?

Just imagine—it wasn't there! No, no, the box was the only item which could not be found anywhere in the house among the luggage we had brought in, nor was it still in the carriage. It was nowhere to be found...The cashbox was obviously still there and was now—in Selivan's possession...Or perhaps he had stolen it during the night. After all, he could have done so; as the host, he was in a position to know every nook and cranny of his decrepit house, and there were plenty of those!.. Maybe there was a loose floorboard and a plank in the partition which could be removed.

No sooner had our Police Chief who was experienced in the investigation of criminal affairs mentioned this possibility—a loose panel through which Selivan could have extracted the cashbox—than my aunt covered her face with her hands and collapsed into an armchair.

Anxious for the safety of her cashbox, she had hidden it under a bench which was placed against the partition separating our night quarters from that part of the hut where Selivan and his wife were.

'Well, now, there you are!' exclaimed the Chief of Police, enjoying the way that his deductions and experience had proved correct. 'You yourself offered him your cashbox!..but I *am* surprised that neither you nor the servants, no-one in fact, missed it when you came to leave.'

'But, Good God! We were terrified out of our wits!' groaned Aunty.

'That's right, that's right, I believe you,' said the Police Chief. 'You had good reason to be alarmed, but still...such a huge sum of money... such a fortune. I'll go there at once—at the gallop. I bet he'll have hidden himself somewhere, but he won't get away from me! It's our good fortune that everyone knows he's a thief, no-one likes him: nobody will give him sanctuary. But still, now he has money, he can share it with others...I must hurry...People are unscrupulous...Good-bye, I'm off. And you keep calm, take some drops or something...I know the mind of criminals, and I can assure you he'll be caught.'

And the Chief of Police was buckling on his sword, when all of a sudden in the porch unusual movement could be heard among the servants there, and...in through the door into the drawing room, where we were all assembled, came Selivan, breathing heavily, and carrying Aunty's cashbox in his hands.

Everyone leaped to their feet and stood there thunderstruck.

'You left your box behind; here it is,' said Selivan dully.

He could say no more, because he was completely out of breath after his amazingly quick walk and, perhaps also, from strong inner feelings.

He put the box on the table, and then, uninvited by anyone, sat down on a chair, and put his head in his hands.

Chapter XIX

THE cashbox was all there. My aunt took the key from round her neck, opened it, and exclaimed:

'It's all exactly as it was when I left it!'

'I've been looking after it...' said Selivan quietly. 'I was running after you...I wanted to catch you...I'm not feeling well... I'm sorry I'm sitting down in your presence...I'm tired out.'

Father was the first to go up to him. He embraced him and kissed his head.

Selivan did not move.

Aunty took two hundred-rouble notes out and tried to put them into his hand.

Selivan went on sitting and staring, as if he did not understand what was happening.

'Take what the lady's giving you,' said the Police Chief.

'What for? She doesn't need to do that!'

'Because you were honest and looked after the money that had been left behind and returned it.'

'But why, of course I did. Did you think I wouldn't?'

'Well, you...you're a good man; you didn't think of keeping what was someone else's.'

'Keep someone else's money!' Selivan shook his head and added: 'I don't need other people's property.'

'But you're poor—take it to help you out,' said my aunt kindly.

'Go on, take it,' my father tried to persuade him. 'You have a right to it.'

They told him about the law which says anyone who finds and returns lost property is entitled to a third part of its value.

'A fine law that is,' he replied, fending off my aunt's hand and the banknotes once again. 'You shouldn't benefit from others' misfortune...No need! Good-bye!'

And he rose to make his way back to his wretched dilapidated inn, but Father would not let him go: he took Selivan into his study and locked the door. An hour later he ordered the sledge to be harnessed to take him home.

By the next day all this was known in the town and in the region, and the day after that Father and Aunty drove over to Kromy, stopping on the way at Selivan's to drink tea in his hut and to leave a warm fur coat for his wife. On the way back they again called on him and brought some more presents: tea, sugar and flour.

He accepted it all politely, but unwillingly, and he said:

'What's going on? Now for the last three days people have been calling...I've started earning again...We've been making cabbage soup...People aren't afraid of us as they once were.'

When I was driven back to boarding school after the holidays, I too was given a present to pass on to Selivan, and I had tea with him, and I looked long into his eyes and thought:

'What a beautiful, kind face he has! Why did I and others so long imagine he was a *bogeyman*?'

I could not get this thought out of my mind; it would not leave me in peace...After all, he was the same person that everyone had imagined to be fearsome, whom all considered a sorcerer and a criminal. And for so long the idea was that he did nothing but plan and set up misfortunes for others. How could he all of a sudden have become so good and likeable?

Chapter XX

I WAS very fortunate in my childhood in one respect: my first lessons in religion were given to me by a superb Christian. This was the Orel priest Father Efim Ostromyslensky—a good friend of my father and a friend to all us children, whom he wisely taught to love truth and mercy. I never told my friends anything of what happened to us that Christmas Eve in Selivan's house, because I had no reason to be proud of my bravery, but rather the reverse: they would have laughed at my fears, but I did confide all my adventures and my doubts to Father Efim.

He stroked me with his hand and said:

'You're very lucky; your heart on Christmas Day was like the cradle of the Holy Child, who came down to earth to suffer for us sinners. Christ sent light into the darkness that surrounded your imagination—the stupid, empty words of unenlightened people. The bogeyman was not Selivan, it was you yourselves,—your suspicions of him, which didn't let you recognize his good conscience. His face seemed dim to you all because your eyes were dim. Just watch out so you aren't so blind another time.'

This was wise and beautiful advice. As the years went by, I came closer to Selivan and had the pleasure of seeing him loved and respected by everyone.

On the new estate which my aunt purchased there was an inn in good condition situated at an official staging post. She offered this property to Selivan on conditions very favourable to him, and Selivan accepted the offer and lived there until he eventually died. Here it was that my distant childish dreams came true: not only did I get to know Selivan very well indeed, but we both nurtured real friendship and full trust in each other. I watched his position change for the better—how peace and tranquillity became established in his household and little by little he came to earn enough for his needs; how it was that, in place of the grim expressions on the faces of people who met Selivan previously, now everyone seemed to enjoy meeting him. And, truly, it turned out that as the eyes of Selivan's neighbours shone when they met him, so did his own face become bright and animated.

Among Aunty's servants, the one who certainly did not like Selivan was Boriska, whom Selivan had nearly strangled on that memorable Christmas Eve.

People occasionally joked about that incident. It was explained that, just as we were all suspicious that Selivan was going to rob

Aunty, by the same token Selivan had the strong suspicion that the coachman and footman had lured us to his inn deliberately, intending to steal my aunt's money in the night and then throw all the blame onto the already suspect Selivan.

Mistrust and suspicion on the one side gave rise to mistrust and suspicion on the other, and everyone thought they were enemies who had reason to believe the other was inclined to evil.

Thus ever does evil engender evil and is countered only by good, which, according to the Gospel, makes pure our eye and our heart.

Chapter XXI

ALL that remains to be explained is why, after Selivan left the baker's employ, he became so gloomy and secretive. Who was it at that time who angered and rejected him?

My father, who was well-disposed towards this good man, none the less imagined that Selivan had a *secret* which he obstinately concealed.

This was so, but Selivan revealed his secret to my aunt, and then only several years after he had been living on her estate, and after the death of Selivan's invalid wife.

Once when I visited my aunt as a youth and we started to reminisce about Selivan, who had only recently died, my aunt told me his secret.

It was that Selivan, by reason of the goodness of his heart, was moved by the sad fate of the helpless daughter of the hangman who had died in their town. No-one wanted to give refuge to the poor girl, as the daughter of a man held in general contempt. Selivan was poor, and he moreover could not bring himself to take in the hangman's daughter in the town, where everybody knew who she was. He had to conceal her origins from everyone; she could not be blamed for them. Otherwise she would have had to put up with reproaches from people who were quite incapable of being merciful and fair. Selivan concealed her because he was ever afraid that she would be recognized and reviled, and this concealment and fear communicated itself to his whole nature and to some extent imprinted itself upon his character.

And so everyone who called Selivan a 'bogeyman' was to a much greater degree a 'bogeyman' to Selivan.

A Pygmy

THIS is a story about an event which really happened; it came to light recently when a circle of close friends was reflecting on the excessive growth in our society of cold and heartless egotism and indifference. Several of those present felt that it had not always been so,—the others admitted that in the recent past, even, hearts had been a little warmer and souls more sympathetic than they are today, and one of the interlocutors, a man from my own part of the country, an elderly and highly respected person, said:

'Well, now, gentlemen, I can say that I still have a friend, a little old fellow, a gentleman of very little substance indeed, a real pygmy, who never in his life played a significant part in anything, except that once, when he lived here in St Petersburg, he was impelled by the most honourable motivation to do a deed which maybe you will find hard to believe. And if I tell you the story, you will see what a really unimportant little man can do for his neighbour when he seriously *wants* to help him; our great sadness today is that no-one ever wants to do anything for a fellow human being, unless he can see some advantage in it for himself.'

And this is the story our narrator told.

I

THE small landowner who is the main character in my story was called S., he is still alive and well and is living out his years on his little old farmhouse in the district of K. Before he retired he worked in government service here in Petersburg, in the City Police Department, in a very humble capacity; it was his responsibility to arrange for the public administration of corporal punishment. At that time—until very recently in fact—in Holy Russia people from unprivileged classes of society used to be flogged with the lash and branded. In the course of his long service, our old—as he now is—gentleman must have 'set in motion' such countless numbers of these punishments, that he had become completely hardened to this unpleasant duty, and he carried out his function unemotionally and without any misgivings, as if it were the most ordinary matter of professional routine. But then once an incident happened of such a nature that he betrayed himself, and, in his own words, 'instead of doing his duty rationally—did something stupid'.

This incident occurred in 1853, when relations between Russia and France were very tense and there was serious talk in the capital of the possibility of breaking them off altogether. At this time Mr S., our official, was handed papers 'for action' concerning the flogging by the public executioner of a young Frenchman called N., who had been condemned for an act of the most disgusting indecency towards a young girl, a minor. I shall not tell you this Frenchman's name, because he is still alive and quite well known; and since his name was protected from unpleasant publicity by the discretion of the 'pygmy', well, I'm no giant myself, so I'm not going to give it away.

'I read the paper,' said S., 'noted its contents, and since we flog young and old and there's an end to it, I just instructed the contractor to set up the scaffold in the public square ready for next day, and ordered the prisoner to be brought in to have a look at him: was he fit and could he be subjected to the procedure without too much harm?'

They brought in a man who was extremely feeble and half dead; he was pale, weeping, trembling and wringing his hands, and babbling piteously.

Oh, good lord, I thought: why did a French wretch like this have to come over here and commit a filthy deed like this, so we have to beat the living daylights out of him in good Russian style?

And I suddenly felt sorry for him.

'What have you done?' I said. 'What possessed you to attack a poor little child?'

And he fell at my feet, raised his shackled hands to heaven, rattled his chains and wept.

'Monsieur, monsieur! Heaven knows...'

'What has heaven to do with it? You've defiled the good earth by what you did, and now is not the time to appeal to heaven; you'd better get ready: the flogging is tomorrow: you'll get what you deserve.'

'I was falsely accused.' (He had learned some Russian during his three years in prison.)

'That's enough of that, *mon ami*, you're lying; no-one found you guilty for no reason: the court knows what it condemns you for.'

'Really and truly,' he said, 'it's all a false accusation. May God, *Dieu, Dieu,* strike me dead...' and he went on in this style, and wept so bitterly, so bitterly, that he got me really worried. I'd seen plenty of tears of all sorts before floggings, but tears of this sort: hot, burning and violent, I have to say I had never experienced. So I saw that it was the false accusation that forced them from him.

Now, just tell me, what could a pygmy like me do for him? My job was simply to have him beaten, branded and exiled 'to carry out the decision of the court', that was all, and there was no more to it. And I nodded to the guard to take him away, because what was the point in my keeping him there? Get all worried myself and make him nervous to little purpose before the event?

'Take him back to prison,' I said.

But when he heard this, he clung to my feet and went silent; and his tears or his face, I'll swear, were so hot that I could feel my foot burning through my boots.

Pooh! Go to the devil! I thought, I've upset myself by talking to him and I couldn't shake him off from my feet; but something started to whisper in my ear:

'Question him, question him, and when you hear, you'll be on his side.'

But, for heaven's sake, what's the point of a nobody like me, an insignificant administrative official, standing up for him, when the matter has been decided by a criminal court, and when the contractor, the inspector and the executioner have all received their instructions? What good is there in standing up for him? But, dash it all, that same invisible whatever it was was whispering in my ear: 'Question him, and stand up for him'.

And I gave in just a little: I'm not going to take up his case, I thought, but I'll question him, there's no harm in that.

'Pull yourself together,' I said, 'Tell me the truth about what happened! But mind you, don't you dare tell any lies!'

II

AS far as his tears and sobs would allow, he told me that he had been lodging in the apartment of a hairdresser on the Morskaya Embankment; a young girl used to call at these haircutters' from the laundry—she was barely fifteen and very pretty. And, he said, she closely resembled his little sister, or rather, as he said, his *cousine*. Well, now he, as a Frenchman..., well, of course he had taste and imagination: he liked the child; one day he would give her a ribbon, the next an orange, then a rouble or a fifty-copeck piece, sweets—in other words, he spoilt her; and her mother was a wastrel: she invited him in and saw that he and the girl were locked up together, and she'd trained the girl to scratch his face and scream, as if he had intended to do her serious harm. A crowd came running, a charge was brought, they kept him in prison for three years and condemned him to a flogging and exile.

I listened to all this, and it all seemed to hang together just as he told it, and I paid particular attention to the wound that the girl had caused on his face: it had been a deep injury, which had healed, but a white scar remained. It was an extremely strange scar: as if some thought had gone in to where it should be placed. For the most part it doesn't quite happen like that: most women in these circumstances go straight for the eyes, and even more often they scratch the man's cheeks,— since women, once seized, instinctively bring up their hands to the man's face, while this girl had, rather like a cat, gone straight into the centre, directly to the nose and down to the upper lip...

I thought, so what? God knows there are shameless people about; if you work for the police you see far more than enough of them, so I said to him:

'Well, Monsieur, if it *is* as you say, maybe God won't let the false accusation stand, so say your prayers and hope.'

He kissed my hands and rattled his shackles; he left and I stayed put where I was and thought: a right pair of fools we have here. First there's him, because he thinks I'm going to save him, and then there's me that's given him false hope.

But I just couldn't get it out of my head that he'd been wrongly condemned, and what's more we were going to flog him the next day, and his puny little French torso'll writhe in the wooden pillory, the blood will flow, and he'll yelp like a live sucking-pig on a spit. My God, I thought, it won't do you any good to be flogged, and anyway I wouldn't like to have to watch!

I can't; it's just that I got all so worked up about him, that I couldn't bring myself to deal with the simplest bits of paper on my desk.

I called my underling and said:

'Will you see to everything? I've got a nasty headache and I'm going home.'

I went home, I paced round and round the room, and cursed and went wild with everyone, my wife and the servants: I couldn't rest, that's all there was to it! That accursed Frenchman stood before me, and I simply couldn't banish him from my mind's eye.

My wife tried to get me out of it: 'What on earth's the matter with you?'—because I was never like that, but she only made me worse.

Dinner was served; I came to the table, but got up again straight away, I just couldn't, and that was that. I was sorry for the Frenchman, that was the long and short of it.

I couldn't bear the thought that everyone at home was seeing the state I was in, so I grabbed my hat and fled the house, and it was from that moment that I was no longer in control of myself, and some new idea started to take possession of me: *I was contemplating treachery.*

III

I WENT straight to the police officer in whose area the case had arisen; I asked him what the facts were three years ago and what sort of a woman the girl's mother was.

The policeman said:

'The devil take it, I don't know: it happened before my time, but that harridan, the girl's mother, is a right bitch, and,' he said, 'she's tried it on once or twice more with her daughter since then. But still,' he said, 'how can we know the rights and wrongs of it?'

Well, fair enough, I thought, you and I, my good fellow, aren't going to decide that, let God decide—so I set off to Konyushennaya Street straight away, to the rank where you can hire a carriage: I bargained for a large one, with four seats, the type they carry invalids in, and I told the driver to take me at the gallop to the Izmailovsky Regiment barracks, where a friend of mine, a family man, lived; he kept a French tutor for his children. This

Frenchman had been living in Russia for a good long time and understood Russian quite well enough for my purposes.

I drove up to my friend's and said:

'Be a good chap and lend me your little Froggy for a while, I need his services for a special reason.'

'What are you up to?' he asked.

'Nothing much,' I said, 'I just need him, for a very short time —only a couple of hours.'

And the way I said it, it must have been clear to my friend that I was far from calm, as I was breathing heavily, I was in a hurry, and anxious, and the harder I tried to conceal it, the more —to my fury—I must have put him in a quandary about my state of mind, and the more he inevitably wanted to know, 'What the devil's going on and what's the matter with you?'

Somehow I managed to cut short any long interrogation by him by pretending I was worried because I had received news that my brother was ill, and I couldn't wait to consult a French fortune-teller with her Lenormand cards to see whether he was going to get better or not, and, well, since I'm more or less totally ignorant of French,...and so on, and so on, and so on.

I've no idea if he believed me, but at least he stopped asking questions and let me have the Frenchman; I got in the carriage with him straight away and said:

'Well, now, Monsieur: you won't know why I've got you here.'

He looked a me and went pale, because, as you know, our police service doesn't dispose freedom-loving people in our favour. At that particular juncture I might have been a particularly unwelcome visitor for a Frenchman, since, I remind you, relations between France and Russia were deteriorating rapidly, and in the police we had what were often secret instructions to keep a very close eye on various people from that nation.

'What's the matter,' I said, 'are you shy?'

He flew into a panic.

'Please,' he said, 'I'm innocent!'

'What's up with you? Who said anything about you being guilty of anything? In fact, my good man, it's me who's guilty, because I'm a *traitor*. I'm getting involved in an affair that I have no right to stick my nose into; well, I can't escape from it now, God sees fit that I put my oar in.' And, can you believe it, I really did feel like that, *that God saw fit* that I should do what I was doing. Needless to say, it was just my odd way of thinking.

'Now, listen,' I said. 'It's like this: one of your compatriots is in a situation where tomorrow he's faced inevitably with nothing less than the lash, and I'm going to save him from it.'

My companion gaped: though he was a foreigner, as I said, he'd been living in Russia for ages, he knew the way we do things, and therefore he must have thought it lunacy for a minor police functionary to try to overturn a judicial verdict which had been confirmed by the highest authority. But I said:

'Please, my good friend, don't gape at me with your mouth open like that, don't oh and ah, but do your duty to God in the affair I've asked you to help with. Do you know where I'm taking you now?'

'No,' he said.

'Well, I'll tell you. Any minute now we'll stop outside your Embassy: I wouldn't be allowed in on any pretext, because I'm a police official, and the law forbids us to enter embassy premises, but you go in, and since your ambassadors are so free and easy that they'll receive their compatriots at any time, do all you can to see that the Duke sees you straight away,[1] and tell him the whole story. Meanwhile I'll sit in the carriage—I'll be waiting for you, and if the Ambassador should tell you to summon me, well, you can fetch me, and I'll confirm everything; but probably he'll believe it anyway and will know what to do.'

We drove up to the Embassy and stopped; my French friend got out and went through the glass doors in the main entrance, and I told the driver to move the coach on a little way, while I hid in the corner of it—and waited. And then all of a sudden it came to me, the whole extent of my treachery, and I started to panic.

---

[1] In Petersburg at this time the French Ambassador and Minister Plenipotentiary was the Duc de Guiche, who handed over office on 10 (22) August 1853 to Baron Burineau de Varennes, who had been chargé d'affaires. [Author's note]

IV

SUDDENLY, you know, all at once I realized that I'd got into a business that was quite beyond me, and this...I was a police official, and, sort of, I was complaining against my own government...and then a foreign embassy...and then it had to be the French Embassy and at such a political time...A nasty business! I'm a traitor, nothing more than a traitor! And the more I thought about it, the worse it all seemed...A nasty business! And my little Frenchie just didn't seem to be ever going to come out of those glass doors, and I could see on the other side of the street, on the opposite pavement, a policeman pacing out his beat. I think to myself: he's not walking around here by chance...And then, you know, if I'm unlucky, he might be one of those sharp ones, you see, looking to get a medal, wants promotion, and he's standing there now, perhaps, and thinking, what's that carriage that's just driven up to the Embassy? Is something going on there? And the beggar will go and look in the window, and there I'll be! The wretched fellow will recognize me, because everyone in the force knows me, and he'll say: 'Ah, your Excellency, so you're a traitor!'—and he'll put in a report to the top brass; and that'll be the end of me...I'll never see home again, I'll be straight across the Trinity Bridge and into the Peter and Paul Fortress, and there, for traitors like me and the others, 'there are many mansions'...I was overcome by such fear that I lay in the corner of the carriage curled up like a damp dog, and, like a dog in cold weather, I was shivering, and cursing myself roundly for having brewed up a stew like this to boil myself in...And all this time through the window of the carriage I was watching the policeman out of the corner of my eye, as he walked up and down on the opposite side, while all the time I was crouching down under the level of the seat on the floor of the carriage and trying to kick open the door with my heels with the intention of making off into the basement shops; fortunately—I knew a building nearby with a courtyard with a way in and a way out the other side—so I wouldn't be easy to catch.

Then I managed it: I left two roubles on the seat to pay the driver, and opened the door—and edged out backwards onto the roadway, when I suddenly heard, 'Look out!'—And then, missing my back by inches, a pair of black horses and a coach drove up to the front door, and I saw the French Ambassador in full uniform wearing all his medals climb in quickly and gallop off, and just then my own little French ambassador seemed to appear from the ground beside me, also very agitated, and said:

'Why have you got out?'

Having such a bad conscience, I got all mixed up and started acting stupid and talking nonsense.

'What do you want? I don't know who you are, and I haven't got out from anywhere.'

'Did you see?'

'What was there to see? Will you please go away; I saw nothing at all.'

'Our Duke has just left,' he said.

'What has your Duke to do with me...Why don't you just go away?'

'What do you mean, what has he to do with you? You know where he's going?'

'No, I don't. I don't know anything at all; there's nothing for me to know, and if you don't go away at once I'll call the police.'

He gave me a look to suggest that I was acting very oddly in what I said, and whispered:

'The Duke has gone to the Winter Palace.'

'Now, go away,' I said, 'I've already told you I don't know what you're talking about.' And I pushed him away and made off through the courtyard I knew, and went back home to my nestlings, in order, while there was still time, to press them to my heart perhaps for the last time in my life. And I'd scarcely managed to do that when suddenly a messenger arrived with a note from the General to say that tomorrow's flogging of the French prisoner had been cancelled.

Good Lord! I thought, things really are hotting up now.

V

ALL I did was bite my lip and write immediately to all who needed to be told about the cancellation of the ceremony and didn't go to bed that night; I paced up and down the room in an odd state of mind. I still couldn't work it out for myself how I'd done it and what would happen next. And it was not only frightening, but at the same time there was a feeling of bliss in my heart. I was also of course thinking about whether something or other might happen to me and what the consequences of my betrayal might be, but I couldn't feel glad for the sake of the wretched Frenchman either. It was only just before dawn that, with these difficult thoughts still in my head, I forced myself to doze in an armchair, when suddenly I heard a din and loud voices in the porch at the door; my wife was asking someone to hang on for a minute, saying that I'd just dropped off; but the other voice, a stranger, insisted that she should wake me up at once, and I fancied I heard him mention the name of the Tsar. At that point I remembered my treachery, and I was immediately fully awake.

I dashed out, just as I was, in my dressing-gown, and looked: a courier was standing there with a very fearsome-looking ugly face on him, like those they send on business to do with prison camps, and he handed me a package without speaking.

So, well, I took the package, and my hands were trembling violently, I burst open the seal and saw a white sheet of paper, and right in the middle there was nothing but the words: *'Thank you'*, and inside there was some money...I counted it: fifteen hundred roubles in cash.

You don't take it all in in the first moment, you know, you don't see what it is and who it's from; and then you don't know who you should go to in a puzzling situation like that for enlightenment. So of course I wanted to ask the courier, but he'd gone, leaving not a trace...Then I looked at the package to see whose handwriting my name was written in, and the 'thank you' message which was so sacred to me, and I remembered whose writing it was...and, can you believe it, I gave vent to my feelings: that is, I tell you straight, I howled like an idiot, and sobbed my heart out, if you don't mind my saying so...I've only wept like that twice in my life: the second time was when Tsar Nikolai Pavlovich died, and I came to his sarcophagus one night to say my own 'thank you' for the fact that *we were a pair*: he, my Emperor, and I his traitor. And there was a third time I cried the same way, on another occasion which resulted from this whole story.

VI

WE never did flog the little Frenchie, and the order was simply given for him to be deported from Russia on the written condition that he never returned within the borders of the realm. You might well ask why anyone but a complete fool would want to come back, and, anyway, there was no reason for him to do so:

he made his fortune in a wonderful way in Paris. I, on the other hand, put aside the fifteen hundred roubles that had descended from heaven in case I ever needed a trip for the good of my health, and in the few years before my retirement the money even grew a little, and the fifteen hundred became a couple of thousand or a little more. So I went to Vichy to take the waters to recover from my sedentary life...Napoleon III was still Emperor then, and everything ran in the old-fashioned way; and when I felt better, on the way back, I stopped off in Paris to look at any interesting places I fancied seeing, and to pick up a few things, you know—fancy goods and perfumery, to take home to my womenfolk. In Petersburg everyone favoured Pineau, the Paris perfumer, so I said to my guide:

'Take me to Pineau's shop, Sir, I want to buy some of his best perfume and pomade.'

But the guide objected.

'Why do you want to go to Pineau's?'

'But isn't he the best?'

'Goodness me,' he replied, 'heaven knows how long ago it was that he was thought to be the best, but it's not Pineau now, it's another perfumer who's considered the very best,' and he told me the name, which was so familiar to me that it just hit me in the face.

'What did you say his name was?'

He repeated it.

Gracious me, I thought, as I recalled that my one-time protégé bore the same name! So I asked:

'Wasn't your famous perfumer in Russia at one time?'

'Oh, yes,' he replied, 'he was, only in 1853, before the Crimean War, he was expelled from St Petersburg for political interference.'

Hm, I know all about what politics he means, I thought.

'All that may be so,' I said, 'but I think I'd better go to Pineau's, I don't want to have anything to do with the other.'

The guide tried to persuade me to the contrary, but I stuck to my guns.

'No, no, no,' I said, 'I'm not going to him...maybe he's doing very well at present, but there's plenty of people in France who become all the rage for a short while, and Pineau,' I said, 'is a firm with a long-established reputation, and he's famous in Russia too; so, please—you take me to Pineau's shop.'

I was being awkward, needless to say, because I didn't want to meet the man...After all, what's the good of reminding a fellow about something unpleasant that's long gone?

But here I have to confess to a little weakness of mine: the guide started telling me how rich the man was; what a prosperous-looking factory he owned, and what an opulent store he had, and how he lived in a house of his own,—I can't remember the name of the street, only that it was near the Vendôme Column... And I thought I'd like to see the house.

So well, then, I thought, if not the man himself, then at least I'd like to look at his property: why not go and have a look? It'll be nothing to him—he won't even know I've been there. Of course, it wasn't a good idea, and I shouldn't have done it, because it was just pointless. But, you see, I thought it would be interesting, because even if it was only a small service I did him, when I'd done it, he went off and started his life again.

So we went: we drove past, deliberately slowly—in the carriage, and what did I see?—a house like a palace; the name-board of the factory you could see three streets away, and the shop window was big enough for you to turn around in a coach and six.

'It can't be the same man!' I said.

'Yes, it is, the very man that was kicked out of Russia for politics.'

I think: what are you talking about, you fool, how do you imagine you understand what I'm thinking? According to you, he's the same man, but I can't see it could be the 'politics' man I've got in mind.

But, then, I start telling him about the black mark against my protégé; it's just that I don't believe that fate could play with a man like that, giving him first degradation and then enormous riches.

'If I could just get a look at him,' says I, 'it would be so interesting!'

'Why, of course,' says he, 'it's quite possible.'

'Only I don't want to go to his shop, that's out of the question...If I could look through a crack somewhere, so he couldn't see me, but I could see him?'

'That's not difficult,' he says, 'but he rarely goes to the shop himself, and doesn't live in the house in summer.'

'Well, where does he live?'

'At his villa, in Passy.'

'He's got a villa as well?' I ask.

'Not just one,' he says, 'two; one's only good for half the year, what they call *demi-saison*, not far from here above the Trocadéro, and the other one, a real one, in Passy,' he says, 'is an out-of-town house, and you don't see many like it, and,' he says, 'every evening at seven o'clock he has a cup of coffee with any visitors there might be on a veranda above a flower bed, and sometimes he plays hoopla with his wife and children; we can drive surreptitiously by a couple of times and you'll get a peep at him.'

'Oh, good! That's excellent!'

It was exactly six o'clock, and I'd already had my evening meal by Russian time; my guide had also eaten, so I said to him:

'Well, now, Sir, let's not put it off: tell the driver to go straight there.' 'Hey, there, driver,' I said, '*cocher*, let's be off to Passy, and don't delay, and there'll be a good tip for you.' The guide interpreted this, and we set off.

VII

WE set off, and since the route lay past the Trocadéro, my guide pointed out the other villa belonging to my old acquaintance,—a very worthy house, a prince of the blood royal wouldn't have been ashamed to live there: while at Passy, it was simply a little château, stone walls, tall ones, overgrown with ivy, and a front entrance from a narrow little alley, while the other side of the railings you could see a flower garden, and behind the garden the house and the veranda. And what do you think?— we found everything just as the guide had said we would: the children were romping around the garden, guests were sitting on the veranda and the master of the house...I hid behind the corner of the wall, got my binoculars out of my pocket, focused on him, and there was no doubt,— *it was the very man*, my protégé! He had matured and filled out too, you won't be surprised to hear, with his prosperous life; but you could still see the white scar on his nose.

'Do you happen to know, Sir,' I asked my guide, 'is he a good husband?'

'An exceptional one,' he said. 'He leads a blameless life; his wife's marvellous, the children are all good-natured, he's good-natured himself, and he never fails to help poor people.'

'He's a really good fellow if he helps the poor,' I said.

Just at that moment, as we were whispering to each other round the corner, he must have noticed we were there, and he shouted to his daughter:

'Alina!'

And suddenly the wrought-iron gate rattled, and a lovely, angelic little girl approached me, wearing a little pink dress, and I scarcely had time to collect myself, when she put a franc into my hand, saying, 'Au nom de Jésus,' roughly equivalent to our Russian: 'Take it for Christ's sake,'—and she went.

I was in my ordinary Russian coat, you know, and I had a soft furry hat on my head, and, really, I must have looked like a vagrant from the streets; and so, well, she gave me a franc from her father for Christ's sake. So, what do you think? Of course I took the franc she gave me, and I keep it to this day; they say that money given you in charity is lucky, but I don't keep it for luck out of superstition, but as a keepsake...

Well, then, and so, then, when I was riding back to my little room, I betrayed myself again; once again, for the third time in my life, I shed tears that were sweet, ever so sweet. I thought, the guide must think I'm an utter fool, and he's quite right. Only I couldn't help it, because, as it says in the ancient doggerel verse:

When kindness and good nature please us,
Our hearts are richer far than Croesus.

What better way is there to thank God for such an undeserved sensation of pleasure than with a tear?

Wrong Done at Christmas

Events that Really Happened

I HAD been intending, dear readers, to tell you on this occasion about something quite different from the story here. I had wanted to use the occasion of Christmas to discuss one of the social evils of which we have been guilty for ages and which we cannot remedy. But then one of my friends, a person who is known to many in Petersburg, happened quite unexpectedly to suffer a great wrong done at the time of the Festival, and he reacted so strangely and untypically to this wrong, that it deserves to be considered by any thoughtful person. So that is what I am going to tell you about, so just you listen, as it is something that can happen to anyone, and what is more, not everybody takes it the same way.

I HAVE a good long-standing friend. He is in the same line of work as I am. I shall not tell you his real name, because he would find that embarrassing, and as far as you are concerned it doesn't matter what he is called; what is important is the sort of person he is, how he was wronged, and how he reacted to the wrong and to those guilty of it.

The man I'm talking about is neither rich not poor, he is solitary, unmarried, and he could well afford to employ two servants, but he doesn't keep any. The reason for that is not that he is mean, but he is simply reluctant: he says—what sort of a person might take up employment in his home, and anyway what would such a person find to do working for a solitary employer? The servant would get bored through inactivity and might start nagging and quarrelling; no good would come of it, only irritation. My friend is a calm and accommodating sort of man who likes a joke, but avoids argument and quarrelling.

For his comfort he arranged to rent a small apartment in an annexe to a large and imposing building on a riverside embankment, and he lived there happily for many years. As I said, he kept no servants, and all essential help at home was offered by the caretaker. When he needed to go out, he locked the door of the flat, and kept the key in his pocket.

The flat was small, but it did have three rooms and was on the first floor, right in the middle of the building, and the staircase led to it from outside the caretaker's quarters. It was so situated that you would think there was no need to fear anything, and, as I have said, for many years he had no trouble at all, but then, all of a sudden this Christmas, something went badly wrong.

HERE I'll take a moment out of my story to say that I see this friend almost every day, and a few days ago we were speaking about something that happened once in our native town. What happened was that a merchant who lived there absolutely refused on one occasion to sit on a jury to try some robbers; and this is how they say it came about.

Once upon a time, long ago in that town, there lived three robbers. Our town has long been famous for robbery, in fact, it's proverbial for it. These thieves got the idea they would rob the store-room in the house of a rich merchant. The store-room was built of stone and there were no windows low down in the walls; there was only one very small window right at the top, just below the roof. There was no way of getting to this window without a ladder, and even if you could reach it, there was no way of getting in, because a grown man would not be able to squeeze through the window.

But the thieves who wanted to rob this merchant were not going to be put off their idea, because the loot was well worth working for: the store-room contained a great many goods of all sorts—summer clothing, fur caps, sheepskin coats, down pillows, canvas and cloth—it was absolutely stuffed with good things from floor to ceiling. How could any self-respecting robber drop such an enterprise?

Then the thieves thought of a daring scheme.

ONE of the thieves, who had no family himself, said to the other, who had:

'I've thought of a good way to do the job: you've got a little son who's only five—he's only little and his body's still supple—he can get through that window. If we take him with us—we'll carry it off perfectly. Get the boy away from his mother and bring him along on Christmas Eve—tell her we're going to church for the service, and we'll all go into action together. Then when we get there, one of us will stand below the window, the other'll get up on his shoulders and the third will stand on *his* shoulders, so we'll make a pillar, and we shan't need a ladder to get to the window; then we'll tie the rope fast round your little boy's waist, give him a dark lantern and a light, and we'll lower him down through the window right into the middle of the store. Then he can have a look around, undo the rope, pick out all the best things, tie them into a loop in the rope, and we'll pull them out, we'll strip the place bare, then the boy can fasten the rope round his waist again—we'll pull him out and share the loot three-and-a-half ways: us two one each, and you and the boy a one-and-a-half share, and we'll give him some sweets for his pains—he'll be pleased at that and it'll encourage him to take up the trade when he's older.'

The father-robber—obviously a good fellow—didn't refuse this offer, he agreed: and when it came to Christmas Eve he said to his wife:

'I've promised to go to the monastery to the all-night vigil,—the singing there's lovely, go and find the lad. I'll take him with me—it'll be good for him to hear some decent singing.'

The wife thought that was all right and let the boy go with his father. But the thieves didn't go to the monastery; they called in at a tavern by the gate on the Moscow Road and started drinking—vodka and beer, but not too much. They laid the child on the floor in the corner so he could have a little nap; and as night advanced and the innkeeper began locking up the premises, they all got up, lit the lantern and left with the boy, and everything they had planned they carried out. At first everything went far better than they could have wanted: the little boy turned out to be very resourceful and agile; he just took one look round the store-room and fastened the most suitable things to the rope, and the adults hauled it all out, until in the end, they saw that they had removed so much that three of them wouldn't be able to carry it away. In other words, there was no further point in continuing the robbery.

Then the man at the bottom said to the one above him, and he said to the one on his shoulders:

'That's enough, fellows. We don't need any more. Tell the lad to tie the rope round his waist, and we'll drag him out.'

The thief standing at the top on the others' shoulders whispered to the boy through the window:

'That's enough, we don't need any more. Now make sure you tie the rope really tight round you, hold on to it with both hands, and we'll pull you up.'

The boy tied the rope round his middle, and they started pulling. They got him almost right to the top, when suddenly,—something they hadn't noticed in the dark,—the rope had become frayed by rubbing against the brickwork, and it suddenly snapped, with the result that the boy fell back down into the plundered store-room, and the robbers, taken by surprise by this unexpected eventuality, lost their balance and fell in a heap...This caused some noise, and at once the guard dogs started charging about and set up a frightful barking...Then all the servants woke up and leapt out of bed, and this, needless to say, was the thieves' undoing. In any case it was near the time when people would be getting up anyway to go to church for the early Christmas service, and the robbers would certainly be caught red-handed.

The thieves grabbed each what they could and took to their heels. Inside the merchant's house everyone leapt out of bed, came running about with lanterns and arrived in the store-room. And as they entered, they saw the disorder and realized that a great many goods were missing. On the floor, the little boy was sitting, badly bruised, and crying.

NEEDLESS to say, the merchant's staff guessed at once what had happened. They raced out into the street, and found there under the window, almost untouched, all the things that the robbers had tried to steal, because the frightened thieves had only been able to take a very small part with them.

And they all started fussing and shouting about what should be done: should they report what had happened to the police, or chase the robbers themselves? But they were afraid to chase around in the dark without knowing which direction to go in, because thieves carry guns as a last resort and can kill a man in the dark like a chicken. We have some resourceful robbers in our town: they would come out at night to steal people's fur hats, but not with their bare hands; they'd use a device something like tongs with a little loop of twine-known as a 'cricket'. (It is mentioned even in Shuisky's reminiscences.) However, the merchant who had been robbed was an excellent fellow—intelligent, good-natured, reasonable, and a Christian; so he said to his lads:

'Forget it, there's no need. What more do we want! My goods are pretty well all here, and there's no point in chasing after little things.'

And the lads replied:

'That's right: God's left us the child to catch the thieves with. It's a clear sign; everything will show who his parents are—it'll be clear as day.'

But the merchant said:

'No, that's not right. The boy's a innocent young soul, he's been led into crime by others—we shouldn't report him, we want to put him on the right track. Don't abuse him and don't touch him: the boy's a messenger from God, we must take him in from the cold and look after him in the Lord's name. Just look at him now, he's frozen stiff, he's shivering and terrified. We mustn't ask him questions about anything. It's not a Christian thing to do, to make a child tell tales on his father...They can keep what little of mine they've got, they haven't done me any real harm at all, but God has brought this child to me, so you keep quiet—maybe he'll stay with me.'

And so they none of them said anything, and no one came to ask for the little boy, and he stayed in the merchant's house, and the merchant treated him like his own son and taught him the business. And since he had a good and just heart, the child was brought up in a good spirit, and he turned into a splendid and intelligent young man, and everyone in the household loved him.

Now the merchant had a daughter, but no sons, and this daughter grew up alongside the robber's son and fell in love with him. This became obvious to everyone. Then the merchant said to his wife:

'I was going to say: our daughter's reached the age when she should soon be thinking of getting married, but why worry about finding her a young man? It's a serious matter, especially as we're well off and everyone will be thinking they'll pick up a great big dowry, and there'll be so much nonsense talked and so much pretence that we'll be sick of it.'

His wife replied:

'That's right: it's always the same.'

'Indeed,' said the merchant, 'some twisted fellow will turn up making himself out to be a good chap when he's anything but. You can never get inside someone's mind: and we could spoil the girl's life for her, and then we'll regret it and wish we hadn't, but we won't be able to do anything about it. No, we'll go about it more carefully.'

'How do you mean?' asked the wife.

'Well, let's do it this way: we'll let her marry our foster-son. He's part of the family already, we know him well, and our daughter—no point in denying it—seems to have fallen for him completely, or so everyone thinks. If we let them get married we shan't regret it.'

And so they agreed there and then to let the young couple marry: and the parents lived out their allotted span and died, the young people lived on and had children who grew up too, and they themselves grew old. And they lived happily and were respected by all, but then the new courts were established, and the foster-child, by this time an old man, was summoned for jury service. The first case he had to hear was a robbery. He trembled as he sat listening, he went pale and then he flushed and suddenly closed his eyes, but tears ran down his face from beneath his eyelids, and sobs burst from the old man's breast.

The Chairman of the court asked:

'Tell us, what is the matter?'

And he replied:

'It's this, It's not right for me to do this, I'm a thief myself who's never been charged, and I beg you to let me confess my sin to you all.'

They thought he was overwrought and would not allow him to confess in public, but later he told his story to some respectable citizens: how as a child he had been lowered into a storeroom on a rope and had been caught and forgiven, and had stayed with his benefactor like a son in the household, and this confession greatly touched everybody, and not a single person in the town thought of condemning him for an offence he had never been tried for. Everyone continued, as before, to treat him with the respect he had earned by reason of his righteous life.

MY friend and I discussed this and reflected with pleasure on the way we sometimes meet tender and good-natured souls.

'We should be reassured,' I said, 'that there's so much good in people.'

'Yes,' said my friend, 'it's fine to be reassured, but more than that, you've got to be ready yourself to cope when necessary.'

That was the sort of thing we used to say to each other (and this was just the other day), but on the very next morning something happened which fitted in so well that you would think it was all part of a stage play.

My friend arrived and said:

'Something's happened.'

'What?'

'Something unpleasant.'

I thought: 'I bet it's nothing very much, he's an over-sensitive fellow.'

'No,' he said, 'it's enormously unpleasant: someone's wrecked my apartment. I was only out for an hour, but when I got back and put my key in the lock, the door opened on its own...I looked in, and there on the floor was a drawer from my desk on the floor, and everything all over the place...a gold chain lying around and something else valuable just discarded, but certain things of sentimental value gone: the gold watch my late father gave me, and my collection of six hundred old coins, and an envelope with five hundred roubles in it for my funeral and the title to a burial plot next to my mother's grave...'

I could not find any words, I was so astonished.

What do you make of it? The previous day we had been talking about the story of the robbery, and now today one of us had experienced something of the same.

It was just as if he had been summoned to take an oral examination.

Now, then, I was thinking, here we are, yesterday you were reassured by someone else's good heart, and now it's your turn to show whether you've got enough spirit in you to match it.

But I sat down and didn't say anything. Then I asked,

'What have you done about it?'

'Nothing,' he answered, 'nothing yet, because I don't know whether I should do anything. People say I should report it.'

And he asked me as a friend to advise him. What advice could I give? To report it had already been suggested, but in another sense, what right had I to propose any course of action? It wasn't my property that had been stolen, and you can easily forgive a wrong done to someone else.

'No,' I said, 'I can't advise, but if you like I'll tell you about the time something similar happened to me.'

He asked me to go on and tell him.

And I told him about my adventure with a thief.

I ONCE had a sheepskin coat made, which set me back three hundred roubles, but it was very heavy. It weighed so heavily on my shoulders that I could scarcely move my arms. So I got into the bad habit of walking with it off my shoulders, and in consequence the hem got worn. In the morning of Christmas Eve my maidservant said:

'The coat's worn: I don't know how to repair it the way a tailor would; if I get to work with a needle, the hem'll get all wrinkled. The caretaker says there's a tailor friend of his living in the house next door—he's very good at repairs; shall we send the coat to him by the caretaker? He'll bring it back by tonight.'

I said, 'Very well.' The maid passed my sheepskin to the caretaker, who took it straight to his friend the tailor next door.

But as Christmas Eve wore on there was a thaw, and the snow was melting and dripping everywhere: by evening I didn't need the sheepskin—an ordinary overcoat was all I wanted.

I forgot about the sheepskin and didn't ask for it, but on Christmas Day I heard a terrible argument and upset in the kitchen: the caretaker, pale and scared, didn't so much as wish me a happy Christmas, but told me my sheepskin had gone and that the tailor had disappeared too...The caretaker asked me to report it. I didn't, but he reported it himself.

He made his report, but of course there was no sign of my sheepskin, and they said there was no tailor either...His wife was left with two children to care for—one was about three years of age, the other was a babe in arms...They were in abject poverty: the woman and the children looked frightfully haggard—they lived in a corner room, but they couldn't pay the rent, and they had nothing to eat. And as for my sheepskin, the woman said her husband had mended it and had gone out to return it, but she had never seen him from that time on...They searched for him in all the places he might have been, but couldn't find him...The tailor had vanished into thin air...I was angry, and had another sheepskin coat made, and had just begun to forget about the loss when, unexpectedly, in the first week of Lent, the caretaker came running to me, all out of breath and gabbling:

'Come to the magistrate, I've spotted the tailor...I saw him, the blackguard, visiting his wife on the quiet, so I caught him and took him to the justice. He's there under guard...They're going to investigate now. Hurry up, please, you'll have to make a statement about the loss of your sheepskin.'

So I went...I saw that in fact the guard had detained a man, thin and emaciated, his hair looking like felt, with bandy legs, and all in rags that no-one could have mended, and giving the general impression that he was half dead.

The magistrate asked me: had I lost a sheepskin coat, what was it like and what had it cost?

I answered truthfully: it was such-and-such a coat, I'd paid three hundred roubles for it, but then I'd worn it, and how much it was worth at the time it disappeared I couldn't say: it might have fetched less than a hundred roubles in the market.

The magistrate began interrogating the tailor, who admitted everything straight away. He said: 'I mended it and took it to the caretaker for him to return to its owner and get the money for the repair...But the caretaker was out and his door locked, and I didn't know the gentleman's name or where he lived, and it was Christmas Eve and we didn't have a copeck to buy things with. So I went out and took the sheepskin to a pawnbroker, and with the money I got I bought some tea and sugar, beer and vodka, then next morning I took fright and fled, drank the rest of the money and since then I've been all mixed up.' By this time he'd lost the receipt and couldn't remember which pawnbroker it was.

'I'm sorry: the sheepskin's lost.'

'How much do you think it was worth?'

'I was a good one.'

'But how much exactly might it have been worth?'

'It was an expensive one.'

'Shall we say it might have fetched a hundred roubles?'

The tailor excelled himself in good nature.

'More,' he said, 'it might have cost more than that.'

'A hundred and fifty?'

'It was worth that.'

To put it simply, the tailor was a good lad and embarrassed neither himself nor me.

The magistrate played it 'by the book' and sentenced the tailor to three months in gaol, and in addition decreed that he was to repay me for the coat.

In short, I was meant to be completely satisfied and nothing more could have been expected from the magistrate.

I returned home, the tailor was taken off to prison, and his wife and children lamented in unison.

What else could be expected?

BY ill luck, I soon contracted rheumatism, for which the Russians used to have a word: 'nightmaritis'. A very good name for it! During the day it was not too bad—you could put up with it, but when night came, the pain would start to nag away at you, and you couldn't get a minute's sleep. And lying there sleepless, heaven knows what thoughts and imaginings you have, and I couldn't get my tailor and his wife and children out of my mind. There he was in gaol on account of my coat, and what would become of his wife and children? Even when he had been there, there hadn't been much to spare, but now their sufferings were beyond measure...And what good had it dome me to go through the trial and the investigation? There was no hope of this tailor ever paying me for the lost coat, and if I had wanted to extract a petty sum from him, it would have reduced him to beggary.

There was no chance of my doing that.

So why was the offence ever reported?

And this thought started upsetting me so much that I sent to find out whether the tailor's wife was still alive, and what was happening to her and her two children.

The caretaker found out, and told me: 'She's been evicted—they're going to turn her out today: someone else will pay six roubles to live in that corner.'

'What a mess! God help us!'

The 'nightmaritis' gave me no rest that night and kept reminding me: I would drop off with exhaustion, but the tailor would suddenly appear and start passing a cold smoothing iron over the painful spots as if I were his ironing-board...And he kept on ironing, pressing the sharp point of the iron into my joints...

And he 'ironed' me until I paid up six roubles, which did my body no good, though it eased my conscience a bit,—because I was sure that the misery of the tailor's family was all my fault.

The tailor's wife turned out to be a woman of sensitive character, and she came to thank me for the six roubles...She was all in rags, and the children had no clothes...

I gave them another three roubles...

No sooner had night come than the tailor reappeared with this cold iron...So why had I done it?...

You get angry at times like this and start thinking: well, what else could I have done? After all, can you give money to every rascal in creation? Anyone would say 'No'. But then it was nearly Easter...The tailor still had six weeks to serve in gaol. And while I had given his wife one or two roubles on many occasions, I felt

I had to raise the allowance for Easter...And so I did increase it as far as I reasonably could, but then the tailor's wife got rather different ideas about what she expected and became dissatisfied and angry with me.

'He's had our breadwinner locked up,' she would say, 'and what am I supposed to do with the children? You've done for us—God will do for you one day!'

It was comical, and infuriating, and wretched and shameful: incomparably better would it have been if my sheepskin had disappeared along with the tailor and I'd never seen it again. It would have been more merciful and more to everyone's advantage: and now if you want to keep the mother of some cold and hungry children quiet—you'll have to support the thief's family, or what'll happen to your conscience? Not to feed them puts you on the level of the hangman, and you don't want to sit at the same table as a hangman, or as a talebearer...

And so, I supported the tailor's family, and very objectionable I felt the whole thing was...It seemed as if I had done something much worse than steal someone else's overcoat...And I couldn't escape the consequences whatever I did.

And then it was Easter and everyone went to the Easter service, but I was too ill and stayed at home alone. I was only just dropping off when all of a sudden I seemed to have a visitation from Ivan Ivanovich Androsov, the merchant from Orel...He was an old man small in stature, very stout, with hair that was white all over, and he had died forty years previously and was buried in Orel. In his last years he lived in extreme poverty, but he had a very rich son-in-law who had managed by some shady dealing to gain control of his property. My father greatly admired the old man and used to call him 'a righteous man', but all I remember about him is that he would stroll in the orchards propagating apple-trees, and that, in our house, if he sat in an armchair he could never get out of it: when he stood up the chair was still sticking to him like a snail's shell. He never had a care in the world and always spoke cheerfully about everything, and if people reminded him about the wrong done to him by his daughter and her husband, he would always brush it off, saying:

'Well, then, there you are!'

'But, Ivan Ivanovich, you should lay a complaint.'

And he would reply:

'That's it, then, isn't it!'

'But what if you starve to death?'

'Well, then, there you are!'

'There'll be nobody to see to your funeral.'

'That's it, then, isn't it!'

People said he was stupid.

But he was not stupid: one Christmas he came to visit us. As he was eating curd dumplings, he said how much he was enjoying them:

'It's just as if I'd been stuffing myself with warm snowflakes, and I never want to get up.'

And he never did get up out of the chair; he simply died where he sat, and we buried him.

A man like that must surely have known what he was doing! 'God abides in a heart free from fear.'

That's the view I should have taken: 'My coat's been stolen!' 'Well, then, there you are!' Should I report it? 'That's it, then, isn't it!' And how much better that would have been for all of us concerned, and I should have been calmer in my mind.

AT this point in my story my friend who had been burgled took me at my word.

'That's it,' he said, 'that's what I thought, and that's what I'll do. I won't report it to anyone: I don't want to plague anyone with complaints and poison Christ's Nativity. I've lost my property, and that's it: "Well, then, there you are" and "That's it, then, isn't it?"'

That is where he left the matter, and I didn't dare make any objection, but later I could not let the matter rest, and I spoke about it to many people, all of whom took a very different attitude to me and him. They all said:

'What a stupid thing to do! You just let people get away with crime. What about the rule of law? It's everyone's responsibility to correct other people and see they're punished. It's a matter of first principle.'

READER! Be gentle: enter into the spirit of our story and remember what you were taught by the One who is born today: should we punish or be merciful?

If you want to be 'with Christ' one day—then you should decide firmly, and what you decide—stick to it...Maybe you have suffered a 'wrong done at Christmas', maybe you've nursed the resentment in your heart and are planning to pay someone back?...Maybe you're afraid that if you don't, you'll feel ashamed...That's very likely, because we don't find it easy to remember what the real 'matter of first principle' is...But you work this out very carefully, please, today—whose side do you choose to be on: those who stand by the word of the law, or His, who gave you the 'words of eternal life'?...Just think! It's well worth a little thought, and you won't find the choice hard to make...Don't be afraid to appear laughable and stupid, if you act according to the principle of Him who said, 'Forgive thine enemy and make him thy brother.'

I've told you a story full of silly things, but you be clever—and find among the silliness something useful that you can take with you into eternity.

Vexation of Spirit

A reminiscence of youth

All is vanity and vexation of spirit
Ecclesiastes 1:14

AMONG those who took part in my education there was a tall, thin German called Ivan Yakovlevich, whose nickname was 'the Goat'. I do not know what his real surname was—he looked like a nanny-goat, and we all called him the Goat behind his back.

This all happened in a village in the Province of Orel, at the home of my rich relations. I grew up among them, and was tutored there until I was sent off to grammar school in the city. We had a number of tutors in the country—there was a Russian, Ivan Stepanovich Ptitsyn, and his wife, living in a cottage near the house, and a Frenchman, Monsieur Louis, who also had a wife and a son called Alvin, who was taught along with us. They lived in another cottage; there was also a German, Herr Kohlberg, a lonely man who was often drunk and very quarrelsome. So often did he fall out with the servants, that my uncle got tired of it and dismissed him summarily; whereupon the Goat was engaged. He had previously lived in several households in the neighbourhood, but had never settled anywhere for long. People said he was very gentle and upright, but that he had 'odd ideas'. He was employed on the firm understanding that he would live with us and teach us German, but never be so bold as to give us any of his 'odd ideas'.

He agreed to this condition and for three months or so did very well, but then all of a sudden he lost his patience and revealed such an odd idea that you would have thought he had never given the promise he did.

One summer we had visitors: the Provincial Governor's wife and son, a boy of about eleven who was very spoiled and disobedient, called on the way to their country estate. We went into the orchard, where this young visitor pulled down a rare plum tree to get at the fruit, which was greatly prized by my uncle. We were alarmed at what he had done and swore an oath to keep quiet about it and say absolutely nothing at all. That evening my uncle went into the orchard and saw that the tree had been damaged. He was furious and summoned the gardener's son, a boy called Kostya, and started to question him: who had pulled down the tree? Kostya did not know, and the suspicion was that he had done the damage himself and wouldn't admit it. They ordered him to be flogged with gooseberry branches, but he took fright and said that it was true he had eaten the plums. Then they flogged him anyway. But we knew who had pulled the tree down, though we said nothing so as not to break our oath and not to disgrace our visitor, but some of us were acutely disturbed by what had happened, and as we were getting into bed, I could not hold out any longer and I told Ivan Yakovlevich that Kostya had been punished for no reason, that he wasn't the thief and I said who the thief was, but that we had all taken an oath to shield him.

Ivan Yakovlevich turned livid and exclaimed:

'An oath! How could you do such a thing? You're supposed to be Christians! Who told you you could swear oaths? Now you see how much trouble has come from that, and now I shall have to leave you.'

We were now even more frightened and started to beg him not to go, but he insisted:

'No, I shall leave, I shall have to, not because I want to, but because they'll kick me out, and that will be good...It'll be all for the best.'

That is what he said, and he wept, and then suddenly put his forehead against the window pane, sighed, and rushed out of the room.

Where he had gone and why we could not imagine, and we waited so long for his return, that we dropped off to sleep. In the morning, when the elderly maid Vasilisa Matveevna brought us our clean linen, we discovered that Ivan Yakovlevich would not be coming back, because he had gone out of his mind.

Good heavens! We were stupefied...Poor, kind Ivan Yakovlevich had gone mad!..And it was all our fault! But what on earth had he done?

'He appeared where the ladies and gentlemen were with an inhuman look on his face, and did something quite crazy, and they punished him for it.'

The 'crazy' thing was this. Very disturbed by our double misdeed, the Goat had gone downstairs, and with that 'inhuman look on his face' had gone up to the Governor's wife and said to her calmly 'in an inhuman tone of voice':

'Your son is a thoroughly bad boy: because of what he did, a poor boy has been flogged and forced to tell lies about himself... Your wretched son was brazen enough to allow this to happen, and, what is more, taught other boys to swear an oath—which is specifically forbidden by Jesus Christ. I feel sorry for your uncivilized and uneducated son. You should help him to open his eyes and see the light and remedy himself, or else he'll turn into an evil man who'll ruin his own character and might spoil a lot of other people's too.'

The Governor's wife came over queer and went into a fit of hysterics.

My uncle was fearfully outraged by this scene and he kicked the Goat out of the room, gave instructions for him to be locked up in the office and sent off to Orel that day in a peasant's cart.

We were enraged by this insult to the Goat and wanted to know 'Why in a peasant's cart?'

'What should they have sent him in, then?'

'They could have made it the trap we go to the post in.'

'Oh, yes, of course! Any other luxury he should have? They use that cart to take the priest around with holy water...Why should a stupid German like him have the same treatment as the Holy Father. The Father prays for our sins at the altar, but that fellow would have been all right if they'd put him in the manure waggon, never mind the cart.'

'Why do you hate him so much?'

'Because he's a fool and talks stupid nonsense.'

'He talks sense and always tells the truth.'

'And that's just what you don't always need to do! What has truth got to do with it? Truth's all very well in its place, but shouldn't be spoken every minute and to everybody. Let him tell the truth for himself, but there's no point in chucking it straight into everyone else's face. Our way of doing things is much better than those Germans': if we tell lies we can do penance; *and* we have saints and self-sacrificers, martyrs, and Praskovyas. That's why he's got nothing to teach us. And that's why they showed him "where God is, and where the door is".'

'How do they show anyone that?'

'Where God is?'

'Yes.'

'They make him face the door, give him a good slap on the back of the head, and then he can clear off.'

'And that's what you mean by showing someone where God is?'

'Yes. He cleared off and that was that.'

'So they showed him where God was?'

'Yes, of course they did, and that was it.'

'What, then: he would see God and...I suppose he'd be glad that they'd kicked him out.'

'Well, then, he can be as glad as he likes; we don't have to be sorry for him.'

I FELT very sorry for Ivan Yakovlevich, and M. Louis's son Alvin was even more affected. He came into our room in tears and told me we should run off outside the village across the peasants' hemp-field, and hide among the hemp until they passed in the cart with Ivan Yakovlevich, so we could stop the cart and say goodbye to him. And that's what we did: we ran off and hid, but the cart was a very long time coming. It turned out that Ivan Yakovlevich felt sorry for the peasant whose job it was to give him a lift, let him off the task, and set off alone on foot. He was wearing his green frock-coat and grey cloak, and dangling from his hand was a very small bundle of clothes and an umbrella with a teak handle. The Goat walked along, not merely calmly, but with a rather solemn air, and you might even say his face was cheerful and expressed pleasure. When he saw us, he stopped and shouted out:

'That's marvellous, boys, marvellous! I'm really delighted to see you just now!'—and he opened his arms to embrace us, and there were tears in his eyes.

We hurled ourselves into his arms and we cried too, saying over and over: 'Forgive us, forgive us!' For what offence we were asking forgiveness we did not quite know, but he helped us to understand, as he said:

'It wasn't a good thing to do when you didn't preserve your freedom and allowed yourselves to swear an oath...You see, you weren't free any more to tell the truth, you were prisoners of your own oath...Yes, you weren't free to tell the truth, and because of that they accused the poor boy of being a thief and they flogged him. That needed to be put right, and I put it right. Someone had to rebel, and I rebelled.' Ivan Yakovlevich became angry. 'I couldn't do anything else...My spirit rebelled within me...my spirit came to life...a spirit free of any oath...I went...I spoke...I wiped the slate clean...I overturned the oath...No-one should swear...Speak the truth without swearing any oaths, that's what people should do. Don't be false in words or in actions! Fear no-one! If you're told you should hold someone in awe by convention, that's all rubbish! Jesus Christ knows better than convention...I know very well, that he knows more! What do you think. who knows more?'

'Christ does.'

'Of course he does. Christ knows more, and he said, "Fear no man." He conquered fear! Fear is all nonsense...There is no such thing as fear! Even me! I've rid myself of fear...And you should, too!..It'll go away. Where is it now? It's not here. There's three of here, and is anything between us? Well? What? Fear? No, fear isn't, but Christ is. He's here with us. Can you see him? What? Do you see, do you feel, do you understand?'

We did not know how to reply to this, but we did 'understand' that we 'felt' something very wonderful, and so we told him so.

The Goat was delighted and said:

'That's what is needed, and may God grant that you never forget it. For that to be so you must always be honest in all your dealings in life. A clear conscience displays God at all times and places, but lying always separates you from God, wherever you are. Don't be afraid of anyone and don't tell lies for any reason.'

'Oh, no, no, we won't,' we said, 'we won't tell lies or swear oaths, but how can we put right the wrong we've done?'

'Put it right? Only God can put it right. Putting wrongs right isn't our business. Be good to Kostya and remind everyone that he wasn't to blame and that he only confessed out of fear.'

'We'll do that, but what about you, Ivan Yakovlevich, where will you go? Have you got a home of your own somewhere?'

He shook his head and said,

'Why should I have my own home?'

'Well, have you got family, people who love you?'

'Family? What do I need with family?'

'Well, have you got any friends?'

'Friends, who are they? Who are they? At the moment, you are my friends. What are "friends"? They're the people who share your love for the same things.'

'Surely you have some people who are special to you?'

'Why should there be anyone special? What does it mean? You should do things as they become necessary, not specially.'

'But where are you going now?'

He shrugged his shoulders and said cheerfully:

'Where? To blessed eternity; but how I'll get there I don't care.—The thing is always to do God's work.'

We understood what he meant by "God's work", and tearfully clung to the Goat.

'We're sorry they got rid of you for no reason at all.'

He shook his head in silence and then said:

'No, it wasn't for no reason at all.'

'How can you say that? You behaved better than any of us and didn't do anything wrong at all.'

'Well, there you are! How could I have done anything wrong? I wouldn't have done that, but I caused an upset: I rebelled against the darkness of this age, and I had to be got rid of. That's the way things are, and it's a very good way too!'

'You say that as if you were quite glad.'

'Glad? Yes, I am glad! I'm very glad! You see, our struggle isn't with flesh and blood, but with the darkness of the ages,—with the spirits of evil living on earth. We are carrying on a war against the darkness of the ages and against the spirits of evil, and they are pursuing us and trying to kill us just as they pursued and killed those who were better than us in all respects.'

'But, why? Why do they chase people who haven't done any harm? It's terrible!'

'Never mind,' said the Goat, looking ever more radiant. 'On the contrary, it's very good. It's good that the chasing is all in vain: it teaches people, it strengthens them. Surely you wouldn't want me to have been sent away not because I rebelled against the evil of the ages and the spirits of evil, but because I'd done something wrong?'

'Oh, no!'

'Well, then, what's the trouble? Everything is just as it should be...everything's fine. As time goes on...if you discover what life is all about, and if you want to live the best way possible, that is, live so that the spirits of malice pursue you, then you'll understand. When they chase you, it's pure joy...it's happiness! But...

He grasped our shoulders and continued in a lower tone of voice:

'But when they flatter you and praise you...That's when...'

'What you say sounds terrible...'

Yes, it *is* terrible. You should be fearful and take care...make sure that our Heavenly Father saves you.'

'Our Heavenly Father! But we don't know how to make sure of that, what we have to do...'

'What do you mean, "do"?'

'So he can save us.'

'Aha! I don't know either...and I'm not even worth...but He...'

Tears welled up in Ivan Yakovlevich's breast and it was as if his words were spoken in ecstasy.

'I'm a poor sinner who came from nothingness; I'm a worm that came crawling out of the dirt, and my Father holds me on his knees; he carries me in his embrace like a son who can't yet walk, but he doesn't let me fall, and he isn't angry that I'm such a fathead, and though I'm stupid, he still tells me everything a man needs to know, and I believe I can discover from him just as much as I need and no more, and...you'll understand too, the spirit will speak to you...Then salvation will come, and you won't ask how it came...And it's all got to be done...quietly... Shh! God moves in silence...*still*!

The Goat suddenly bowed his head, put his hands together on his chest and began to say the Lord's Prayer in German. Without his asking us, we took off our caps and joined in. He finished the prayer, laid his hands on our heads, and with tears in his eyes prayed in Russian.

'Father!' he said, 'I thank Thee that Thou hast again granted me the joy of being cast out for fulfilling Thy will. Strengthen the hearts of those who suffer for their obedience to Thy will and illuminate with reason and mercy the eyes of those who persecute us. Leave not these children long in the wilderness: grant that they may enter into understanding and taste that same bliss which I now feel in my heart on account of Thy blessing. Grant them understanding of Thy will!' And again he embraced us, and strode off towards the town, with nowhere to go, yet totally happy, while we, who had everything we could need in abundance, remained kneeling on the dusty path, weeping and watching as the Goat receded.

It was as if he had cast before us something which was bitter as well as ecstatically joyful. The Goat had called down something upon us, he had surrounded us with something, we wanted to understand how to fulfil the prayer about softening hearts, and suddenly we both leaped up and raced after him, shouting:

'Ivan Yakovlevich, Ivan Yakovlevich!'

He stopped and turned round, and it seemed to us that he had changed in some way: he had grown taller somehow and become radiant. Most likely this was because he was standing on a mound, and the sun shone directly upon him. But his voice had changed too. It was as if it was pouring through the air.

'What else do you want? What is it?'

But we did not know what it was we wanted to say to him, and so we asked:

'Will we ever see you again?'

'You will.'

'When will that be?'

He said in a more muffled tone:

'It may happen, perhaps, quite unexpectedly, and then it won't happen again, and then it does sometimes happen again...'

We ran after him, as it seemed, but he strode on ahead alone, while we fell behind and shouted:

'Where will we meet again?'

But he replied from even further away:

'Anywhere, it doesn't matter,' and he gestured in all directions as if he wanted to say that it did not matter at all where we might meet again 'sometime'. Space did not exist in his mind. 'It doesn't matter, sometimes we'll see each other...and again, sometimes we won't', and he said something else of the sort as he receded further and further from our view, and suddenly it was almost funny the way he shook his arms and set off at a run; he ran and ran, and eventually disappeared. Since those days many years have passed, and for a very, very long time the Goat never came to me in my imagination, but then suddenly he appeared once, then again, and then a third time, and he became as close as if he had never been away, but at the same time he was ever running onward. And in those moments it seemed to me as if I had not been completely static myself. It was as if sometimes I was trudging along and only moving forward very slightly, while at the same time I was conscious that I was weak and tired and could scarcely even crawl. And it is finished! I shall be left behind and never see him again!...But then unexpected help always arrives; someone arrives from somewhere and shows me 'where God is'. And when that happens, you take stock once more, you become conscious again of all *your own* people in your heart, and you are not afraid to part from any of them, because 'all those filled with the same spirit shall be united in their understanding of life.'

A Response to 'The Kreutzer Sonata'

Any young woman is morally superior to a man, because she is incomparably more pure than he. When a girl marries, she is always superior to her husband. She is superior to him both as a maiden and when she becomes a woman in our society.

Lev Tolstoy

I

IT was the day of Dostoevsky's funeral. The weather had been severe and overcast. I was far from well that day, and it took me the greatest effort to make myself follow the coffin as far as the gates of the Alexander Nevsky Monastery. There was a tremendous crush at the gates. Groans and cries rang out in the press. Averkiev, the dramatist, appeared standing raised above the crowd and shouted some indistinct words. He had a loud voice, but it was impossible to make out what he was saying. Some people said he was trying to marshal the crowd, and approved of his efforts, others were annoyed. I was among those who were not allowed into the grounds, and seeing no point in staying any longer, I came home, drank some hot tea and dropped off to sleep. Because of the cold and all the impressions of the day, I felt very tired, and I slept so long and soundly that I did not get up for dinner. I did not manage to get any dinner that day, because in addition to all the various experiences of the day I underwent yet another, one that agitated me considerably.

It was getting very dark that evening when my maid aroused me and said that a stranger, a lady, had arrived and was refusing to leave. She was insisting on being shown in to see me. Visits from ladies to the likes of me, an elderly writer, are not an unusual occurrence. Plenty of young girls and ladies call to seek advice about their literary efforts, or to try to get us to intervene on their behalf with unknown publishers. Consequently the arrival of a lady, and even her persistence, were no great surprise to me. When distress is great and need unavoidable, a person inevitably becomes persistent.

I told the maid to admit the lady to my study, and I set about tidying myself up. When I entered the study, my reading lamp was lit and was standing on the big desk. It brightly illuminated the desk, but the rest of the room remained in semi-darkness. The stranger who was paying me this visit was indeed unknown to me.

When I met her eyes and invited her to sit down in the armchair, it seemed to me that she was avoiding the more brightly lit parts of the room and was trying to stay in the shadow. This surprised me. Persons who are a little shy and inexperienced sometimes play this game and seem similarly embarrassed, but what surprised me most of all was the agitated condition of the lady, which I sensed and which was communicated to me in some way. She was beautifully dressed, but modestly, everything she wore was rich and elegant: a beautiful plush coat which she had not discarded in the hall, and which she wore all the time she was talking to me, a smart black hat, obviously in the Parisian fashion rather than the Russian, and a black veil, folded in two and tied at the rear in such a way that I could see nothing but her white round chin and her eyes which shone occasionally through the double thickness of the veil. Instead of giving her name and stating the purpose of her visit, she began by asking me:

'May I rely on your not being interested in knowing my name?'

I replied that she could rely on that completely. Then she asked me to sit down in the armchair in front of the lamp, and without asking permission, adjusted the circle of green taffeta on the lampshade in such a way that all the light fell on me while shading her face, and she sat at the other side of the desk. She asked again:

'You are alone?'

I replied that she was not mistaken: I was alone.

'May I speak to you completely frankly?'

I said that if she trusted me, I could see no reason why she should be prevented from speaking any way she liked.

'Are we alone?'

'Completely.'

The lady got up and took two steps towards the next room, where all my books are kept, and beyond which is the bedroom.

In the library at that time a heavily shaded lamp was burning, by the light of which the whole room could be seen. I did not move, but pointed out for the lady's reassurance that she could see there was no-one in the apartment except the serving woman and a little orphan girl who could play no part in her consideration. She then resumed her place again, adjusted the green circle again and said:

'Please forgive me, I am in great agitation, and you must think my behaviour very strange, but please put yourself in my place!'

Her hand, which she had stretched out again to the circle of taffeta on the lamp was covered by a black kid glove and was shaking violently. Instead of answering I offered her a glass of water. She refused, saying:

'There is no need, I am not as nervous as all that, I came to see you because that funeral...those chains...that man who has made such an unusually powerful impression on me, that face and the recollection of everything of which I have had to speak twice in my life, all that has disturbed my thoughts. You shouldn't be surprised that I have come to you. I shall tell you why, it doesn't matter that we do not know each other: I have read a lot of your works and so much in them is akin to my own feelings, so close, in fact, that I cannot prevent myself from approaching you. Maybe what I have been intending to do is utterly stupid. I want to ask you about it first, and you must answer candidly. What-'ever you advise me, I shall do.'

Her deep contralto trembled and her hands, which she did not know what to do with, were shaking.

II

I CANNOT say I have had frequent visits and approaches of this sort in the course of my literary career, but I have had some.

They have been more from people of a political cast of mind, and it is rather difficult to satisfy them, and doubly risky and unpleasant to offer help, all the more so because in such cases you never know the sort of person you are dealing with. On this occasion my first reaction was that the lady was stirred by political passions, that she had some grand idea, which unfortunately for me she had taken into her head to impart to me; the prelude to what she wanted to say had a lot in common with that sort of thing, and so I said to her unwillingly:

'I don't know what you are going to say. I dare not promise you anything, but having said that, if your personal feelings have impelled you to trust me on account of what you know of my life and reputation, then I can say that I shall not in any eventuality betray what you obviously want to confide in me as a secret.'

'Yes,' she said, 'a secret, an absolute secret, and I'm sure you will keep it. I don't need to tell you why; I know that you sense the reason; I can't be wrong about this: your face tells me this better than any words could, and in any case I have no choice. I repeat, I am ready to commit an act which one moment seems honourable and the next an act of crass folly: the choice has to be made at once, now, and it all depends on you.'

I had no doubt that there would immediately follow a revelation of a political character, and I said reluctantly:

'I understand.'

Despite the double veil, I sensed the firm gaze of my guest directed straight at me. She was looking at me at point blank range, and she said firmly:

'I'm an unfaithful wife! I'm deceiving my husband.'

To my shame I have to admit that when she said this a great weight fell from my heart; obviously, this had nothing to do with politics.

'I am deceiving a fine, good-natured husband; it's been going on for six...no, more!..I must tell the truth, or there's no point in talking at all: it's been going on for eight years, and it's still going on, or rather, no, it began in the third month of our marriage; nothing in the world could be more shameful! I'm not old, but I have children, you understand?

I nodded.

'You understand what that means. Twice in my life I went to see the man we buried today and whose death has affected me so greatly. I confessed my feelings to him, once he was brusque, and the second time, tender as a friend. But now I'm...not in the state I was in when I went to see him, and, anyway, I want you to give me the advice I need. Deception is worse than anything in life, I feel it, it seems better to reveal your foul deed, to bear the punishment, and be humiliated, crushed, thrown out into the gutter,—I don't know what will happen to me—I feel an overwhelming need to go and tell my husband everything; I've been feeling that need for the last six years. Since I first began to be unfaithful, there were two years when I never saw...the man; but then it all started again and it's going on the way it did...for six years I've been trying to say it, but I never have, and today as I was following Dostoevsky's coffin, I wanted to have done with it, have done with it in whatever way you advise me.'

I said nothing, because I did not see the sense in her story and could give no definite advice; she picked this up from the look on my face.

'Of course, you have to know more, I didn't come to play at riddles, but to tell you, to tell you everything. In fact, I'd be a shameless liar if I tried to make excuses. I've never known any hardship, I was born in plenty and I live in plenty. Nature hasn't denied me my share of good sense, I got a good education, I was free to choose a husband for myself, so there's nothing more to say; I married a man who had never damaged his own reputation until that moment, on the contrary. My position was fine when that man...I meant to say, my husband, my legal husband... proposed to me. I thought I liked him, I thought I could love him, but I never dreamed in the least that I could deceive him, even less deceive him in the most disreputable, foul way, while enjoying the reputation of an honest women and a good mother, since I'm not honest and I'm a dreadful mother, and it was the Devil himself who brought me to this level of deception,—if you want to know, I do believe in the Devil...In life an awful lot depends on circumstances; they say—there's filth in towns, but cleanliness in the villages; but it was in a village that it happened, because I was alone face to face with this man, with this accursed man who was brought and placed in my care by my husband. I should do penance, if penance has any purpose at all, I should do eternal penance for this deed, for which I am obliged to my husband, but the fact is that I don't remember that moment, I only remember the thunderstorm, a fearful thunderstorm, and I've always been terrified of thunderstorms since I was a child. I didn't love him then, I was just afraid, and when the lightning flashed and lit us up in the huge hall we were in, I grabbed his hand in fear...and again I don't remember the way it continued... Then he went on a trip around the world, he came back and it all began again: now I wish it could finish once and for all. I've wanted that more than once, but I've never been able to hold to it. Any decision I took has always flown out of the window as soon as he appears, and the worst thing of all—I don't want to conceal anything—is that it isn't him, it's me who is the reason, me, you understand, I'm the one who spoke out and got my way and acted spitefully if it was hard to get my way,—and if I'm going to go on like this, the deception, my degradation will never come to an end...'

'What do you want to do?' I asked.

'I want to tell my husband everything, I want to do it this very day, I want to leave here and go straight home...'

I asked what her husband was like, and what sort of a character he represented.

'My husband is a man of the highest reputation,' said the lady. 'He has a good job and adequate means; he is regarded by everyone as a man of nobility and honour.'

'Do you share that opinion?' I asked.

'Not entirely, people attribute too much to him; he is too talented and decent, he has too little of what one might call heart, however stupid that word is, recalling as it does the spirit of music, but I can't put it any other way; the promptings of his heart are all correct, specific, exact and unvarying.'

'And the man you love?'

'What were you going to ask?'

'Does he inspire your respect?'

'Oh!' the lady exclaimed, and waved her hand.

'I don't quite understand how I should interpret the meaning of your gesture.'

'You should assume that he is the most heartless and worthless egotist, who inspires respect in nobody and who wouldn't care in the least whether they respected him or not.'

'Do you love him?'

She shrugged and said:

'Yes. Love is a strange word, you know. It's on everyone's lips, but very few understand it. To love is the same as being inclined to poetry, to righteousness. Very few people are capable of such feeling. Our peasant women, instead of using the word 'love', say 'feel sorry for'; they don't say 'He loves me', they say, 'He feels sorry for me.' To my mind that's much better: it gives a much simpler meaning to the word; the expression 'love-feel sorry for' means to love in the everyday sense. And that is, to want; people talk about my 'desired' person, my 'dear', the one I want...you understand, to desire...'

She stopped, breathing heavily; I offered her a glass of water, which she took from my hands this time; she did not flinch and seemed to be grateful that I did not look closely at her.

Neither of us said anything; I didn't know what to say, and her torrent of frankness dried up. Obviously she had said everything, the most important things, and only the details remained. She guessed my thoughts and said softly,

'There we are, then, if you tell me I should tell my husband everything, I shall do so; but perhaps you will tell me differently? Anyway, what makes me feel sympathy and confidence in you is your practical attitude. I read your works very carefully; we women sense things that dedicated critics don't notice. If you wish, you can tell me your frank opinion: should I or should I not go home and confess my shameful and long-established offence to my husband?'

III

DESPITE the fascinating nature of her story, I was conscious of my awkward position. Although an answer such as that required by my visitor could be given much more easily than appeasing a political activist or granting him whatever assistance he sought, none the less my conscience was sensible of having been summoned to intervene in a very serious matter. I had experienced enough of life and seen enough women who were cunningly concealing misdemeanours of this type—or if not concealing them, then at least not admitting to them. I had also met two or three frank women, and I remembered that they had appeared to me to be not so much frank as hard and affected. It had always seemed to me that, with all this frankness, a woman might temporize, and before announcing her offence to whomever would be made to suffer by the revelation, might decide not to. I had never cared for what the world might think of the inner life of the person concerned. It is not the world, but the human being which is important to me, and if it is possible not to cause suffering, why cause it? If a woman is as whole a person as a man, an equal member of society, and if she experiences all the same feelings, the same human sense, as Christ gives us to understand, and as the best people of our own century say, as does Lev Tolstoy, and in all this I sense an incontrovertible truth,—then why should a man, who has broken the vow of chastity before a woman to whom he is obliged to be faithful, be able to remain silent, silent about this, conscious of his offence, and why should he contrive to smooth over the unworthiness of his passion? Why on earth should a woman not be able to do the same? I am convinced that she should. There is no doubt that the number of men deceiving women exceeds the number of women, and women know this; there is scarcely a single rational woman who, after a more or less long separation from her husband, would nurture the confidence that he had been faithful to her for the whole of this separation. But none the less, when he returns, she forgives him so sincerely that her forgiveness manifests itself in the fact that she never even asks him about it, and frankness on her part would not be a favour but a cause for pain; it would be an action which revealed what it was that she did not want to know. In ignorance she finds the strength to continue her relationship, as if it had been interrupted unintentionally. I confess that my reasoning contains a good deal more pragmatism than abstract philosophy and elevated morality, but nevertheless I am inclined to think the way I do.

With all this in mind, I continued the conversation with my visitor, and I asked her:

'Do the bad qualities of the man you love inspire you with any lack of respect?'

'Very strongly, and perpetually.'

'But sometimes you try to find excuses for him?'

'That may be, unfortunately; there *are* no excuses for him.'

'Then I am inclined to ask, does your dissatisfaction with him remain the same or does it sometimes decline and at other times increase?'

'It increases constantly.'

'Then I must ask—if you will permit me?'

'By all means.'

'While we are sitting here together, where is your husband?'

'At home.'

'What is he doing?'

'Sleeping in his study.'

'And when he wakes up?'

'He'll get up at eight.'

'And what will he do then?'

The visitor smiled.

'He'll wash, put his jacket on, go to see the children and play bagatelle, then the servant will bring in the samovar and I'll pour him a glass of tea.'

'Well, there we are,' I said, 'a glass of tea, the samovar and the lamp—they are splendid things that we make the centre of our lives.'

'That's beautifully put.'

'And everything will go reasonably...pleasantly?'

'Yes, as far as he is concerned, I think it will.'

'Forgive me, but in the matter which you have chosen to reveal to me, he alone has the right to be considered, not the children, who both may and should know nothing about it, and certainly not yourself, of course...Yes, you have no right, because you have done him harm, and he is the injured party. Therefore we have to consider him and save him any suffering, and just imagine, instead of him finishing his tea as is his custom, and then maybe graciously kissing your hand...

'So what do you suggest?'

'And then, when he goes to get some jobs done...and after that has his supper and wishes you good-night in a perfectly calm frame of mind,—instead of all that, he'll have to listen to your confession, and he'll discover that his whole life, from the first month of marriage, maybe even from the very first day, has been acted out in an utterly senseless setting. Tell me, will you be doing a good or an evil deed by telling him?'

'I don't know. If I did know, if I could make up my mind, I shouldn't be here talking about it. I'm asking your advice: what should I do?'

'I can't give you advice, but I can express the opinion which is beginning to form in my mind. However, so that I can clarify it more exactly, I'd like to presume to ask you another question... People's feelings never remain the same for long...Is your distaste for him fading?'

'No. On the contrary, it is getting sharper.'

She let out this exclamation in heartfelt anguish, and she even rose briefly from her chair as if she wanted to escape from something, or so I imagined. Despite the fact that I could not see her face, I felt that she was undergoing terrible anguish, and that this anguish had reached such a pitch that it had now to be resolved.

'Consequently,' I said, 'you despise him more and more severely?'

'Yes, more and more often.'

'Excellent,' I said. 'Now I'm going to allow myself to tell you, that I should consider it rational, if you went home and sat down at the samovar, just as you always used to.'

She listened in silence; her eyes were fixed on me, and I could see them shining through the veil. I could hear her heart beating loudly and more quickly.

'You advise me to continue my concealment?

'I'm not advising you, but I think it would be better for you, for him and for your children, who *are* after all your children.'

'But why is that better? It means this will go on for ever!'

'It's better, because if you were open and honest everything would be worse, and if *that* went on for ever, everything would be much more unhappy than what you are imagining now.'

'My soul would be purified by suffering.'

I felt I was seeing into her soul: and sensitive and impetuous it was, but not one of those souls that are purified by suffering. In consequence I made no reply about her soul, but mentioned the children again.

She wrung her hands so tightly that the joints cracked, and she let her head fall in silence.

'And how will my saga end?'

'It'll end well.'

'What do you anticipate?'

'That the person you love, or, as you say, do not love, but whom you have got used to...will become ever more loathsome from day to day.'

'Ah, yes! I do find him loathsome.'

'It will get worse, and then...'

'I understand.'

'I'm glad you do.'

'You want me to drop him without saying anything?'

'I think that would be the happiest way out of your anguish.'

'Yes, but then...'

'Then you could give back...'

'It would be impossible to give anything back.'

'I'm sorry, I meant that you would give redoubled attention to your husband and your family; that will give you the strength not to forget, but to preserve the past and find sufficient reasons to live for others.'

She rose, unexpectedly, let the veil down even further over her face, held out her hand to me and said:

'Thank you. I'm glad I obeyed the impulse which led me to come to you after I had endured the frightful experience of the funeral; I was out of my mind when I got back, and it's a very good thing I did not do all I intended to do. Goodbye!' She held out her hand again and firmly gripped mine, as if to stop me on the spot where we were. Then she bowed and left.

IV

I REMIND you that I never saw this woman's face; it was difficult to arrive at any impression of her face from the chin alone, concealed by the veil as if by a mask, but her figure left me with an impression of grace, despite the plush overcoat and hat. I should say that it was an elegant figure, slim, unusually lively and it left a particularly strong impression on my memory.

This was the first time I had ever met the lady, and her voice was not familiar. She did not disguise her voice, a light, low contralto, very pleasant; her manner was very elegant; one would take her for a woman in fashionable society, more exactly from the highest ranks of the civil service, the wife of a head or deputy-head of a government department, or that sort of position. However, she was unknown, and remained unknown, to me.

Three years passed after Dostoevsky's funeral and the event I have just described. I was ill during the winter, and in spring went abroad to take the waters; a friend and one of my female relations saw me off at the railway station; we were travelling in a carriage with all my luggage. As we passed along one of the streets adjoining the Nevsky Prospekt, at one of the corners, by the front door of a large official building I saw a lady; despite my short-sightedness I recognized her as my stranger. I was not prepared for this in any way, I was certainly not thinking of her, and in consequence the striking resemblance surprised me greatly; the idiotic thought crossed my mind that I should stop the carriage, accost her and ask some question, but since I had other people with me, I fortunately did nothing, but exclaimed;

'Good heavens, it's her!' and this made my two companions laugh.

And indeed it was her; and this is how I discovered it. Like all Russians, or the majority of Russians, I had chosen a circular route; I first called in at Paris, I took the waters in July, and only after that, in August, did I turn up where I was meant to have been in June. I quickly made the acquaintance of most of the other Russians who were taking the waters and knew nearly all of them, so the arrival of any new face was not unnoticed.

Then once while I was sitting on a bench in the park through which the road to the station ran, I noticed a carriage in which were sitting a man in a light-coloured coat and hat and a lady in a veil. With them was a boy of about nine.

And the same thing happened as when I was leaving Petersburg.

'Good heavens, it's her!'

And it *was* her.

The next day in the restaurant in the park where I was having coffee I saw her handsome but gaunt husband and her unusually pretty child. The boy was somewhat of the gipsy type with black curly hair and very blue large eyes.

I allowed myself to descend to some slight cunning: I bribed the waiter to find me a table closer to the lady; I wanted to have a good look at her face.

She was pretty, with a rather pleasant but not very striking expression; she certainly recognized me, two or three times tried to turn round in her chair in such a way that it would have been awkward for me to look closely at her. She then stood up and went over to a lady whom I knew, had a few words with her, then moved away and returned to her husband.

That evening, over coffee after dinner at one of the informal concerts, the lady acquaintance of mine to whom the new visitor had spoken told me that she wanted to introduce Mrs N., who was just passing by us at that moment, and the introduction was immediately effected. I made a conventional remark, to which she replied in similar vein, but by those words, by her voice and by her manner, I knew her; it was undoubtedly she, and she was wise enough to realize that I had recognized her; she decided not to conceal the fact and pretend she did not know me; she could rely on my rectitude and discretion with regard to what she had told me on the earlier occasion.

From then on we saw each other occasionally, and even went on a few excursions together with the ladies of my acquaintance and with her son. Her husband did not seem to like trips; he had a painful knee and limped, and besides, I cannot make out what he was up to, whether he was ill at ease with his wife, or whether he wanted to be free to pursue one or maybe more than one of the visiting ladies of dubious reputation. But at none of our meetings did she ever say, or mention that she had visited me or that we had met before: only I had the strong feeling that she was confident we understood each other. Then suddenly into this situation came a completely unexpected occurrence.

One delightful morning she did not appear in order to accompany her husband to the pump room to take the waters; he sat alone at coffee and said that their son Anatoly was unwell, and that the mother was out of her mind with worry.

At eight in the evening the porter in my lodgings told me the dreadful news that a child had died of diphtheria in one of the hotels; of course, it turned out to be the son of the unknown lady.

I am not an over-cautious person and therefore immediately took my hat and set off to the hotel; I had the impression that the husband had not shown much concern that morning; if the child with diphtheria was her son, then perhaps some help or sympathy on my part was not without purpose.

When I entered the hotel where she was staying...I shall never forget what I saw. There were only two rooms; in the first, where the hotel furniture stood, all upholstered in red plush, stood the lady, with her hair in disarray and a glazed expression; she held both hands, with fingers outspread as if defending the little divan on which something was lying covered with a white sheet; from under this sheet could be seen one blue leg; it was the body of the boy, Anatoly. By the door stood two men I did not know, in grey coats, and in front of them lay a box, not a coffin, but a box, rather like a large candle-box about four foot deep, half full of some white liquid, which looked to me at first like milk or starch; among them stood a senior police officer and a civic official wearing a badge of office; they were conversing loudly; the lady's husband was not at home, she was alone, she was disputing what these people wanted to do, defending herself, and when she saw me she exclaimed:

'My God! Protect us, help us! They want to take the child; they won't allow him to be buried properly; he has only just died.'

I tried to stand up for her, but it was completely useless, even if we had had the strength to resist the four men, who, without any show of sympathy pushed her into the next room and locked the door, against which she beat with her fists in vain, groaning horribly. They picked up the child, who seemed to in the bloom of life, placed him in the lime solution and quickly left.

V

IN small bathing places and spas people are mightily averse to fatalities. Proprietors of hotels and furnished rooms do everything possible to avoid accommodating tenants whose health gives rise to the fear that they may soon die.

In none of these towns are funeral processions allowed, and if anyone dies, then he is concealed from all other persons and removed by railway most definitely without any funeral rites.

Infectious diseases with a fatal outcome occur very rarely, and in the place where the son of my acquaintance died, it was the first time this had happened, and the news spread among the populace with incredible speed. It produced frightful alarm, particularly among the ladies. The local doctors, who comprise the most important class of shapers of opinion in such places, tried to calm anxious minds, and, vying with each other in their zeal, fell out and divided into two camps: one of these, to which belonged two consultants who had treated the boy, did not deny that the cause of his death had been a genuine case of diphtheria, but stressed that they had taken all possible measures against infection, that they had visited him in special clothing which had been scrupulously disinfected afterwards; two of them had even shaved off their hair and beards to show how seriously they took the matter. The others, a much bigger party, asserted that the case was rather dubious, even that there had been some counter-indications, and accused their colleagues of incautious exaggeration of the boy's illness, which had led to a great and unnecessary panic, disturbing the peace of mind of patients and most of all threatening the economic interests of the local population. This second medical coterie were critical of the local civic authorities, who had treated Mrs N. extremely rudely and abruptly; they had supposedly torn the child from her arms with brutal force more or less at the moment of death, and submerged him in lime solution, maybe even before the very last spark of life had been extinguished. By pointing to such cruelty the doctors wished to distract attention from themselves and direct it at others, whose behaviour had indeed been extremely unfeeling; but the ruse did not succeed. Human egotism at moments of danger becomes particularly obnoxious, and no-one could be found among the public who had much sympathy for the plight of the unfortunate mother. After all, if it was really diphtheria, there is no point in undue formalities, and the more decisively and firmly the authorities acted, the better. You really could not expose others to danger! One thing was of the greatest interest: where had they sent the box with the dangerous deceased? And the information on this matter was fairly reassuring. The box had been transported to a black bog from which at an earlier time curative mud for bathing had been extracted. The box had then been lowered into this bog and submerged in one of its deepest parts, after having been loaded with stones and filled with disinfectant. It seemed that an infected corpse could not possibly have been dealt with more decisively and punctiliously; but then began the reckoning with the hotel, from which almost everyone fled except for those impoverished persons who were not in a position to allow themselves the luxury of deserting rooms they had paid for a month in advance. The whole hotel had to be disinfected, or at least those rooms which the N. family had occupied, as well as the adjacent suites; the passageway in which the boy played was also to be disinfected, along with the corner of the dining-room where the N. family had their meals. This all represented a considerable financial outlay, more than three hundred gulden if I am not mistaken, since the soft furnishings of three apartments, as all recognized, had to be burned to ashes, while in all the others the curtains at the windows, carpets and door-curtains had to be replaced. On this account Mrs N. was presented with financial demands by the proprietor of the hotel, and the civic authorities supported the right of the owner, who, in spite of the compensation required, had still lost by reason of the events concerned, since most of his rooms would remain vacant all season and in future the hotelier risked loss of custom from many patrons if they found out that there had been a case of diphtheria in the house.

Claims of this sort were new to the visitors, and everyone was interested to see how it turned out. Some thought it was a pettifogging demand, while others found it entirely reasonable, although excessive; everyone was talking about it the whole time, and Mr N. became a centre of interest. But it was surprising that no-one was afraid of him. People approached him, since it was well-known that, being a sick man, he had left the hotel room as soon as the illness had been discovered, and did not return until after his son's death. No-one asked about his wife, and she was not seen for several days. It was thought that she had gone away or that she was ill. Mr N. himself was of the greatest interest to people who were interested in foreign ways of doing things. Mr N. told everyone every day what demands were being placed upon him and how he was responding to them. He did not deny that the hotel-keeper had suffered loss and that the death of his son had been the cause of these losses, but he resisted the notion that anyone had any right to demand payment arbitrarily, and was not intending to pay anything without due process of law.

'Supposing I am obliged to pay,' he said, 'at least that has to be decreed not by some police officer and three local citizens, but laid down formally by a court, the decision of which I can accept. Anyway, what does it mean to say I must pay? It'd be all right if I had the means. They can take my suitcase and welcome, but that's all. Supposing some pauper was in my place, I bet you there'd be no talk about compensation.'

And everyone was intrigued by the intricacies of the problem, and Mr N. was forever surrounded by circles of people arguing about his rights and the associated unpleasantness. The matter, however, was soon settled peacefully: the municipality did not want to go so far as to take him to court, because if they did, talk about the case of diphtheria would become more widely known, and so they decided upon an arrangement whereby Mr N. was simply to pay the bill presented by the disinfection contractors. The matter ended there, but then suddenly a new event occurred: Mrs N., after spending a week in a large room in the hotel and daily visiting the marsh into which her son's body had been sunk, went there on the first day of the next week and did not return. She was sought in vain; no-one had seen her in the wood or in the park, she had not called on any of her friends, had not taken tea in any of the cafés—she had simply disappeared, as had the brass dumbbells which her husband used for his private gymnastics. A search continued for two or three days, but then the suspicion was expressed that she must have drowned herself in that same marsh—which, people said, was later proved to be true, but her body, which was supposed at one stage to have risen to the surface, was sucked down into the depths again. And so she perished.

This event was remarkable for its tragic nature, and for the quiet way it had all happened; Mrs N. left no note when she departed and had given no sign of wishing to do away with herself. Mr N. aroused the sympathy of many; he behaved very modestly and maintained a cold and proud silence; he would say, 'It would be best if I went away,' but he did not leave, because his own health was very poor and required him to hold to his original intention to remain until the end of the course of treatment at the spa.

My acquaintance with him did not prosper: it was obvious that we were not compatible in character. Despite my being privy to a family secret which should have disposed me to be sympathetic towards him, he seemed to me to be far more disagreeable than his wife, who had been guilty of a marital offence against him. I had no reason to seek his friendship, but out of some motivation on his part which was incomprehensible to me, he suddenly sought my company, and in the conversations which took place between us, he very often and very gladly recalled the memory of his late wife.

On Translating Leskov

THE American scholar, William B. Edgerton, has called translating Leskov 'the almost insoluble problem'. This refers to the difficulty of malapropisms and folk etymologies, what a French translator of Leskov, Jean-Claude Marcadé, has called '*barbarismes étymologiques*': the amusing confusion of words which Leskov's characters perpetrate deliberately or accidentally in speech. These figure in some of the stories in this volume; but these are not the only challenging problems for the translator.

A good title is an asset: it may intrigue the potential reader and provide motivation to pick up the book and read. Leskov was accused of choosing titles which were *vychurnye*: 'forced', 'mannered', even 'conceited'. Yet if some of his titles are puzzling, it is all to the good. They are often not easy to translate neatly into English. *Soboryane*, the title of his novel usually rendered 'Cathedral Folk', is not a usual Russian word: it means 'the people associated with a cathedral': even so, a '*sobor*' is not the same as a West European cathedral. Trollope called *his* famous novel *Barchester Towers*, and so totally have we come to accept this title, that it never occurs to us to wonder—why 'towers'? Would not some have refused to accept this 'clever' title if the novel had been a translation from another language?

The titles of the stories in this book present no insuperable difficulties, but my versions may require some justification. 'A Pygmy' is a literal translation of the one-word Russian title (though the question of 'a' or 'the' is always with us, Russian having no such words). 'Vexation of Spirit' is a direct quotation from Ecclesiastes. *Dvorianskii bunt v Dobrynskom prikhode* is straightforward: 'Rebellion among the gentry in the parish of Dobryn' includes a necessary slight degree of explanation. It is, of course, ironic, since the gentry rebellion is spurious and the real one is among the peasants; but that is not the translator's problem. The literal translation of *Nekreshcheny pop*, 'The unbaptized priest', felt rather abrupt: 'who was never baptized' seemed to be more euphonious and non-translational. The problem of the word *pop* is explained later.

A liberty was taken with *Pugalo,* 'The Bogeyman', as 'Selivan, the Bogeyman' appealed for its rhyme and rhythm; there is a precedent in Leskov for a rhythmic and rhyming title: *Malanya, golova baranya,* 'Malanya muttonhead'. *Po povodu 'Kreytserovoy sonaty'* literally is: 'on the subject of the Kreutzer Sonata'. 'Re' is too bureaucratic, 'apropos' too foreign, 'concerning' or 'about' not unsuitable, but a little casual. 'A response to' accurately reflects the author's stated intention and makes a neat and comfortable title.

The most difficult is *Pod Rozhdestvo obideli.* The first two words 'at Christmas(-time)' are straightforward. *Obideli* means 'they insulted/offended/hurt [him or them—understood]'. Scholars use 'Insulted at Christmas', or 'Offended before Christmas', which are satisfactory for reference purposes, but, as the title of a version, will they really do? No-one in the story is 'insulted', 'offended' or 'injured' in the English sense of the words, but wrongs are done to more than one person. 'Wrong done at Christmas' uses 'wrong' in the general singular, without saying who was wronged. This title reflects the content of the story and appears less uneasy in sound than any other possibility.

The linguistic medium of some of these stories raises issues for decision. The 'Priest who was never baptized' serves in a Cossack village, where the inhabitants speak a version of Ukrainian, a language familiar to Leskov, who began his career in government service in Kiev. Other stories contain elements of Orel dialect. How should a translator convey this? Should the peasant characters speak in a regional dialect of English? This was rejected on principle: it creates more problems than it solves. One thinks of Hollywood films about the Roman Empire in which the Roman oppressors speak with upper-class English accents, while the noble freedom fighters sound like honest all-American boys. The consequence, at least to English ears, is hilariously funny. My solution here is not a solution at all: all the Cossacks, peasants and workers speak in colloquial English with slight rural or working-class elements to it, and the reader has to take my word for it that in the original they are speaking local non-standard versions of Ukrainian or Russian.

Cultural elements are both interesting and taxing. Non-Russian readers may find themselves in a very unfamiliar world. This applies in particular to the church. Russian parish clergy (in contrast to some extent with monastic orders) of the time were mainly from a low class in society, often of very poor educational attainment (barely literate in some cases), and it was not unusual for them to be held in near-contempt by their parishioners and by society in general. Father Savva, clearly a scholar, confounds expectations by refusing to enter the training courses for episcopal orders and insisting on being a village priest. The very word *pop* ('priest' in the title of 'The Priest who was never baptized') is untranslatable, since it has several nuances: friendly familiarity, lack of any very great respect, or perhaps even contempt. 'Parson' has some, but only some, of the same feeling to it, but will certainly not do as a translation. We read in these stories that some of Leskov's priests the respect of their parishioners, despite all this.

Parish priests invariably married upon ordination; if widowed, they were not allowed to marry again and were normally expected to enter a monastery—though several of Leskov's priests avoid this fate, and either 'live in sin' (which seems to be what the Cossacks expected Savva should do) or simply carry on as a single person. The bishops and archbishops were all unmarried and better educated, and may possibly—though it was very rare—have come from the ranks of the nobility. The point is that the words for clergy can only be translated by their dictionary equivalents, and when we read of the 'rural dean', the priests, archpriests, bishops and archbishops, we should put all thoughts of the cultured Oxford-educated, upper-class clergy of rural England right out of mind—likewise the Scottish minister with his MA from Edinburgh or St Andrews. Such people in Britain were certainly not always comfortably provided for, but even Chaucer's fourteenth-century poor parson of a town was 'a learned man, a clerk'. Such learning was rare in Russia among the village clergy. Moreover, unlike British clergy, Russian priests were entirely dependent on fees from their parishioners for their support: they had no other stipends.

Other terminology creates little difficulty even if unfamiliar: the attire of an Orthodox priest, for example, or the layout of an Orthodox church, though one should know that the sanctuary is gated and the laity were not allowed to enter it; the 'ambo' is a raised dais from which the Gospels are read. 'Old believers', as any Russian reader would know, were the often passionate adherents of traditional religious practices which were reformed in the mid-seventeenth century. The biblical Christians, the *Shtundists*, would, however, have been unfamiliar even to many contemporary readers, as Leskov's explanations in the text indicate.

Another 'cultural'-historical difficulty for the reader concerns the classes in Russian rural society, especially before the freeing of the serfs in the early 1860s. Some of Leskov's remarks in the stories indicate that not every reader even in Russia at the time of these tales' publication would be fully familiar with the situation and the relationships involved. The serfs were bound to their masters and largely at their mercy; the peasants traditionally held the belief that all the land was theirs originally and had been taken from them. They could be removed from their own land and forced to work in the manor house as a house-serf. Leskov mostly uses the archaic word *muzhik* to refer to the peasants, usually neutral, but which may sometimes bear the nuance of 'clod' or 'yokel'. The role of the village elder was to organize work on communal land; he was usually a respected figure who was something of a link between landowner and peasant. And the Cossacks? The word is Tatar for 'free men' and Leskov's Cossack characters were the fiercely independent-minded descendants of those who had established themselves in the 'wild' fringe areas of the Russian Empire centuries ago.

The gentry covered a wide range as regards their wealth and possessions. Leskov's father owned an estate with only two families of peasant serfs, which left the Leskov family in a state bordering on genteel poverty; there were other squires with hundreds or even thousands of serfs, and the famous Sheremetiev (referred to in passing in 'Selivan') owned hundreds of thousands of peasants. Leskov himself had to work in government service before first taking employment with an uncle and then setting up as a writer. The 'pygmy' was in such service. Some of Leskov's tales are set among the merchant classes, as is 'Wrong done at Christmas'.

A strong challenge for the translator and the source of the greatest delight to the linguist comes in handling the eccentric speech of some of Leskov's characters. We have splendid examples of malapropism in these stories. Father Vasily's wife, for example, in Dobryn, says that her husband, when recovering from one of his drunken 'benders' would weep and pray '*do uzhasti*', by which she meant 'to a frightful degree'; however, she was combining *uzhas*, horror, with *uchast'*, fate. The trouble is that the English equivalents rarely match in the same way as they do in Russian. Readers may have better solutions than those proposed to the various examples here. The best I could do with *do uzhasti* was mix 'dread' with 'destiny': 'till you thought he would meet his dreadstiny'. One that does actually come together is when the peasants hear that Father Illarion is expected to receive an order (of knighthood, or the like), and they mix *orden*, order, with *morda*, snout, ugly mug, referring to his order as a *morden.* The obvious English equivalent is 'mawder', but the word 'maw' is too literary to be convincing in the context; I first chose 'defecoration' for its humour and crudity. But it is open to several objections, not least that a decoration and an order are not the same thing. The 'insignifia of an order' at least indicates the contempt in which the idea of honouring the slimy priest is held.

In Kromy, the 'Bordeau wine cellar', *bordosskii pogreb*, suggested *barbos* to the locals. 'Barbos' is a name given to dogs; by extension it takes on the meaning of a 'dog'—a rude or coarse person. *Barbosskii pogreb*, then, might perhaps be rendered as the 'Bordello' wine cellar, but I chose to call it the 'Bawdy-o cellar': this is a mixture of words an accomplished Malaprop might produce, and it is closer to 'Bordeau' than 'bordello'.

When Father Vasily is recovering from his drunken stupor, he requests olives: 'Mazulinku daite'—give me olives. The Russian for 'olive' is *maslina:* what is he confusing it with? Surely not *mazurka* (the dance); more likely *mazurik*, a simple-speech word for a swindler. Readers' suggestions are invited: I could find no English word with a related meaning which might be confused with 'olive', so chose 'oliverive'—a malapropism which suggests the state of Father Vasily's internal organs. The peasants refer to the Governor, a Count, *Graf*, as 'grap'. Is this any more than peasant pronunciation of *p* for *f*, common enough in Russian dialectal phonetics? But *grap* in South Russian pronunciation is very close to *khrap*, either 'snoring' or another word for 'snout', and this may be part of the joke. There is a way of mangling 'Count' in English which is too obscene to use; 'Clownt' suffices.

Readers may like to try their hand at one or two more and see if they can improve on my versions. The peasants drink *grom yamaisky* (Jamaica 'thunder'-*grom*, rather than *rom*—rum), and a group of squires are praised for being *proizvoditeli dvoryanstva* ('producers' rather than 'marshals'—*predvoditeli*—of the nobility). In this last case I was tempted by 'martyrs' in view of the unpopularity of that post, but it clashed strongly with the context. Is there a solution to the 'empty innkeeper' (*pustoy dvornik*), Selivan, so called because no-one ever stayed at his inn? The word *pustoy* is, however, a pun on *postoyalyy*, the adjective which defines the *dvor*, household, as an inn. What about the 'Outkeeper'? The 'Nobody-in-keeper'?

Leskov's vocabulary is in general diverse and unusual. On dozens of occasions when translating these stories words were encountered which were not in any easily-accessible dictionary, and when locating them in the seventeen-volume Academy Dictionary of the Literary Russian Language it was discovered that the example given was the very sentence from Leskov I was trying to translate. Were they words Leskov coined, or did he give them currency by using them?—one cannot always be sure. He uses regional words (there is at least one even in 'A Response to the "Kreutzer Sonata"'), dialect, simple speech and technical language—sometimes explaining it, but often not. An interesting example is the tool used specifically in Orel by thieves to remove the headgear of their victims in the street, in Leskov's words 'a device something like tongs with a little loop of twine-known as a *kobylka*.' Now, the Russian word *kobylka* has numerous meanings, as a trawl of dictionaries reveals: a filly, the bridge of a stringed instrument, and 'an insect of the genus of locust'. This last meaning seems to be the clue, and the back legs of a locust or cricket suggest the construction of a nefarious tong-like device.

All translations are flawed, since the very act of translating deprives a work of a major part of its essential flavour, which depends not only on the language, but on its setting and on the cultural assumptions and the mind-set of its originally-intended readers. However, as an enthusiast for the writings of Leskov over many years, I refuse to be deterred from making these translations available by a false sense of perfectionism. Imperfect they doubtless are, but they are offered here for what they are worth.

J.M.

Notes

Sources. Major collections of Leskov's works: (1) *Collected Works* of 1889-90, one volume of which was banned by the censor; (2) the same reissued in 1897; (3) reissued again in 1902-03 as *'Complete Works: Third Edition'* in 36 volumes. It was far from complete, but contained most of his stories. (4) *Collected Works* (11 vols, 1956-58), with essays and annotations; later reissued. (5) *Complete Works* (30 vols planned) under way since 1996.

The Priest who was never baptized

Russian title: ***Некрещеный поп***: first appeared in *Grazhdanin* [Citizen] in September-October 1877; substantially revised for a book version, 1878; appears in vol. 6 of 1956-58, from which this translation has been made.

Leskov strongly implied elsewhere that the story of the unbaptized priest was a real-life event.

p.1. *Buslaev* (1818-97): Moscow University professor; scholar of immense reputation. Leskov worked with him on the journal *Russkaya rech'* in 1861.

trepak: the popular and highly energetic folk-dance.

p.2. *Archbishop Ignaty Bryanchaninov* (1807-67): monk who became a bishop; figures in Leskov's story 'The Disinterested Engineers'.

Tsar Nikolai Pavlovich (Nicholas I) reigned 1825-1855.

p.4. *flocks of Laban:* the story begins in Genesis 24.

p.20. *'Be not drunk with wine, wherein is excess'*, Ephesians 5:18.

p.21. *St Barbara's Day:* 4 December. *Feast of St Nicholas:* 6 December.

p.26. *as the ram awaited Abraham:* Genesis 22:12-13.

p.28. *'what it should be according to the church book'.* St Nicholas's day is 6 December; by the Russian Orthodox Church calendar two Saints Savva are commemorated on 3 and 5 December.

p.30. *'in whom he made his abode'*: John 14:23.

'from His hand no-one should ever pluck him': John 10:28.

p.31. *'tradition of men':* Mark 7:8.

Shtunda: 'Shtundism' was a religious movement, which originated probably among Protestant German immigrants in the Ukraine in the early nineteenth century. The word comes from the popularity of *Bibelstunden* (German: Bible study sessions) among these Christians. Their faith was biblical, and it was characterized by Christian fellowship and mutual caring.

'whomsoever shall do and teach': Matthew 5:19

p.32. *'God setteth the solitary in families':* Psalm 68:6.

'hope towards God that there shall be a resurrection...': Acts 24:15.

p.33. *'a living sacrifice':* Romans 12:1.

'a friend to God': James 2:15-23.

p.34. *'house empty, swept and garnished':* Matthew 12:43-45.

'a sacrifice [acceptable], well-pleasing to God': Philippians 4:18.

p.35. *'Is he worthy?'* The ordination of an Orthodox priest requires the assent of the whole people of God, who express their approval by shouting: 'He is worthy' when invited to do so.

p.37. *'a false balance is abomination to the Lord':* Proverbs 11:1.

p.39. *'God desireth not the death of a sinner, but rather that he may turn from his wickedness and live.'* Words from a liturgical declaration of the forgiveness of sins based on Ezekiel 18:23.

p.43. *the name of St Savka in the calendar:* see note to p. 28 above.

p.49. *'I would not that ye should be ignorant...':* I Corinthians 10:1-4.

p.50. *St Gregory the Theologian,* (AD 310-390): a father of the Church held in great respect by Russian Orthodox Christians.

Vasily the Great (AD 329-379) of Caesarea; theologian responsible for a marked influence on the composition of the Orthodox Liturgy.

Rebellion among the Gentry in the parish of Dobryn

Russian title: ***Дворянский бунт в Добрынском приходе***; published in *Istorichesky vestnik* [Historical Messenger], vol. IV (no. 3), 1881. The many articles Leskov contributed to this journal must surely have enlivened its staid scholarly pages. 'Rebellion' was not republished in the Soviet era.

p.52. Of these families, the *Trubetskoys* are probably the best known, though the Trubetskoy referred to here is not particularly eminent.

Marshal of the Nobility: elected by an assembly of the nobility of a province or region to serve as a representative of the interests of the gentry class. The post was as eagerly sought by some for its prestige as it was avoided by others for its responsibilities.

p.54. *Old believers:* known also as 'schismatics', these Christians stood fast in observing the religious customs of the Orthodox Church before the reforms of Patriarch Nikon in 1655. The 'reforms' were, to modern eyes, slight: small changes to the liturgy and the making of the sign of the cross with three fingers instead of two. Nevertheless, the bitterness engendered by the decision to make changes lasted for centuries.

p.55. *Vasily the Great:* see note on p. 50.

p.57. Vorontsov madeira: properly made from the grapes in the Crimean vineyard of the Counts Vorontsov. The Orel imitation referred to here was perhaps of less elevated quality.

Monsieur Yard, known in Russia as 'Yar', was a French restaurateur, founder (in 1826) and proprietor (till 1867) of a fine restaurant in Moscow. After changes of name in the Soviet period, it is still open and again bears the name of Yar.

p.58. *'bearers of spikenard':* see John 12:3.

p.61. *'this was not my doing'.* A good number of Leskov's later stories explored the 'righteous' man or woman, taking the notion from Genesis 18:23-32 which tells of the ten 'righteous' for whose sake—if they could be found'—God would reprieve Sodom. The word became so clearly one of Leskov's 'trademarks' that he feels obliged to explain here that in this case it was really the villagers and not he who dubbed Marfa Tikhonovna a 'righteous woman'. (See also p.165.)

p.69. *struggle under Ivan the Terrible:* the massive upheaval which began in the mid-1560s, whereby Ivan expropriated lands from his boyars (hereditary nobility) and established his own lands which were ruled by his own appointees.

p.70. *'cholera year':* Leskov's father died in the epidemic of 1848.

p.72. Turgenev's novel *Fathers and Sons* was indeed set in the 1850s. The 'scenes of misunderstanding' are of the type portrayed between the main character Bazarov and the peasants he seeks to cultivate, when no meeting of minds materializes. Leskov is not quite right in stating that the clergy play no part in the novel: an intelligent and witty Father Aleksei appears in Chapter 21.

p.73. *Levashov, Nikolai Vasilievich,* Count (1827-88); served in St Petersburg after relinquishing the governorship of Orel.

p.75. *Diebitsch-Zabalkansky,* Ivan Ivanovich (Johann), Count, 1785-1831; German soldier who joined the Russian army in 1801, fought against Napoleon; Adjutant-General to Tsar Alexander I, Chief of Russian General Staff; famous for his campaigns against the Turks 1828-29; promoted Field Marshal and given the name of Zabalkansky to commemorate his Balkan exploits.

p.81. *in Rama:* Matthew 2:18.

p.82. *Collegiate Assessor:* civil service rank equivalent to army Captain.

p.83. *'...a decent ignoramus.'* The first quotation is from Pushkin's *Evgeny Onegin* (II, 7, line 5), it is correct, but changed in context. The second is adapted from an anonymous verse published outside Russia in 1855. Leskov regularly misquoted to serve his purposes: here he takes lines with general political import and applies them to a particular person.

Third Section: the security police of Nicholas I's Imperial Chancellory, which established censorship and paranoid investigations of real or imagined dissident groups and activities.

p.87. *Filipp Kolachev and Ivan the Terrible:* Kolachev was, as Metropolitan of Moscow, a strong clerical opponent of Ivan, who had him arrested in mid-sermon and imprisoned in a monastery, where he was killed in 1568.

p.90. *Yakushkin's peasants:* I. D. Yakushkin (1793-1857) was a liberal would-be reformer, educationist and associate of the Decembrists who attempted a 'revolution' in 1825. His social outlook was too advanced for his peasants, whose docility in the incident referred to is legendary.

p.91. The *'layman in a position of authority',* was the Chief Procurator of the Holy Synod, who had ministerial rank, and who exercised control over the running of the Russian Church. The most famous holder of this office, from 1880 to 1905, was Konstantin Pobedonostsev (1827-1907), who was despised by Leskov. Thomas Masaryk wrote: '[His] desperate attempt to suppress the progressive movement of Russian youth was largely responsible for the deplorable state of the country.'

Archbishop Agafangel of Volyn (died 1876) was an outspoken opponent of the synodal system referred to in the note above.

Makary Bulgakov (1816-82) was Metropolitan of Moscow 1879-82. *Count D. A. Tolstoy* was Chief Procurator 1865-80.

'What will ye give me, and I will deliver him unto you?' See Matthew 26:15 (Judas Iscariot's negotiation with the chief priests).

p.92. *'Where art thou?':* Genesis 3:9.

Selivan, the bogeyman

Russian title: *Пугало*; written and first published in 1885 in the journal *Zadushevnoe slovo* [Sincere Word]; described as a 'story for young people'. Later Leskov called it as a story half of childhood and half of the life of the people. It proved popular both with adults and children. This translation was made from vol. 8 of the Soviet collection.

p.107. *Bucephalus:* legendary steed of Alexander of Macedonia.

p.111. *rhetorician:* rhetoric was the principal study in the first year at theological seminary; hence the title enjoyed by students.

p.113. *'at Sheremetiev's expense':* that is, at someone else's expense. The noble family, and particularly Count Boris Petrovich Sheremetiev (1653-1719), was famously generous to the poor and needy, and their reputation for hospitality thus entered the Russian language.

p.116. *Quintilius Varus:* the unfortunate Roman general defeated by Herrmann (Arminius) in the Teutoburg Forest in AD 9.

p.128. *hut on hen's legs:* the dwelling of the mythical Baba Yaga in the folk legend—an unlikely sanctuary for our travellers!

p.139. *Father Efim Ostromyslensky* was teacher of religion at the Orel Grammar School; his pupil Leskov more than once expressed gratitude for his 'good lessons'.

A Pygmy

Russian title: *Пигмей*; first published with the title 'Three Good Deeds' in *Grazhdanin* [Citizen], 1876; appeared in the 1903-03 collection. This translation was made from Leskov, *Ottsovskii zavet*, Moscow, 2000.

p.146. *Lenormand cards:* named after their inventor, a Mlle Lenorman or Lenormand. They are fortune-telling cards, still used by aficionados of the occult in Russia and elsewhere today.

p.148. *'There are many mansions':* John 14:2.

p.150. Tsar Nicholas I lay in state for a few days in mid-March 1855.

Wrong Done at Christmas

Russian title: *Под рождество обидели. Житейский случай*; first published in *Peterburgskaya gazeta* [Petersburg Gazette] in 1890, and not included in the 1902-03 or 1956-58 collections. This translation was made from Leskov, *Ottsovskii zavet; rasskazy*, Moscow, 2000.

p.156. *proverbial for robbery:* Leskov is referring to his native Orel, the setting for his amusing story 'Robbery' of 1887.

p.158. *Shuisky's reminiscences:* which of the many members of the Shuisky family the author is referring to remains obscure.

p.160. *new courts*: reform of 1864 established public trial by judge and jury.

p.165. *Androsov:* Leskov refers to Androsov several times in his works. The remarks are not consistent; here he is described as a merchant, elsewhere as a peasant. His biblical wisdom is praised in *Schism in High Society*. In 'Deathless Golovan' we learn of his naivety in believing he had a cure for plague—while he is said to have died of it. Here Leskov gives a different account of his death, further illustrating the liberties he took with 'facts'.

righteous man: another of Leskov's hints at Genesis 18:23-32; see note to p.61.

p.167. *words of eternal life:* John 6:68.

make him thy brother: not a direct biblical quotation, but see Matthew 18:15 and Luke 17:3.

Vexation of Spirit

Russian title: ***Томление духа. Из отроческих воспоминаний***; first published in 1890 under the title *Koza* (The Goat) in the journal *Igrushechka* [Plaything]. It appears in the 1902-03 collection; this translation was made from Leskov, *Ottsovskii zavet*, Moscow, 2000.

p.170. *Praskovyas:* the servant is referring to St Paraskeva, martyred under Diocletian for refusing to renounce Christ. Her cult was widely practised in old Russia.

p.172. *No-one should swear:* the Biblical precept prized by Tolstoy. See Matthew 5:34-37.

fear no man: probably an inexact reference to Luke 12:4.

A Response to 'The Kreutzer Sonata'

Russian title: ***По поводу 'Крейцеровой сонаты'***; written in 1890, never completed, not published until 1899, after Leskov's death, in the journal *Niva* [Cornfield].

Before publication in 1891 Tolstoy's story, 'The Kreutzer Sonata', was circulating in manuscript copies to which Leskov would have easy access. This translation was made from vol. IX of the Soviet collection.

p.177. *any young woman:* this epigraph is from an earlier unpublished version of Tolstoy's story, and it has been slightly altered by Leskov.

Dostoevsky's funeral was held on 31 Jan 1881 (old style).

Dmitry Vasilievich *Averkiev* (1836-1915): writer.

an elderly writer. Leskov was no more than fifty in 1881!

p.179. *those chains:* the mysterious visitor is doubtless referring to the chains Dostoevsky had to wear when in prison and in exile.

p.186. *my soul would be purified by suffering:* The lady has clearly taken this Dostoevskian notion very seriously.

Bibliography of translations into English of works by Leskov

This list indicates the extent of work undertaken over the years by English translators of Leskov, and it may interest readers who wish to explore his writing further in translation. Collections exclusively of his works are listed first in chronological order of publication.

Translated by Isobel F. Hapgood: ***The Steel Flea.*** Boston: privately published, 1916

Translated by A. E. Chamot, with an introduction by Edward Garnett: ***The Sentry and Other Stories.*** London: John Lane, 1922
  Includes also: 'The Lady Macbeth of the Mtsensk District' 'The Make-up artist' 'On the Edge of the world'

Translated by Isobel F. Hapgood: ***Cathedral Folk.*** London: John Lane, 1924; Reprinted: Westport, Conn: Hyperion, 1977

Adapted from the Russian by Babette Deutsch and Avram Yarmolinsky and illustrated by Mstislav Dobujinsky: ***The Steel Flea.*** New York and London: Harper, 1943

Translated with Introduction by R. Norman: ***The Musk-ox and Other Tales.*** London: Routledge, 1944
  Includes also: 'Kotin and Platonida', 'The Spirit of Madame de Genlis', 'The Stinger', 'A Flaming patriot', 'The Clothes-mender', 'The Devilchase', 'The Alexandrite'
  This volume is said to be The Tales of Leskov Vol. I. *No vol. II appeared.*

Translated by David Magarshak: ***The Enchanted Pilgrim and Other Stories.*** London, New York, Melbourne, Sydney: Hutchinson, 1948
  Includes also: 'Iron Will', 'Deathless Golovan', 'The Left-handed artificer', 'The Make-up artist'

Translated with introduction by David Magarshak: ***The Amazon and Other Stories.*** London: George Allen and Unwin, 1949. Reprinted: London: Four Square Classics, 1962, and Westport, Conn: Hyperion, 1977
  Includes also: 'A Little mistake', 'The March hare'

Translated by David Magarshak with an introduction by V. S. Pritchett: ***Selected Tales.*** London: Secker and Warburg, 1961
  Contents: 'Lady Macbeth of the Mtsensk district', 'The Enchanted wanderer', 'The Left-handed craftsman', 'The Sentry', 'The White Eagle'

Translated by George Hanna (illustrated): ***Lefty.*** Moscow: Progress, 1965

Translated, edited, introduced and annotated, by William B. Edgerton: ***Satirical Stories of Nikolai Leskov.*** New York: Pegasus, 1969

Contents: 'The Steel flea', 'The Archbishop and the Englishman' (extracted from *Trivia from the life of archbishops*), 'Single Thought', 'Journey with a nihilist', 'Deception', 'Choice grain', 'Notes from an unknown hand'—'A Clever respondent', 'How it is not good to condemn weaknesses', 'Superfluous mother love', 'Female aspirations toward understanding lead to vain distress', 'On the harm that exists for many of reading worldly books', 'About the folly of a certain prince', 'About the rooster and his children', 'Fish soup without fish', 'Figura', Night owls', [translated by Hugh McLean], 'A product of nature' [tr. McLean], 'Administrative grace', 'A Winter day'

Translated and annotated by George H. Hanna with an essay by Yuri Nagibin: ***The Enchanted Wanderer and Other Stories.*** Moscow: Progress, 1974, reissued 1983

Includes: 'Lady Macbeth of Mtsensk', 'Lefty', 'The Make-up artist'

Translated with introduction, notes and index by K. A. Lantz: ***The Sealed Angel and Other Stories.*** Knoxville: University of Tennessee Press, 1984

The volume includes also: 'An Apparition in the Engineers' Castle', 'A Robbery', 'The Mountain', 'The Cattle pen'

Translated and annotated by Harold Klassel Schefski: ***The Jews in Russia. Some Notes on the Jewish Question.*** Princeton NJ: The Darwin Press, 1986

Translated with introduction and notes by David McDuff: ***Lady Macbeth of Mtsensk and Other Stories.*** London: Penguin, 1987

The volume includes also: 'The Musk-ox', 'The Sealed angel', 'Pamphalon the entertainer', 'A Winter's day'

Translated with commentary and notes by James Muckle: ***Vale of Tears and 'On Quakeresses'.*** Nottingham: Bramcote Press, 1991

Translated with preface and notes by Michael Prokurat, illustrated by Tatiana Misijuk: ***On the Edge of the World.*** Crestwood, NY, 1992

Translated, annotated and edited with bibliography and index by James Muckle: ***Schism in High Society. Lord Radstock and his Followers.*** Nottingham: Bramcote Press, 1995

The following translations have been traced in anthologies:

'The Clothesmender' in *Russian Stories*, edited by Gleb Struve with translations, critical introduction, notes and vocabulary, New York: Bantam, 1961, pp. 182-219, translated by Gleb and Mary Struve.

'The Sentry' in *Anthology of Russian Short Stories* vol. 1, Moscow: Raduga, 1985, pp. 410-31, translated by Olga Shartse.

'The Ghost of the Engineers' castle', in *The Masterpiece Library of Short Stories* vol. XII, edited by Sir J. A. Hammerton, London: Educational Book Co. Ltd, no date, pp. 586-596.

'Lady Macbeth of the Mtsensk District' in *Six Russian Short Novels*, selected with an introduction by Randall Jarrell. Garden City, NY: Doubleday, 1963